The Itinerant

THE

ITINERANT

William Herrick

SECOND CHANCE PRESS   Sag Harbor, N.Y. 11963

7/1984
gen'l

Originally published by McGraw/Hill Book Company
First republication in 1985 by
SECOND CHANCE PRESS
RD2, Noyac Road, Sag Harbor, New York

Library of Congress Catalogue Number: 83-051499
ISBN: 0-932966-45-0 (cloth)
         0-932966-46-9 (paper)

To Jeannette

The Itinerant

I

It snowed slush that February day he was born. In itself not unusual, but the sun shone red and black splashes through the winter clouds. Commentators of the day, an ignorant lot, hinted the freakish weather was the result of the mighty blasts of the Big Berthas shelling Paris clear across the sea on the 49th parallel. Nonsense, of course. His mother knew better. Even as she felt him fight his way free of her impatient yet stubborn loins, she knew her son would be a challenger. He was a Gurevich. In her extreme labor and pain she spat out an obscene oath as he broke his way into the world, and though he was only one full second old when he heard it he remembered it a lifetime. Or so he always said. She cuffed him with oaths until he was a man, to protect him, she thought, from the devil and to accustom him to the rudeness he must encounter. Her oaths drove him into the streets, the alleys, the East River wharves to bite his lips and stare out his yellow eyes at the comings and goings. Or to fight with an overwhelming anger. Or yet to contain it in himself, pretending he hadn't heard or seen or noticed, biding his time to become a man. But the image of himself which he retained longest was of a bony, scruffy, redheaded kid perched on a capstan, picking his nose, eating his snot, and watching the ships go by.

The doctor passed the bawling and brawling infant over to the aunt, the mother's sister, a short, chubby woman with wispy red hair and a fatigued cherubic smile. The aunt had eight of her own and another two-thirds on the way, one who when born would be called Joshua if a boy, Judith if a girl, as this one would be called Samuel Ezekiel after his father's grandfather, still restless in his grave, a former itinerant peddler of novelties in Europe. Before the doctor left, he looked again about the small, drafty, overcrowded flat and said to the aunt, "Advise her husband to refrain for six weeks, tell her to stay off her feet for at least a week, and try to impress them both with the importance of cleanliness. Cleanliness is Godliness, you know," the latter said with smug knowledge that the sarcasm would not be lost since this family was notorious in the neighborhood for its boastful impiety and the infant's mother for her obscene tongue and slovenly habits —but only in English. In Russian she was very clean; in Yiddish almost elegant.

Child and man, Zeke was to be obsessed by whatever it was he loved or hated. He demanded his mother's breast with a cry which shook her bones and once her thick nipple was in his mouth he refused to let go so that he had to be torn from her with great vehemence—and an oath followed by another cry so loud it brought the neighbors running, hoping to be audience to murder at the arrogant Gureviches; held in his father's arms, he hugged the man's throat as though he wished to strangle him; when Rebecca, his sister, played with him, he took her fingers to his mouth and tried to bite through to the bone, only to become enraged because he didn't have teeth with which to succeed in his purpose.

His father was a painter—not an ordinary house painter, one who painted billboards, none too high for his daring. All his life Zeke Gurevich was to think of his father as an heroic figure—not of course because his father painted billboards high above the street but because his father had fought in the woods against cossack pogromists and in the streets of St. Petersburg during the Revolution of 1905 together with Leon Trotsky and had a long scar on his left thigh from a Czarist officer's sword to prove it. While his father painted billboards, his mother, like her sister, chunky and red-haired, unlike her sister in that her mouth was far from cherubic, being in fact bitter and angry and very tough-jawed, sold sour pickles and sour tomatoes from a brine barrel in the street market. His sister Rebecca, slender and black-haired, with long slanted eyes and a short, fine nose, went to P.S. 63, as ugly a Victorian Gothic temple of learning as ever defaced a brilliant island. As he sat high in the gallery, Rebecca hogged the center of the stage in company to her father's and mother's idolatrous applause. She never had to be asked twice to recite or to dance or to put on a show for visiting dignitaries to the household such as aunts, uncles, friends, gas meter readers or the like. Zeke hated her her glory and loved her and at one point in his childhood wanted to marry her, making a ghastly attempt which she turned aside with a sneer. Infuriated, he flew from her bed.

He was to become a great flyer—a bignosed red-haired Icarus. With wings of wax, daring the fires of dragons. Fortunately, he was also like a cat—curious, arrogant, with a quick-change temper—and had numerous lives.

At six, his mother's lady friends already knew it was dangerous to sit him on their lap: he pinched. At nine, he began to sprawl behind hallway stairs with every girl from six to ten in the tenement in which his family lived on Hester Street. At twelve and a half, their boarder, Lamiel Forté, a huge man with a blue beard and great biceps, a cellist by trade, caught Zeke taking a shower, invited himself in, and before Zeke had a chance to yell slipped to his knees and, though half drowning, played a charming pavanne on the boy's flute. In the following months Lamiel, a versatile and indefatigable musician, repeated the performance quite often. Though Zeke felt terribly guilty, not knowing exactly why, he found Lamiel's attentions exceedingly pleasant. And it did save wear and tear on his fist which had just recently discovered one of its *raisons d'être*. The boy's affair with Lamiel terminated soon enough: his cousin Miriam Gurevich whose father had just died came to live with Zeke's family for the summer and Lamiel Forté departed for Paris, France, from which for a time he sent his young friend sensitive, poetic letters which Zeke showed to his cronies. Howling with laughter, they would amost choke to death on the smoke from the Italian stogies they had picked from the gutter. Lamiel stopped writing when he married a man his own age.

Lamiel Forté became a world-famous cellist and lived happily enough until the Nazis conquered France in 1940. Asked to play a concert in honor of Hermann Goering, he heroically refused, for which act a swinish but beautiful SS lieutenant had his fingers chopped off to the knuckle. Lamiel died in Dachau.

Miriam, a year Zeke's junior, rescued him from the charming fate of a spent rake before he reached the age of thirteen, an age which tradition said brought manhood. It was for obsessive love of Miriam that he temporarily adopted celibacy as a way of life, stopped stealing pennies from the blind newsdealer on the corner, and learned not to call Steve Wojeczewski, who wore braces on his shriveled legs and had a hare lip, "Hey, cripple."

Zeke was a skinny, red-haired, bignosed cock of a boy and Miriam a sturdy, pretty, red-haired serpent of a girl. No one—child or adult—knew which way to turn with her, she took one coming and going: gentle, sweet, courteous; tough, obscene, bitter. She could upstage Zeke's sister Rebecca, three years her senior, with dauntless arrogance (within a week Rebecca retired, a has-been) and the next flatter her with audacious hypocrisy. Of course Miriam had an advantage no one, especially Zeke's sister, could match: she had been born with two perfectly formed feet, a sturdy round body with a behind as round, as hard, as sweet as two pomegranates, and one perfectly formed hand. The other, the left, ended at the wrist. A stump. Soon after her arrival Zeke reached under her skirt to snatch her almond: down came that stump on his bony head. The boy lost his senses and flung himself at her. She brought up her knee so hard he sat choking on one testicle for a full twenty minutes as she danced a wild fandango around him holding high her stump, the victory smile on her pretty face so carnivorous he felt certain she was preparing to eat him. He fell madly in love.

Miriam was born in Trenton, New Jersey, to Zeke's Aunt Rose and Uncle Charlie, his father's youngest brother, on the second floor over their wallpaper store on Union Street. Uncle Charlie was a paperhanger, a sick man who always smelled of medicine and paste. His wife Rose was a petite, coquettish woman who ran the store, her husband being far too sick and too tired. Rose had a wry, abrasive tongue feared by family, friend, and stranger. After Miriam's birth, Zeke's entire family (paternal and maternal branches) spread across the breadth of the earth wept as only his family knew how to weep: nobody in the entire world ever suffered the troubles they did, which might well be true. After Miriam's stump came to light, they cried so loud even God in heaven heard and turned His other cheek, or so Zeke's father, Solomon Gurevich, said to his wife with an impassive smile. Wrung dry, the family forgot about it. When remembered at some family celebration, wedding, birth or death, they would cry again, "Woe is Rose. What a misfortune. Who will marry a cripple?" Everyone was sweet to Miriam, especially the housewives on Union Street in Trenton who had to pay in some measure for their secret gloating at Rose's misfortune. Instead of asking, "Damn God, why?" they muttered, "Thank God, not mine. Serves her right —with her whorish ways," by which they meant that Rose was prettier than they and too often the recipient of their husbands' leering smiles.

Rose hated her daughter Miriam and took every occasion to prove it. In the kitchen upstairs above the store after a tiring day, she would scream, "Take it away. This ugliness, my misfortune. All my life I'll have to take care of her." The upbringing of the one-handed girl fell to her sister Rebecca, named after the same deceased grandmother as Zeke's sister. Rebecca diapered the baby, bathed her, fed her, and stuffed a woolen glove with absorbent cotton and pinned it to Miriam's left sleeve to simulate a hand. Miriam couldn't tie her shoe laces, cut her food with a knife, uncap the tooth paste and spread it on the brush without wasting half of it, all of which Zeke offered to do for her. No fool, she accepted. In winter, she told him, her greatest difficulty was the putting on of overshoes, snowsuit, leggings and so on, but with kids, she boasted, she had no trouble at all. If another kid was too brash, she'd rip off her padded glove and stab her stump into his eyes.

But what could she do with her mother's scorn? As Rose screamed, "My misfortune, my ugliness," Miriam would dance and sing, ignoring the screams, Rebecca adding to the din by howling obscenities at her mother in Yiddish and English, the first as expletive and explicatory as the second—coarse, short and to the heart, until Charlie, more tired and more sick as the years flung by, pleaded with all of them for some peace. "What's keeping you, vile angel of death?" he would sob, full of self-pity and despair.

Not for long. Soon he died, was placed in his box and buried, Rose now having another misfortune to scream about. The family found itself spread-eagled, one foot on grief and the other on joy, since on the very same day Charlie died, one of its far-flung progeny in distant Buenos Aires, Argentina, gave birth to twins. They resolved the difficulty by laughing and crying simultaneously, a family invention, they trumpeted with self-serving smugness.

Samuel Ezekiel fell completely in love with Miriam as soon as she banged him with her stump—anyway, as long as it took for her to usurp stage front and center from his sister. For that alone he promised her lifelong fealty. Besides, she could hit a Spalding rubber ball a sewer and a half—she hit line drives, using the stump like a bat—and had absolutely no fear of cops, cars, or devil's curses which she warded off with her crippled limb raised over her head as if it were a holy relic. In addition she could sit for hours in the shabby little kitchen embroidering doilies on a wooden hoop as he stood wide-eyed, dazzled and hypnotized by the swift agility of the fingers of her good hand.

She would ignore him for hours, and then, her timing perfect, would gaze up at him and smile her serpentine smile so that his heart jumped. He was supposed to have a heart murmur: since his parents never remembered it, neither did he: but to elevate himself to Miriam's high estate he rediscovered it and now they were cripples together.

[9]

Once, as if to answer what the adults in the family were always saying, she looked deeply into his eyes—he looked like a skinny, long-beaked rooster with a red coxcomb—and said in a strong, vibrant voice, "Don't you worry, Zeke, when I find the boy I want to marry, I will," and he thought for sure she meant him.

He blurted, "I'll marry you any time y'say, Mimi." She smiled a brilliant smile, lay her embroidery aside, and kissed him till his head whirled.

It was a good summer, Coney Island swimming with Rebecca, the movies and ice cream cones, but Friday nights were special and exquisite. His father and mother would go to a basement tearoom down the block to drink tea with homemade blackberry brandy and spread the socialist enlightenment among neighbors and friends, his sister would sit on the stoop flirting with the second baseman of the Avenue C Aces, and Zeke and Miriam would go to the Yiddish theatre on Second Avenue, where they discovered early that summer they could sneak in after the second-act intermission. No matter what play it was, the third act always was the same, or so it seemed to them, and they loved it. The entire audience would be extremely quiet, just a little anticipatory sniffling from those who knew what was coming. And though Zeke and Miriam knew what was coming no matter what new title shone in lights on the marquee, they stood there expectant and ready to sniffle with the rest. The third act always started with the daughter coming to her parents' house on Friday night. There they'd be on the stage set up to look like a parlor, the old father and mother drinking tea, whitehaired and in Sabbath clothes because the time of all Yiddish third acts is Friday night, after *shul*. And the daughter, who had been thrown out of the house in the middle of the first act—Zeke checked this with the people he got to know in the balcony—because she was pregnant out of wedlock, returned to her parents' home with her little *momser* in her arms, and she cried and her mother cried, and her father yelled and yelled. Then the daughter would suddenly put the baby in her father's arms and he wouldn't know what to do with the baby. And the baby howled. The mother and daughter cried and the father kept getting redder in the face. And everyone in the audience sniffled and sniffled. Suddenly the baby smiled at the old man. The old man, fighting his own lips, then smiled too. The baby then wet the old man, and he began to laugh and the baby laughed back. And the mother and daughter both laughed and cried. The entire audience began to laugh—sniffling, laughing, hiccoughing—the whole theatre in an uproar. And Zeke and Miriam both stood there in the steaming balcony watching this scene for the thirteenth time, laughing and crying, sniffling, tears running into their nose and mouth. Then the old man on the stage began an Hasidic dance with the baby in his arms, then his wife and daughter joined him and soon they were dancing round the stage faster and faster and everyone in the theatre was stamping, everyone's face shining from the tears and the sweat, and hiccoughing from the laughing and the sniffling, Miriam and Zeke stamping and laughing and sniffling along with them, Zeke hiccoughing the loudest. Then the curtain began to fly up and down for twenty bows and everyone in the theatre was saying it was the best play they ever saw, and this was the best third act because they had never laughed and cried so much together, even though they had all seen this act and said the same thing for every play of the last thirteen shown in the Yiddish theatre.

Miriam and Zeke would run outside as the laughing-crying people began to leave the theatre to go to the Café

Royale or to Ratner's, and Zeke would stand alongside Miriam, a long sad look on his bignosed face, and she would hold out both her stump and good hand, "Gimme a nickel, mister, we're little *momsers* too." The people would sniffle and hiccough and some would drop a penny or a nickel into her hand, and soon they would run off to one of the large hot dog and hamburger palaces on Fourteenth Street where they would get enough root beer and french frieds to hold them till the next Friday night, when they again would sneak in after the second-act intermission just in time to see a different daughter with a different baby, everyone crying and sniffling and hiccoughing.

Afterwards they would return to the flat, to find Rebecca necking on the stoop and his parents still gabbing away in the tearoom, damning the bosses or talking about their latest Caruso record. Miriam and Zeke would run upstairs and drop off to an exhilarated sleep. Miriam slept with his sister—a truce existed between them since Rebecca had abdicated—in a big bed which took almost the entire room next to Zeke's.

One broiling Friday night near the end of August, the house still empty but for them, Miriam fell fast asleep, but not Zeke. He couldn't sleep because it was terribly hot and the window shade kept slapping in the window and it frightened him because there was absolutely no wind and he kept conjuring up ghosts and ghouls. Concentrating, he sent the ghosts and ghouls running, but his imagination turned to Miriam who would soon be leaving. He badly wanted to go look at her, though he knew he musn't. Became obsessed with the wish, fought a losing battle, decided at last to go to her. He slipped out of bed and in his BVDs sticky with sweat he sneaked in. He left the door open so the hall light both dimly lit and shadowed her room. She slept on her back, her mouth slightly open in the way children sleep and he looked down at her with a beating, awesome heart, with no idea at all about why he'd come. She breathed so quietly it was frightening. He bent over her to better hear her breathing and there on her plump and sweaty twelve-year-old chest lay the naked stump which was her left hand. He had never gotten a close look at it, so now under the shadowed light he examined it minutely: an innocent deformed limb, pink and delicate, alive, and he was put into a state of beatitude by it as if it were possessed of a secret holy meaning—a secret which joined all other awesome secrets, those which lay in graveyards or in the Ark or the prophet Elijah's drinking of wine from the silver chalice on Passover in one or another uncle's house. And something even more secret, the secret shining smile which passed between his father and mother which he on occasion had the good fortune to witness and which he knew had a connection with the secret of life that surged from him when he did what boys do in their most secret places. A crippled hand? No, no, Mimi was not a cripple. She soared on the wings of life. He could feel his skin become taut, and the pounding of his heart became so painful he thought he would die. Miriam turned in her sleep, and as she did her deformed limb raised off her chest and there he saw revealed for the first time her newborn, plump girlish breasts. He stood transfixed a moment, gasped, then ran and fell into his bed. Blessed.

A few days later Miriam left with her sister Rebecca who had come to fetch her, and he hid in the basement of the tenement and wept.

II

Miriam was torn from his youthful heart in late August. Peaked and unhappy, he was sent, on recommendation of a short but stupendously broad lady social worker who smelled of warm sat-in leather, to a camp operated by a foundation for poor boys and orphans in Bear Mountain. He was a poor boy: billboards had not yet captured the imagination of the country, and sour pickles and tomatoes were still purely a parochial delight. Most people addicted to these hideous but luscious fruits prepared their own: small wooden barrel, a bushel each of small cukes and tomatoes, bay leaf, dill, garlic, vinegar, a dark, cool, enclosed area, and luck.

An orphan he didn't become until the following year when his father's scaffold broke as he painted a billboard atop a building on the other side of the Brooklyn Bridge. The billboard advertised ladies' hairnets. It was close by the one he had painted the previous week which advertised JESUS LOVES.

Though it was an institutional camp, contrary to everyone's expectations, he enjoyed it. He did not enjoy Friday night services which were held in the social hall, because he'd been reared a non-believer. Besides, the young congregation had to sit on a wooden floor and he was unfortunate enough to be possessed of a nervous, bony behind. The counselor who officiated spoke in a boring sing-song rhythm, and the fatboy of the camp, who sat next to Zeke, kept up a continual silent blast of a particularly noxious gas. Zeke won the camp pennant for cleanliness (he was considered an eccentric in his immediate family), for the Indian leg wrestle, and his ability one rainy day to sing off-key all one hundred stanzas of *Abdul Abulbul Amir*.

He returned home a few days before school was to start. The day after his return he went to Yankee Stadium to see the Babe hit a homer. As one obsessed, he had the entire summer hoarded his wealth to blow on one grand outing before school began—fifty cents for the bleachers, ten cents for a hot dog, and ten cents for a bag of peanuts. For the first time in his life he felt himself fortunate: Herbie Pennock, a lefty like himself, pitched a beaut, Babe Ruth hit one four hundred seventy-one feet and of course the Yankees won. He swaggered from the ballpark. All his life he remained a Yankee fan despite the sneers of his many friends who pointed to his loyalty as proof of his neurotic need to identify with power.

He decided to visit his cousin, Abe Abramson, who lived a few blocks away from the Stadium with his second wife, Viola, his first having died tragically three years before. Abe and Viola kept good things to eat in their icebox and he liked them enormously, as much for the food as for the fact they neither patronized his youth nor his poverty. To be sure, Abe and Viola greeted his arrival with a charming collective smile and a tremendous salami sandwich, pickle, and sarsaparilla. Then Abe, who was a licensed medical doctor, examined Zeke's heart and reassured him—Zeke liked nothing better than to put on an act that he was dying—that the murmur was mythic and Zeke fated to live to a hundred.

"Poor kid," Abe laughed.

"Stop bleeding, yuh crumb," Zeke responded, for which Abe whacked him hard on the ass because he believed (in many ways an old-fashioned man) that kids should have respect for their elders, a theory Zeke also came to swear by when he became an elder, which took some doing since he fought in two wars.

Abe then conned him into remaining to answer the phone while he and Viola went to hear Heifetz at Carnegie Hall. Seated behind Abe's large desk, Zeke managed simultaneously to mangle another huge salami sandwich, guzzle soda, and goggle over Abe's set of *Sexualis Psychopathia*, which of course was more edifying for a boy of his youth than Tillie the Toiler doing a vibrato on Moon Mullins, another classic of the day.

The phone rang, as it usually does, at a most inopportune moment, but he answered it. An anxious mother of a baby girl told him her child had a high fever. Dr. Abramson's assistant advised until the doctor called back the child should be given baby aspirin every four hours and—

"That's all?"

"—and an enema."

"Oh, thank you, doctor."

"You're welcome, I'm sure," Dr. Gurevich replied, smacking his lips lasciviously.

Resumed Krafft-Ebing's sinister tall tale about the squirrel lady who collected burrs which she then scurried about burying in the crotch of men's longies hung out to dry.

Heard the front door open—jumped, grabbing at his fly. It was only Abe's sister, Helen, who lived with her brother, taught school in the Bronx and was Zeke's most favorite cousin because she paid off her responsibility to him as the poor relative in the family with a quarter every time they met. Two girls accompanied Helen, one a blond snatch of a girl who Zeke scanned quickly through gimlet eyes, and the other Rachel Farrell, the sight of whom made his murmuring heart go starkly mute. He had been reading Old-Testament stories that thirteenth summer of his youth and he saw himself as Absalom and her as Tamar: she was blood of his blood and he yearned instantly to know her. She was a slender, graceful girl, with long and wild black hair and large, brooding blue-black eyes. What an Irish knish, he murmured to himself as his cousin Helen handed him a quarter and a pat on his curly red hair. The blond snatch, June her name was, hair cropped to the ears, sneered at something which held her attention on the wall behind his ugly head while Rachel Farrell smiled at him, her large white teeth almost intimate, her dark blue eyes so intent on him he was certain she saw through to the bone. His challenger's heart wanted to hold her hand.

The three young women had been Saturday shopping, it was hot, and they were tired. In Abe's and Viola's bedroom, they kicked off their pumps and sprawled on the big bed to take a nap, the new fancy fan Abe had bought stirring up a breeze in the September twilight, as the sun, in the style of the time, setting over the fabled city, haven to the millions who had come steerage from the slums and ghettos of the world (Orientals excluded), reflected purple gold on the tin roofs of the crowded tenements.

Zeke remained in Abe's office, behind the physician's desk, less entranced now by the psychopath who stole ladies' silk stockings to wear round his neck like a flying ace's scarf. And another Fokker plummeted in flames. He heard the girls whispering, a faint giggle (were they laughing at him?) and then only the whir of the fan.

Krafft-Ebing still open before him, a sick book, the salami sandwich long ago consumed, he munched now on a navel orange and thought of Rachel Farrell. A sweet mick.

How could he so suddenly love her when just last week he
had loved Miriam—when only a few seconds ago he had
loved Miriam? Loved her so much it made him sad. Does
love always bring pain and this pleasant, sweet sadness?
Oh, he loved her, Miriam or Rachel, they were one. As he
had loved Rebecca, his very own sister. Was he also sick
like the maniacs who inhabited this crazy book? No, no,
Abe had once told him not to read his books or he would
begin to find each symptom his own.

Perhaps they were sleeping and he could sneak in and
take a look at her. One look. No, he mustn't. She had
smiled at him intimately as though she had liked him. How
could anyone like him? Didn't his mother always call him
a green, bony herring, just as Aunt Rose called Mimi her
ugliness?

Defeated, always defeated, he hitched up his knee
pants and stealthily entered the bedroom where the fan
billowed the girls' summer dresses, revealing enough leg
to inflame his yellow eyes. He tiptoed round the bed,
searching for an opening he could edge into. Found one of
about two-and-a-half inches between June and Rachel. In
he slipped, his rear to the blond, his nose pointed to the
Irish girl. He held his breath for fear he would wake
them. The young women must have been very tired, for
they snored, atonally though gently, and from Rachel
came a warm, sweet scent. He closed his eyes tightly and
allowed himself to enjoy paradise. Never again would he
find it as he did that late September afternoon. His
grubby, young boy's hand couldn't hold still and he sent it
out in search of peace. He discovered it when his pinky
touched hers. The room was hot and the sweetness from
Rachel overwhelmed him. He forced himself to open his
eyes a moment. Affrighted, he saw Rachel observing him

through dark, mysterious eyes. Then she smiled her white, intimate smile—what a *gauche* child—raised a long delicate finger to her lips, took his hand in hers, pressed it warmly, and was promptly asleep.

His hands in hers, she filled him with life and a terrifying energy. Then he also slept and had violent dreams.

III

Rachel, then eighteen years old, was living with Simon Xavier Farrell, who was about twenty-five. She had gone to live with Simon knowing he had only a few years left to his life.

Simon was a tall, very thin, black-bearded man with green, suffering eyes. Those who frequently climbed into Abe Abramson's small Bronx apartment—and their names could be found daringly perched on the mastheads of the revolutionary magazines of the day, present and recent past, or obscenely carved on the toilet walls of Greenwich Village speak-easies: writers, painters, revolutionists all— said of Simon he was an El Greco Jesus. At the least St. Jerome. They weren't disparaging Simon, though they were the majority of them spitters on God. They were attracted by the tragedy of his birth, congenital rheumatic heart disease. Doctors had been saying since the day of his birth that he would be dead before his next birthday. Dr. Abramson, as unsentimental a man as Zeke was ever to know, a man who never cried, the exception to the rule among the Gurevich family, never spoke of Simon X. Farrell without a soft, gentle smile creasing his large fat face. "Simon is our sad daydream of ourselves. When we die, preferably at a young age, everyone will say beautiful, poetic things about us at our grave. He's the only man I've ever known to whom it seemed exactly right to send persimmons as a gift."

Simon wore work shoes, heavy twill trousers, gray flannel workshirt and a black beard (Zeke believed Simon took it off before he went to bed); Rachel wore flowing Isadora Duncan dresses, diaphanous, brightly colored scarves and a narrow silk bridle for her breasts. When they entered a room, El Greco Jesus arm-in-arm with wild naiad, everyone stopped what they were doing—which usually meant talking—to stare at them. It wasn't merely their beauty, it was the storybook tragedy which hovered about them. Still they managed to float in on a magical carpet woven from the threads of LIFE.

They were anarchists of the Kropotkin school—"Something like medieval Christians, except we don't believe in God" is how Rachel explained it to Zeke as Simon shook his head and compressed his purple-red (blood circulation poor) lips to indicate compassionate intolerance for her oversimplification.

They were comrades of Bartolomeo Vanzetti, and together with Abe, Viola and most everyone Zeke was to meet in Abe's house had exerted their energies, time, and what little money they had on the Italian anarchist's behalf. They had worked also on Sacco's behalf. Doubt about Nicola Sacco's innocence they expressed only among their most intimate friends, but there was no doubt about the irregularities of the trial and the overt bias of the judge. Zeke, who met Rachel and Simon a few years after the execution of the two anarchists, had himself been taken by his father to many protest demonstrations on behalf of Sacco-Vanzetti.

Simon Farrell earned a poor living as a photographer, was a painter and sculptor, not very good, really quite banal, the critics said. But among his friends he was considered very good. Heroic, they exclaimed, except for Abe, an honest, unromantic man, who said, "Irish schmaltz. His friends are seeing him, not his work." Twenty years after Simon died (which was how long it took Rachel finally to give him up to his grave, having meanwhile bored and not a little angered her second husband, Matthew Cahn, and at least one lover with her interminable reference to her first husband) Rachel told Zeke that Simon had been a fake as an artist. "He knew he was no damn good and didn't really work at his craft, just continued the charade at being an artist because he believed it added to his romantic image. He had to hoard his energy to remain alive. Simon used to say he would screw God by extracting every last grain of life from every last second he lived. Romantic faker though he was, he did." For twenty-nine years, which were twenty-nine years longer than had been promised him.

Zeke Gurevich, a poor boy, soon an orphan, alternated a wild gregariousness with a neurasthenic loneliness, unhappy, ugly, consumed by self-pity and self-hatred. No one loved him, he used to cry to himself, which is why, no doubt, he responded so quickly, if not fatally, to sympathetic women and girls. His friends called him girl crazy. It took him many years to accept it and make the best of it. Before Simon he always stood tonguetied, awed by the black figure of death which seemed to be grinning over Simon's shoulder. Simon, gentle, soon put the boy at his ease. And Zeke came to both love and hate him for his possession of Rachel.

Rachel Mary Conyngham was sent by a friend when she was sixteen to model at a painting class Simon gave in his flat on Commerce Street. They fell in love and began living together and were never formally married. Like many of their friends, they believed in free love and granted each other complete sexual freedom. Simon never took advantage of his freedom (he didn't understand free-

[22]

dom to mean license and neither did he have the strength to exercise it), though the women of their *milieu* weren't wanting in willingness to be a receptacle to his slender grace. Rachel, it was assumed by everyone who knew her, was a fervent believer in the practical and immediate application of freedom. It was the impression she gave: freedom to her meant talking and posturing like a man. Not any man. Don Juan, say. Her face and body were constructed to attract the attention of any fit male—or unfit, for that matter: she moved with an easy, opulent grace, and was not afraid of her emotions or of men. Of course, Zeke Gurevich loved her then and there, and henceforth.

A few years after their first meeting, ten months to the day before FDR was elected president for the first time, Abe told Zeke that Rachel and Simon were going to the Soviet Union. Though they were anarchists and therefore suspicious of the bolshevik *newsociety,* still one must go see for oneself. In his secret self, Simon forgave the *newsociety* its apparent distortions and wanted to touch its sacred earth before he died. If he died there, his desire was to be buried next to Jack Reed, a man whose classic *Ten Days That Shook the World* he admired, and whom he felt he knew since Reed had slept with a Radcliffe girl whose husband-to-be had seduced Rachel when she was thirteen, or so Rachel boasted. No one in his right mind believed Rachel even at thirteen had taken the passive role of seducée. Abe, an unchic man, chided Simon and Rachel about going to the bulwark of the vanguard of the future.

"You ought to know better. It's the counterrevolution. It's the time of the Directorate. Of Thermidor."

They laughed at Abe. "You're a bullshit artist, Abe. When all your friends were against, you were for. Now that most of your friends are for, you're against. Abe Abramson, iconoclast."

Abe laughed. "All right, go. That's the best cure."

Abe told Zeke the Farrells were coming to his place for vaccinations and dinner. Zeke came because he wanted one last look at his phantom sweetheart as he referred to Rachel to himself and had even printed those words in the closed parenthesis of a heart on his white sneakers in India ink. The trip was supposed to be for a year, and to his just-turned-fifteen-year-old brain, a year meant forever. Miserable at her going, he was prepared to betray his impiety and go say a prayer for the dead which he hadn't even said for his father, who had left a letter instructing his family to read *The Communist Manifesto* over his coffin if and when. Zeke vehemently disagreed with Abe, whom he considered a Cossack and aberrant mutation to the family strain, for Zeke believed that anyone who had the good fortune to go to Russia would never return to this crummy bastion of world capitalism.

Rachel appeared in a zebra-striped dress, a silken red scarf flowing about her regal column of a neck, colors clashing like lunatics (she had the world's worst taste, Zeke was to discover traumatically years later), her black hair long and unruly enough to strangle her, smiling that damn intimate smile so that his adolescent penchant for love began immediately to frolic in his first pair of long pants. And she kissed him, too, with moist soft lips, for when she kissed it was for real. He tried in his obsessive, fierce way to stick his tongue down her throat, so that she had to bring up her knee, albeit gently, for when he kissed, it was to kill. She and Simon went into Abe's office for their physicals and Zeke made an abrupt decision to stop playing hooky and go back to school to become a doctor.

There were many friends present at Abe's that night (in

fact, every night): teachers, revolutionists, bohemian artists, real artists, even one good artist, musicians, writers, and one businessman, the pariah. They were crowded into the living room, small, sitting on benches, chairs, the double studio bed which no respectable anti-bourgeois household would be without, and the floor, eating spaghetti and meatballs with hot garlic bread and drinking bootleg booze from a motley collection of glasses. Not Zeke; Abe and Viola watched over him closely, and he drank his usual sarsaparilla. One subject was the topic of discussion all evening. Zeke listened, his mouth wide open, his anger pent. It was a shiny copper and gold gadget which Abe produced for everyone's inspection. It resembled a modernistic wire-sculpted work of an insect, a daddy longlegs: a gold oval body to which were attached two long copper wire antennae, to the ends of which were welded round gold buttonlike eyes. The conversation sped about the room one hundred eighty-six thousand miles per second and was apparently hilarious, since everyone seemed to be in stitches. Zeke understood just enough to learn that the long antennae were supposed to be slipped into Rachel's Irish knish, as he lovingly thought of it, all the way up. (Years later, when he remembered the incident, it seemed to him the antennae had been two feet long, but he was certain his memory exaggerated.) The bug was to act as a permanently inserted birth control device until Rachel and Simon returned from Europe. Zeke looked painfully at Rachel, such a slender thing, and wondered how these long wires could get up into her without stabbing her to death. He held on to his anger as long as he could, then, just a boy, he lost control and began to scream at Abe, "You goddam murdering bastard, what yuh trying to do, kill her?" There was a yelp of laughter and Zeke, giving way to the family failing, began to cry. Rachel had to run from her usual perch on the studio couch, where she always managed an elegant sprawl, a proletarian Empress Theodora, to hug and kiss him until his tears stopped, his large nose, as if by itself, making a sweet riotous probe of her very alive breasts.

He was relieved to learn from Rachel that she had refused to have the gadget inserted against the urging of both Simon and Abe.

"*Nyet*," she exclaimed obstinately, the extent of her Russian after a six-week course, being tone deaf. "If I become pregnant, I'll have an abortion."

"She's had five already," Abe said in disgust, turning to the multitudes for alliance. "She and Simon do it like the beasts in the forest, *au naturel.*"

"There's nothing," Rachel shouted to the masses, her white teeth gleaming, her red scarf flung over her shoulder defiantly, loving the words as she articulated them with her tongue, her eyes on every straining face in the crowd, "there's absolutely nothing I'd rather do than fuck bare."

Thus one era came to a close and another began.

IV

Rachel and Simon Farrell returned from Russia in six months, not a year, Rachel pregnant with Sean. "The Hearst press is terribly inaccurate," Simon said through his black beard, his cheeks thinner than ever, to a roomful of friends at Abe's new place on Washington Square. Then he furtively looked about the room to make certain no capitalists were present, because he wanted to tell the truth which a radical couldn't do in the hearing of the enemy. None present, he continued, "It's even worse than Hearst says. It's a charnel house." Everyone started to yell and argue and a couple of leather-coated ladies began to pull each other's hair.

Zeke paid no attention. Love came first, as it always did with him. He sat alongside Rachel, loving her up with his yellow eyes, his thigh pressing against hers, his right hand round her shoulder and under her scarf, sneakily touching her right breast. She spoke animatedly to some forkfaced dame who was heavily rouged. "It's slavery," Rachel said.

"You and Simon have gone completely crazy."

"Slavery. Workers haven't got the right to strike."

"Why should they strike against themselves?"

"Themselves? The Russian state and party are the largest and harshest monopoly in the world."

It was the first time Zeke had ever touched her breast and he was faint with fear she would discover him and make him stop.

"I have a friend who was there just last month who said the children were the happiest she'd ever seen."

"Of course. Why shouldn't they be? All are encouraged to inform on their parents." She turned on Zeke, "Damn you, I thought you were Simon." Then smiling, "You have his touch—you're going to do all right."

He saw them often at Abe's house, where he lived most of the time, sleeping on the couch in the living room, and they were there nearly every evening. They didn't have a dime. Abe, who had a fine practice now that he and Viola lived in Manhattan, never turned anyone from his door. Poor or rich, whatever he had he felt he must share. Those who mooched the most said he overdid it. "He's paying off his guilt for having money in the bank." Abe also carried the burden of guilt for every patient he couldn't cure, for everyone under his care who died before their time, and for every man, woman, and child who went hungry. A thin man when he first went into practice, now he was a big, fat man who thought he had to be everybody's papa. Many of his friends and most of his relatives—including Zeke—called him a reactionary, a white guardist, and soon, with the change of line, would be calling him a social fascist. It had started when Lenin-Trotsky put down the Kronstadt rebellion with bullets and Abe said, "The counterrevolution has come to power. You'll soon see its ugly face in every aspect of Soviet society: farm, factory, art, music, literature. Permanent terror has replaced permanent revolution. As Napoleon discovered to his advantage, the counterrevolution is able to use the energy of the revolution to make at least an attempt at world conquest."

Though his friends called him a reactionary dog, when they were hungry his was the first door they entered, and without bothering to knock, since knocking was a bourgeois custom. Zeke no less than they. He was already a young communist, but one who reserved his activities to May Day parades and Union Square demonstrations. He had other things on his mind—the most important of which was to stay away from home. He believed he and his mother were incompatible, Rebecca, his sister, impossible.

Simon, on his return from Russia, looked about ready to die, thinner and more haggard than seemed possible for any man to be. Rachel looked poorly herself, thick black rings under her eyes, the blue almost lost in the black, terribly fatigued and pregnant. No abortion this time, it was too late.

Yet both found time for Zeke, nearly sixteen, unhappy, and becoming wilder by the day. The truant officer and he were mortal enemies. He now began to seek out violence, alternating between block gang wars—stockings stuffed with ashes, their weapons—and the most riotous communist demonstrations and strikes. He hated everyone—more accurately, envied everyone their better fortune. His father had left nothing but debts, his mother hardly scraped out a living for herself and Rebecca by selling sour pickles and tomatoes out of a barrel on the street. He was the superfluous mouth to feed; he was the bum in the family— or at least so he thought. If not for Viola, Abe, and the Farrells, he might have become a prize hoodlum. The world, he found, was an abominable hoax and he was against everything in it—including himself. Simon even in his dying had time to stop to talk to him, to ask him questions about himself, to proffer some advice. "Come on, tell me what you want most?"

"I want a gun," Zeke said half seriously.

"Yes, I know you want a gun. I'm a pacifist and I want a gun, too. Once in a while when someone crosses you, you hope he dies, don't you?"

Zeke looked at him scared. "Yeah, how do you know?"

"How do I know? I know. There are times when I feel the same way. Everyone does at one time or another." Zeke was delighted to find himself accompanied by the multitudes. Paradoxically, he at once felt safer in the world and with himself.

"Now tell me what you really want?" Simon asked patiently, with a half smile, sad. What an intense boy. *Farouche* is the word for him. Probably will bite his way through life. "Well?"

"I want somebody to love me very much, somebody who always thinks of me, a girl I can love all I want. Not just to feel up, but inside, like Rachel."

She can use you, too, my little cock. "Is that all you want?" Simon asked, no longer smiling. Sixteen years old and already demands everything. A redheaded challenger. Life, damn you, I want everything. "If that's what you want most you'll have it. I prophesy you'll have it. Now what else do you want? Think deeply."

"A better world," Zeke said off the top of his head, thinking Simon would like to hear it.

"No, no, no. No faking. You want it—everybody wants it. It's the fashion of the time. It's important to know what *you* want. Come on, tell me." Simon kept staring at Zeke hard, a cigarette down to the butt burning his full purpled-red lips, the smoke curling about his beard. What did he want from this boy? To live through him, to get some of his vitality?

"I want to live," Zeke said.

"You want to live, eh? What does that mean? Well?"

"I can't explain it, goddam you, leave me alone. I just want to live."

"Then live, dammit," Simon said bitterly, pulling hard on the boy's red hair. He walked away with a smile, a funny smile, just on one side of his face.

Though Simon took time to notice Zeke and to prod him, still the boy threw himself about wildly, mostly muted, fierce—*farouche*—listening wide-eyed to the talk of his elders—that vociferous, articulate, radical and creative crowd which pressed in and around the Abramsons.

Abe's brother Joshua would come up from Trenton, where their parents lived, the mother being Zeke's mother's sister, the very one who had assisted at his birth. Josh was Zeke's contemporary; he had a large head and a tremendous nose, a shy, lisping kid who always had that behemoth of a beak in a book, almost like a teacher's pointer. Zeke counted himself as handsome alongside Josh but still could hardly stand him, so filled was he with envy at his cousin's good fortune, to have two parents, a few cents in his pocket, so many brothers and sisters (eight) who apparently loved him. Once they played chess and Josh won quickly. Shy as he was, he used a pawn like a cannon. So hateful was Zeke, he picked up a large book from the table—it was *Don Quixote*—and bashed Josh over the head with it, and his cousin fell unconscious.

Fortunately, Abe was in the house and administered to his brother. Josh waited for Abe and his sister, Helen, the one who always gave Zeke quarters, to be angry with his attacker. They weren't. They took Zeke aside and spoke to him quietly, remonstrating with him that he must learn to control his temper. No doubt it was the right approach to Zeke for their gentleness made him feel his guilt deeply; if they had been tough or if Abe had smacked him he would have felt he had broken even. But what about Josh, the injured? What little satisfaction he received. Years later, when he was in training analysis (he became a psychiatrist) he told Zeke he hated the lot of them because they'd never lost their tempers with either of them. "Anger's an important emotion," he said to Zeke, as if the latter didn't know it without being told. "If it's not used on your behalf or even against you when you deserve it by those you love and respect, you begin to feel they don't really give a damn about you. My father, who was the most beloved man in the community," he said sarcastically, "never threw an angry word at me—in fact, he rarely uttered any word to me, I thought he despised me, but that's a different matter. Anger's important. You agree, don't you?"

Because it was obvious to him that Josh desperately needed agreement, Zeke said, "Yes, you're absolutely right." But he thought to himself what was true for him wasn't true for Josh. Josh had needed anger and he had needed gentleness. These were gentle people—only violent about their politics or the comparative quality of painters and writers. Not Rachel. When she heard about Zeke's having bashed Joshua's head, she took him aside and tore hell out of him. "If you're going to be an animal, stay away from me. I detest animals." And, there it was, from her he loved it. From her it was as good as a soul kiss.

Rachel, Rachel. Rachel Mary Conyngham Farrell. Later, Cahn.

She was a cubic yard of contradictions made into a unified whole by the cement of time. She made bricks of them to throw at him and then retrieved the bricks to build a house into which to seduce him.

All contained in a body which never sent the scales over one hundred ten. Too perfectly formed, so symmetrical one didn't believe it except when she was naked, then one saw she had a big brown mole off center at the base of her spine. Years later, many years later, it was to grow and metastasize and kill her. Many years later. One also saw when she was naked that her left breast was noticeably

[32]

larger than her right, and she had a very classy, grassy plot. What made her believable was her poor taste in clothes, save for her shoes which were always in elegant taste and about which she was a fetishist. She had superb ankles. In the late twenties and early thirties when bohemia demanded sandals, she refused to wear them. She loved elegantly turned high heels. Her dresses were either too florid or too frumpish, never right somehow, excepting they always had a loose bodice so that when she leaned over one could see her breasts. They were of the round type, not pearlike. She was the despair of her friends, female, who constantly admonished her to buy simply cut dresses or suits, for her body was its own adornment. She was a fancy piece. She never listened of course because she believed her taste unerring—a result no doubt of osmosis since Simon was a man of fine esthetic taste and how many of her lovers? Zeke was certain she never listened to anyone in her life about anything, though she pretended she did to Matt, her second husband. She just didn't care about clothes because she didn't believe in them. "Clothes are anti-freedom," she said. "You should always be ready for a little fun." She smiled that broad, white, intimate smile. Posing. Perhaps she came to this attitude by way of her earning power as a nude model for artists whenever she and Simon, and later Matt, had nothing to eat, though she never quite believed in economic determinism. She was a woman of the future, a free woman, and tried to talk like a man. With an ass like that, Zeke would smile, and a pair of knockers which can strike a man blind.

When a man looked at her he realized immediately how thirsty he was. My, how he wanted to get under that arch. When he went to drink from her, he found she wasn't a public fountain. "A little thirst's good for you, my arrogant friend," she'd laugh. "Just because I believe in sexual freedom doesn't mean I have to sleep with men I don't desire. What makes you think you're so hot?"

When Zeke was a boy and would meet her and Simon at Abe's house, he thought she slept with every man she smiled at or modeled for, and he would get a stomach cramp from jealousy. She had a habit when speaking with a man to poke his arm with her index finger whenever she made a point. "You see what I mean?" It drove Zeke crazy, this constant touching of another man, and he would find a way to wedge himself between her and her adversary until she noticed and stopped. She would kiss his forehead, smile gently, and resume her discussion with her arm round him, and he would close his eyes and forgive her anything. The year they returned from Europe, Abe and Viola gave a New Year's Eve party and Zeke caught Rachel in an embrace with a strange man in the kitchen. He became so infuriated he grabbed a knife off the table. Fortunately, the man, Leo Norton, was the wiliest street fighter in the trade union movement in New York and had no difficulty disarming him. Zeke called Rachel a Gentile whore. This time Abe whacked him and Rachel refused to speak to him for weeks. It was the *Gentile* which upset everyone the most, that someone brought up among them should show this vestigial prejudice. Simon spoke to him for hours and he later apologized to all of them, Gentile and Jew alike. Years later Zeke discovered that during Rachel's life with Simon Farrell she had slept with no man but her husband, with one exception—Abe, the night after his first wife died. The Farrells slept in the room adjoining Abe's the night after the funeral and they could hear Abe's grief through the walls. Rachel told Simon she must go to Abe to comfort him. Simon didn't demur and she went. Abe was in his bed beating his head with his fists. She took him in her arms and let him cry on her breast, hugging his big head to her until they both fell asleep. During the night sometime the most natural thing in the world happened. None of them were ever ashamed.

About a year after their return to New York, Simon became very ill and some doctor advised it might be best for him to live in Arizona. Abe disagreed, but since nothing he did for Simon helped, he said they might as well go and try it. So Rachel packed their valises, placed the baby, Sean, with her mother (it was to be the first of many times that Rachel was to put Sean aside as though he were a doll) and took her husband to Phoenix.

Before they left, Abe and Viola made a birthday party for Zeke—he was seventeen—and at the same time a going-away party for the Farrells. Viola, who was as thin as Abe was fat and as silent as he was vociferous, finally won a battle and no one else was invited. Abe and Viola now had two children, a boy and a girl, with whom Zeke played before they were put to bed. Then the five of them plus a couple of uninvited guests, Joe Gaines, short, stocky, blond, with an ageless broad face, who smoked long Russian cigarettes and sported *pince-nez* glasses in the style of a Russian *intelligent,* and who was a Trotskyite from the West Coast (Zeke considered him a treacherous fiend), and Alonzo Truesdale, a scrawny, bowlegged Negro, with thin lips and a smashed nose, a poet and comrade whom Zeke worshipped for no other reason but that his skin was black (in those days Zeke would have given an arm to exchange his white for Alonzo's black), sat down to a huge steak, Italian red, ice cream, and strawberries. After they put it all away, big, fat Abe and Zeke, to everyone's amusement, shared a long salami. That's the way they ate in Abe's house—Abe and Zeke, anyway. On Abe it showed. Zeke—he was as thin as a nail.

As soon as they were seated they became involved in a passionate political argument about Franklin Delano Roosevelt, then in his first term. Everyone spoke up in Abe's house—loud and clear. No one pleaded the Fifth Amendment—or the First for that matter. You believed in something, you shouted it so that the shiny instruments in the glass cabinet in the next room rattled on the shelves. Each would have been proud to stand on the dock so that he could enunciate in clear, loud tones exactly what it was he believed in. For one brief moment Joe Gaines and Alonzo Truesdale agreed with one another: Roosevelt, they said, was a social fascist. Abe began to yell at both for using that term too freely, intimating neither knew precisely what it meant anyway. But the Stalin-Trotsky alliance didn't last long because somewhere along the line Gaines referred to Stalin as a mediocrity and a mean imitation of Napoleon Bonaparte, and Alonzo called Joe a Judas pig. If Alonzo had been a white man, Joe would have slugged him, Russian *intelligent* pose or not, but he responded in a quiet, patronizing tone, which made Alonzo even angrier and he called the Trotskyite a paternalistic chauvinist, the supreme epithet. Simon, despite the haggard fatigue of the ambulatory sick, was biting his lips to keep from laughing at both of them, and finally caught Alonzo's eye and asked him to recite some of his poetry. Zeke paid little attention, his yellow eyes constantly on Rachel. All were aware of his infatuation, it was stale cake in that house, and no one noticed. He was no longer a little boy, and the age difference between Rachel and him had of course narrowed. He didn't want Simon to die, but he was aware of the imminence of his death and he had to admit

[36]

to a sneaky feeling of impatience. He caught himself thinking about it too frequently. Let's get it over with. Rachel was only twenty-two and she and he could have a whole life together. He for one was never going to die. And though for a couple of years now he'd been running around with his friend Irving Green (a name which was always to bring back golden memories) deflowering Second Avenue from First Street to Fourteenth, Rachel was the dandelion he most wanted to crush.

Truesdale said a few poems, very sentimental stuff about the incorruptible working class, a large section of which was at that precise moment clasping Adolph Hitler to its collective bosom, and one poem about his wonderful girl comrades in their shiny leather jackets (soon to be discarded) and gleaming black and white faces on the picket line. His sentimentality puzzled Zeke because he had once been witness to Alonzo's cruelty. As Zeke grew older he learned—mostly from himself—that sentimentality and cruelty were frequently intimates. Alonzo once brought a girl to Abe's house for a party, then ignored her while he flirted with every woman there. The girl, a shy little Negro with tremendous eyes, was named Clara and this was the first time in her life that she was a guest in a white family's home. Everyone was extravagantly *nice* to her and she wore one of those terribly fatiguing manufactured smiles. Clara tried at one point to recapture Alonzo's attention and he became enraged. In front of the entire crowd (they all pretended they didn't notice, it wasn't even happening, the ceiling and the walls were their primary interest), he took Clara by her thin shoulders and shook her violently. Then he told her to go back to niggertown where she belonged. The girl left in tears and no one admonished Alonzo for his cruelty. Alonzo became a wino, but managed to sober up long enough a few years later, in 1937, to join the International Brigades south of Madrid. On the first day of battle, he grabbed his gun which he had never shot and ran ahead of the entire battalion to within twenty yards of the fascist trenches and was killed. The commissars and many of his comrades called him a hero, but a few of his comrades believed he had committed suicide.

After Alonzo finished saying his poems and was honored with great exaggeration, Abe and Viola gave Zeke his first wristwatch and Rachel and Simon gave him his first book of verse, from which Simon read at random in his deep basso:

" 'Life of life! thy lips enkindle/With their love the breath between them/And thy smiles before they dwindle/Make the cold air fire. . . .' Or 'My soul is an enchanted boat/Which, like a sleeping swan, doth float/Upon the silver waves of thy sweet singing. . . .' Or 'I weep for Andonais—he is dead!' "

And Rachel leaned over and whispered in Zeke's ear so that he got goose bumps, "Shelley was an anarchist comrade, you know."

They drank to one another's health and Rachel said it was time for them to go. She meant it was time to get Simon to bed. He had to remain in bed about fifteen hours a day now and lived under an austere regimen which Rachel supervised with pretended strictness. "What makes the difference?" she asked Abe. And Abe said he didn't know what made the difference. It was all over but the dying.

She rose to go into the bedroom for their coats and Zeke followed her. As she put on her coat, he saw how tired and unhappy she looked. He squared his shoulders and said heroically, "If you need any help out in Phoenix, let me know, I'll come on the run all the way."

She fluffed her hair out over her coat collar, examining him harshly through the mirror of the bureau with her blue-black eyes. "Of course, it couldn't be anyone else," she said kindly. He's waiting for Simon to die, but we all are, aren't we? What an urgent boy; a root trying to break through the hard ground. Abe's kin, the immortal kind. She saw the boy was overcome with love for her and sort of expected what was coming when she turned from the mirror. He took her in his arms and kissed her roughly, aggressively, the way a boy would, and she didn't fight it. When she thought he'd had enough, she began to break away and found she didn't want to, he wasn't a boy at all, he was a man, with a man's wonderful hardness and Simon had been too ill now for about a year to sleep with her, and she was overcome with weakness at the knees and allowed herself to fall hard against him. They kissed deeply, with great feeling. As his hand began to grope, she pushed him away. She stared at him with her cavernous eyes, almost in surprise, and he stared at her with an abrupt, newfound shyness—something had changed. "You're a man," she said softly, caught up with a start at how quickly the years were flying and how deeply she felt for him.

"I love you," he said.

"Yes," she answered. "I know," and left the room.

V

Several months later Zeke decided to go off with his friend
Irving Green to the Newday Co-operative Farm in Michigan founded by a group of anarchists—respectable family
folk who wanted to escape the Depression by constructing
a collective community for themselves and their children
out of the hopes of their utopian daydreams.

Irving he met through Eva Green.

One harsh fall day a few years earlier, shortly after
Rachel and Simon had gone to Russia, Zeke came away
from a broken picket line at one of the laundry plants
downtown extremely hungry. The leader of the strike had
shackled herself to the front gate of the plant and Zeke
and several comrades had ringed her to thwart any police
attempt to cut her loose with a hacksaw. A tough female
Spartacus, she used hysteria as a weapon and had her
praetorian guard and the striking proles jumping about
her like a riot of lean wolverines. They gave the cops an
extremely difficult time that day, but in the end the cops
had to win since Zeke and his comrades weren't prepared
to haul out the red flag and proclaim the city captured by
the provisional committee of revolutionary workers and
peasants. Though if the youthful Zeke had been asked, he
would have said, "Let's."

The cops finally broke through Bessy Dufarge's centur-
ians. Her name was one she chose for herself, a true con-
spiratorial revolutionary. Zeke was fortunate enough to

come away unhurt, though he did almost tear a cop's ear off. Two cops held Bessy while another sawed away. Just to show their contempt, each cop held one of her breasts (which were matters of substance), squeezing so hard she almost bled milk. Very cruelly. The laundry workers when they worked put in sixty, seventy hours a week for about seventeen cents an hour; Zeke, a strong fifteen-year-old, had just quit a job where he had worked seventy-five hours for nine dollars throwing fifty-pound lime sacks around; for overtime his boss had bought him a sandwich and a Coke. Times were cruel, Bessy was cruel, the cops were cruel. Abe said no man need be cruel if he didn't want to. Zeke wondered.

After the cops broke it up, Zeke loped off by himself, hungry and tired. He was on lower Second Avenue, passing a Bohack's which hadn't yet taken its fruits and vegetables in off the street. As he swung past the fruit stand his eyes were captured—and captivated—by a still life of pomegranates on top of a basket of oranges and he almost fainted with boyish delight at the sight. He was immediately obsessed. His salivary gland salivated, his stomach yearned, and his hands instinctively curled into a clutch. He simply must have, hold, and eat one of those dull-shiny red pomegranates. And he didn't have a cent. Since he was a youth of quick decision, he leaned over the orange basket and with lightning speed lifted just one dull-shiny red pomegranate from the bevy of beautiful, thick-skinned navel oranges. Then whirled, he fancied himself a great brokenfield runner in the style of Albie Booth of Yale, and ran smash into the biggest *Poljań* this side of Chicago. The Pole held him by his pants—and he was no little boy, he was six feet tall, everyone believed he was going to be a giant; they jinxed him, for he didn't grow another inch the rest of his life—but the Pole held him by his pants in a grip of iron. "Y'goddamn bum, can't leave piece fruit outside y'don't steal," all in a voice so loud and so proximate to Zeke's eardrums his head blew up like a brown paper bag. Pow.

Caught, too tired after the day's battling over Bessy Dufarge, Zeke was ready to accept hanging as his lot. When out of the store barged the grandest lady he'd ever seen, six feet tall, two hundred pounds and a face so red she must have had a tourniquet twisted round her neck. She stepped up close, and addressing first Zeke and then his captor, she roared, "Whazimadda, Jakie?" which of course was not his name, "Liv my Jakie alone, I tole him buy fruit while I chopped in your lousy staw. How much?" The Pole glommed Zeke, glimmed her, let go.

"Five cents."

She paid and they left, the pomegranate clutched in one of the boy's claws, her package in the other.

"Thanks, missus. You're a lady."

"Kerry peckedge upstez gib yuh kop kawfee."

"Thanks, lady, but—"

"Upstez, pliz. Mahch."

On Second Avenue, near Eighth Street, they marched upstairs. The place smelled of chopped herring and apples.

That's how he met Eva Green, or Chava as she was called.

She was a six-footer all right, two hundred pounds of massive hips and breasts like Niagara, overflowing with a crash. Her red face was pockmarked, her nose like a pitted lump of clay stuck into the middle of her head by a child's hand.

Chava had been born in some little Ukrainian village of Jewish father and mother—peasants—in the 1880's. Time not exact. There weren't many Jewish peasants in the

[42]

Ukraine—or anywhere else for that matter—so Eva had a headstart in eccentricity. A brawny girl, and not dumb either, she enjoyed her girlhood, her only problem the paucity of young men big enough or brave enough.

One day.

A Turk—an aristocrat, or so he said—who had exiled himself from the anger of some reigning pasha, no one knew why, appeared in Eva's village—a big, heavy-muscled man, with bone joints like bowling balls.

They were married—or so she told Zeke over kop kawfee the very same day she rescued him. But it didn't really matter to Zeke, since he'd been around the radical crowd and wasn't tied to the silly convention of making love into an institution, all brick and shiny utensils but no heart.

Eva had two children with the Turk, Irving and a daughter named Bosporus, as sweet a brown licorice stick as one could buy off a pushcart near any school.

World War I—and Eva's Ottoman disappeared. Either the anger of the pasha had subsided or he wanted to avoid the Czar's army. Perhaps he was a patriot, since he claimed to be an aristocrat, and it's widely known aristocrats are absurdly patriotic. So Eva, in bad straits, but full of life, picked up her skirts and Bosporus and left for America. Irving would be sent for.

She duly arrived in Castle Garden, thence to a flat on Second Avenue, down near the cabarets filled with exiles from the Hapsburg empire and Yiddish theatres filled with exiles from pogroms. There she lived a good life, with one headwaiter after another. Only headwaiters—Chava was no fool. Eventually of course there was only one. Kalmon Yentz was his name—an invention, he cried when razzed by his colleagues, of some idiot immigration official. When Zeke met her she already lived with Yentz, at the time headwaiter of the Roumanian Eden, a man half her height but just as round. In the predawn mist, rolling home from the cabaret, he could be mistaken for a wine barrel, spout and all. He loved sweet Tokay.

Irving remained in the Ukraine through the war with his maternal grandfather. He was a lanky boy, with a beak like Saladin's. Fierce. His hair was the color of straw, and why it was, with a mother and father whose hair was black as pitch, no one ever dared ask. Boy and man, he was always hungry, and as obsessive as Zeke. But where Zeke was bold, Irving was shy. Where Zeke was, to be polite, an exaggerator, Irving was as precise and honest as the guards at Fort Knox better be. A big schklump of a kid. Yet a mule.

The revolution.

His village bounced back and forth over the taut net of history like a pingpong ball, from red to white to red to white, life just as precarious under hobbled boots; so the grandfather, a thin knife of a man, loaded a wagon with their bedding, sat himself atop a huge goosefeather pillow, eight-year-old Irving atop another, whipped the skinny nag and off they rumbled for Poland and the Baltic through alternating red and white lines.

They made it to Warsaw, where the old man pulled on his ear lobe, took a sniff of *tabac,* wrapped his phylacteries around his arms and head, said the evening prayer, and died. Irving was on his own in the middle of history. Even then he showed what was to be a lifelong trait—mulishness. Refused to steal. "I'm an honest man," he used to say. "My people before me were honest men. My children will be honest men. And their children too. History will flow. Revolutions, wars, tyrants will come and go. But we'll be honest men." So he refused to steal. Lucky for him he showed some brains. He lived off the kind raggedness of the *shamis* of an old *shul* in the Warsaw ghetto.

When the old *shamis* didn't have enough, Irving searched out some Turks, gave his Turkish name, Ibn Khaldoun (his father loved history books) and lived off them, hoarding the extras to give to the *shul*.

In a short time Irving received steerage money from Eva who had already established herself with Yentz who made a good living stealing from waiters and busboys.

Irving was immense at the shoulders, heavy-boned and long-muscled, with a big jaw and a terrifying nose. A real nose—no dainty nonentity of a nose for him. Curved like a hookah. A scimitar. Zeke was slightly shorter than his friend, less broad and thick in the chest, except in nose where Zeke was just as big though not as fierce—big as a summer squash. Which of course was an irony. Irving looked like a Mameluke who'd just freed himself and was about ready to put the world to rack; Zeke looked like a bignosed, redheaded medieval troubadour, skinny, ragged and hungry.

Irving was going to Cooper Union, majoring in civil engineering, and working at night as a busboy in the Roumanian Eden. Yentz, though a thief, was a good man. "Here, Oiving, from you I can't steal." On the side, for book money, Irving ran errands for a florist. One day shortly after Zeke met him, Irving made a delivery of a dozen American Beauty roses to a sleek Hungarian housewife who lived near St. Mark's Church. Fell in love, the fool. Obsessed. Her husband left for work at 3 p.m., Irving Green *né* Ibn Kaldoun appeared at 3:10. He loved her till one day he got to chatting with the butcher boy down the block. Poor Irving. Found out his mistress loved the butcher boy for meat, the baker's boy for bread—didn't miss a trade.

Irving gave her up—an idealistic youth, a fool. Thereafter Zeke delivered roses to St. Mark's Place.

They became friends, Irving and Zeke, it was immediately after Zeke gave up pomegranates and went in for kumquats and Irving gave up pistachio nuts for Charlotte Russes. Though the Hungarian lady was joyous, it was Eva Green whom Zeke loved—straight, like a mother. He now had three homes—one of which he rarely entered, his own. He sent a few dollars home when he could, sometimes would wait in the street among the pushcarts to intercept his sister Rebecca, hatefully watching her walk down the street like Katherine Cornell making an elegant entrance and wanting to sneak up on her and kick her hard in the pants. Good space between them, communicating with stone-edged words, he would make inquiry after his mother, she would stare down her splendid Canaanite nose at him, declaim a few cold pearllike words, and that would be it. Then he would stare after her, confused and flustered and confounded by a burning passion, that was his sister Becky, dammit, he loved her and he hated her and his mother as well. Terrified, burning and freezing almost simultaneously as one with an exotic grippe, he would begin to run at full speed through the city streets, avoiding people like a halfback on a tear, until tired and empty he would enter Abe's house and cavort about with their growing children until Viola would have to ask him to stop in her quiet voice.

It was at Viola's or at Eva's that he lived. Eva urged him to go home. In her Odessan Yiddish she would say, "What are you, a wanderer? An outcast? When men hate their own, they hate themselves. Look upon my Irving. Perhaps he should hate his father who forsook him. But no. I have taught him that life is strange and the most important element of life is living. His father came, made no promises, gave life and much pleasure and then left, may the devil tear him to shreds. But what has Irving to com-

[46]

plain? Look at him. A giant. A warrior. His father gave him strength. I gave him blood like an ancient wine pressed by God's own hand. And you, too. *Ein held.* Go home and laugh at your mother's ways." Thus, she urged, but after a while gave up. In her Second Avenue English, with a dancing, bosom-shaking shrug, she said, "Awkay. Life's shawt, vy egrivate it. Live a lot, kip it hot." Another time, philosophically, "For a woman it's not nice to sleep with more than one man at a time, but if I were a man I'd sleep with every woman in the world. *Trenn un trenn,* boys." Screw and screw.

Irving and Zeke took her advice—to the very best of their abilities.

It was Depression time, FDR was a prestidigitator who sort of made one forget one's hunger in the excitement of his *legerdemain.* Irving went to college winter and summer, worked when he could; Zeke confounded the truant officers, took out his working papers and worked when and where he could find it. In between they paraded in hunger marches, demonstrated on squares, picketed, yelled themselves red, red, red in the face. They enjoyed an intimate fraternity which actual brothers rarely have, each swiping from the other what he himself lacked. The older boy enjoyed the stolen glory of the younger's precocity and wildness, the younger that of the scholastic brilliance and seriousness of the older. It was the usual intimacy of young men. Amazing how often they were infatuated with the very same girl.

One day Irving phoned Zeke. "Chava's sick." She'd had gall bladder trouble for years, but had refused to permit the probing of her flesh by anything as cold and as unfeeling as a scalpel. Now she was dying.

They stood before her in the Bellevue ward, the ceiling peeling dirty paint, the curtains drawn round her bed, and they cried bitter tears. Their hearts were laden with the ashes of grief, yet they sneered at the gods for beckoning one like Eva Green when there were so many deadheads walking the goddam streets. Eva, atop her bed like a huge white-sheeted volcano, squinted at them through her flaming green eyes. Then like an eruption she roared, "Tonight I paiger (croak) and you should take my Irving out and dance and sleep with girls the whole night through. Live, my children," she roared. "Make of each day a joyous feast." Irving and Zeke, they laughed and they cried and they hugged and they kissed her.

She died.

They didn't dance and they didn't sleep with girls. They cried, Bosporus with them—and Kalmon Yentz too. "Where? Where will I find a woman like Chava?" he screamed, tears like sweet Tokay pouring from his little fat eyes, the barrel shrinking before them. They kept the death vigil, burned candles, and buried her the next day.

Before the coffin was lowered, Irving demanded they raise the lid. It was a pine box and she was wrapped in a shroud. No paint on her face. Plain as she died. Her clay-pitted nose was now stone—her rich full mouth cold. His sister's hand in his, Irving and she bent over the open coffin and kissed Chava Green full on her lips.

Zeke Gurevich could do no less.

A month after Chava died, Irving was graduated from Cooper Union *cum laude* in civil engineering. Bosporus and Zeke attended the exercises, but Kalmon wouldn't come. Since Chava's death the old man had shrunk to nothing. The skin hung from his little body and what had been a round button nose had become long and thin, the way a man's nose becomes when his face begins to shrink. He was always crying and from his nose dripped a pelucid tear. From sweet Tokay he turned to Old Overholt. During her life, Eva Green's energy had been enough for the two of them and he'd waxed fat from her burning candle. Now the world was an empty barrel, he even lost the will to steal. He went on like this for a few years. One day he turned up with a Roumanian woman who looked like a gypsy, a vibrant violin of a woman, and in no time at all Kalmon Yentz was his old rotund self. His instinct for women was of the most discerning, Zeke and Irving were to conclude, and proved to be fabulously self-preserving.

After the graduation exercises, the three of them went to the Café Royale for slivovitz and coffee. Bosporus was in Irving's image, tall, big-boned, yet slender and with a magnificently fierce nose. The only difference was her darkness as opposed to his fairness. Why? one asked. Ask God, another answered. As they sat around sipping brandy and coffee, she and Zeke stared at Irving, waiting for him to say something profound, after all, *he* had just been graduated *cum laude* and *they* were both incorrigible truants. He smiled diffidently under that huge scimitar, those terribly honest eyes embarrassed by his new position in life. "Mom should have been here today," he said and they agreed, bitter tears welling in their eyes, her death still a fresh wound. Then with a start he squared those great shoulders as if he wished to say, I'm an adult now, no more of this nonsense. And Bosporus and Zeke sat at the edge of their wire chairs, her fierce hookah and his summer squash displacing big chunks of expectant and respectful air. "Bosporus," Irving finally said sternly, blushing, "your stomach looks like you've swallowed a canteloupe whole. What gives?"

Startled, Zeke examined her, seeing for the first time what should have been obvious for a good month. She blushed, though her hookah shone like pale ivory. She essayed a little grin. "Yes. I'm carrying Sam's child."

Though Zeke's given name was Samuel, no one ever called him Sam. But Irving didn't wait. He leaned over the marble-topped table and clouted Zeke with one of his cleavers. Bosporus screamed and Zeke just stared stupefied from his seat on the floor. "Not that kid, you big dope. Sam Berger."

Irving apologized, helped Zeke to his feet. Seated quietly again, Irving, the head of their family of two, soon three, attempted a stern, patriarchal mien, and for a moment Zeke was afraid he was going to be his mulish foolish self. But Irving had enough Eva Green in him to smile, the scimitar flashing like a polished samovar. "*Nu,*" he said in his mother's diction. "You feasted? Now suffer. You want or you want not to get married?"

The three of them laughed so hard, taking in such great goblets of Café Royale air, that soon they were hiccoughing like a family of frogs. Then they had to scare the hiccoughs away by telling ghost stories because that's the best way to rid oneself of hiccoughs, or at least that's what Maurice Schwartz, starring in *Brothers Ashkenazi* across the street, told them with an urbane smile.

Bosporus, a curved strait, desired marriage. Sam Berger, broad-beamed and short-armed, a dreamer, wasn't sure, he was just getting started in the butcher trade, "Who knows how long it will take to build the business?" but Irving and Zeke convinced him it wouldn't take too long. Since Sam loved Bosporus, an exceedingly sweet licorice stick, he wasn't too difficult to convince. The lovers were married at City Hall by a bespectacled clerk in shiny serge trousers and for their honeymoon went off to Atlantic City where it was they had conceived their baby in the first instant. Atlantic City is of course most famous for its cherrysmashing industry. A billion dollar business on the Million Dollar Pier.

They went off and Irving and Zeke went to a party on Avenue C. A great party, very successful—the hollering could be heard in Gramercy Park. Aside from the political in-fighting, of which *ad nauseum*, there was Lindy Hopping, hootch, and a regiment of red-kepied fornication on the roof. And Irving met a girl named Volya, a Russian girl who'd been educated in England. She was in Chava Green's proportions—50–10–50—and had a belly like a Turkish dancer. Looking at her, a man's mouth watered, his knees trembled, and everything in between howled for attention.

"She smells like a flower—like Turkish halvah," Zeke said to Irving, edging closer.

"A knish," Irving said shyly, shouldering Zeke aside, his scimitar honed to a fine sharpness. "Like ma."

"You're an obstinate fool. Like halvah, she smells."

"A knish," Irving roared, his oedipal showing, the scimitar unsheathed, swinging wildly, "a sweet *zaftig* knish. Like Chava Green. The kind you can smell ten blocks away."

It proved to be true.

One day after work, Irving went to Brooklyn to a colleague's house for supper. Volya and Zeke were to pick him up in an old hand-me-down car which belonged to Rachel via Abe and which she used for chauffering sick Simon about. This was before they went off to Phoenix. When Volya and Zeke got to Avenue Y, Brooklyn, he asked her for the address. She didn't have it—didn't even know the man's name. Zeke became so angry he couldn't look at her. In fact he had to park the car for fear he would ram it against a fire plug just to injure her, and he was too young to even have a driver's license.

She began to laugh, and as she laughed those fifties boiled over until he thought he'd drown.

"Go ahead, laugh—you—you Turkish delight."

"He always says he can smell me even if he cahn't see me," she said with a vain little smile, the fifties subsiding.

"We shall soon see."

Out she stepped, revealing a monumentally delectable thigh, into the middle of the street. The wind must have been with her, for in a few seconds there was Irving being led by his nose.

So Chava Green's blood multiplied. Bosporus stashed away with child, Irving Green married Volya Tamarovna, an aggressive, loud-laughing, passionate-looking wench from Moskva. They moved into a three-room apartment in the Bronx, near Fordham Road. Soon Zeke had to move in to help pay the rent. In that foreign land. Irving's job as an engineer paid just enough to starve and yet live. Zeke's paid less, but he needed less, he was only one. Eleven dollars a week he earned for pushing a handtruck in the silk market off Seventh Avenue. He slept on the couch in the living room.

Immediately he found Irving had his troubles. Built like a Turkish passion flower, Volya was as cold as iced herring. Late at night he would hear them in the next room, Irving pleading, begging, demanding, threatening, and Volya's bell-like answer, clang, "Irving, all you think about is sex."

"What should I think about?" he'd yell. "Calculus?" Then Zeke would hear him pounding on the walls with his great fists. No patience, Zeke would think. What a fool, that's no way to thaw out a broad.

For a while Zeke thought it important enough to ask his current girl friend to seduce Irving, he needed it so bad, and his girl friend who went to Sarah Lawrence became angry and said in a very cold voice, "Whom do you love, him or me?" and Zeke had to answer, "Stop taking Freud so seriously, you'll take all the joy out of life." But it couldn't have been as bad as it sounded for in a few months Volya's belly became big and hard. And those fifties. Man!

The baby duly arrived—a girl, eleven pounds six ounces. Jennifer, Irving named her; for short, Jennitl. The flat became jammed for space and Zeke removed. But he came often, bringing big brown paper bags full of food. Zeke didn't have to pay rent, he slept at Abe's, or at Rachel's on the floor of the Farrell one-roomer, happy to snatch a glance of Rachel in her nightgown and to see Simon and to talk with him. Simon was a skeleton, beginning that last illness during which they were to decide to send him to Phoenix, perhaps a change of climate would help. Not having to pay rent, Zeke had money for groceries for the Greens and himself. With girls he went out Dutch treat. Most of them were comrades, if not by party card then in spirit, and Dutch treat was in the spirit of the time. He loved Irving and his baby and Volya too, because like Chava Green she could never turn a hungry man from her door. In fact, after the birth of Jennitl, she became very passionate and blossomed to 60–20–60. As for Irving, he walked around vulnerable to the world, shy, gentle, a believer in truth. They shared crumbs together those few years and didn't mind being with each other even when they bored one another; neither felt the need to talk just to prove how clever he was. Still, when they fought, it would be a brawl. Irving began to doubt the validity of the dictatorship of the proletariat, began to debunk its sacredness. "Dictatorship *over* the proletariat," he yelled. It seemed impossible for either of them to talk without yelling.

"Aa, you're too pure."

"Why do I stand for you? You're still an amoral child."

"Don't start pulling age on me, Iron Ass."

So they would argue, and when they argued they fought—lips curled, hands fisted, blood flowed. Then they would break out a bottle of seltzer and drink to freedom of speech.

One Saturday night, several months after Rachel and Simon left for the West, Zeke rolled into Irving's flat after a date with a rich high-school girl from the Grand Concourse. Her father earned seventy dollars a week and she thought she owned the world. "No," she said. "Not until we're married."

"Married?" he said, sliding from the couch and zipping his fly. "I wouldn't marry a girl who said that if her box was gold-plated and lined with mink."

A few minutes later he was banging on Irving's door.

"What the?" the Turk yawned.

"Your fillings are blinding," Zeke said. "Go back to bed. I'll get a blanket and sleep on the kitchen floor."

"Keep your voice low," Irving whispered, "you'll wake Jennitl."

"Then shut up, you're whispering loud enough to wake Edgar Allan Poe up the block."

"Mice in the kitchen," Irving said, scratching his blond Ottoman crotch.

"I'll sleep on the table."

"Naaa," Irving yawned. "Aaa, come on, sleep with Volya and me."

"Okay. Let's go, I'm bushed."

Zeke undressed in the kitchen and went with Irving into the bedroom. They tried to shove Volya over so Irving could sleep in the middle; she wouldn't budge, those sixties like sacks of sand.

"Screw her," Irving said, climbing in on one side, Zeke on the other.

"Not me. She has trouble taking one man, how's she gonna take two?"

"Don't get nasty, she's my wife. And, besides—"

"Yeah, she's become a hot knish," Zeke cut him short and fell asleep.

Not too bad a night, though Volya slept on her back and snored like a shuttle. Zeke made himself as thin as a straw as far away from her as he could get without falling off the bed. Even then he slept all right. In those days he could sleep at the edge of a precipice.

It was a hot May day, and the sun, when it peeked through the window, touched his lids and woke him without opening his eyes. He lay under the sun, half awake, sort of wondering where he was. Pleasant—all quiet—even the Bronx cats in the alley asleep in the sun. Once he tried to open his eyes but the sun beamed too sharp. Ah, he sighed, relaxed a bit more. What a good pillow it was. He rubbed with his cheek—no hurry—Sunday—plenty of time. Rubbed with his nose—ah, it smelled sweet—just like a fat fig. Still half asleep, he turned his head to take a soft nip, and heard a sigh like a whisper far away. Sweet it was on his tongue, like halvah. HALVAH!

He opened his eyes in a squint—opened them wide. There was Irving six inches away—biting the twin of the one he'd just nipped. Irving turned and there they were: scimitar to summer squash.

And Volya asleep on her back sighed with delight.

Zeke released what he'd filched, began to slip from the bed like a thief, when Irving let go what he'd bit and made a grab at his throttle. "SKUNK! TRAITOR! She's *my* wife!"

He missed and Zeke ran. Into the kitchen they raced—round and round the table in the center of the room, their naked bodies flashing with sweat in the Bronx sun. Zeke was faster than Irving, but the big fool wasn't dumb; he braked at the icebox, shoved in his big paw and withdrew it clutching the neck of a seltzer bottle.

With cruel deliberate aim he nailed Zeke to the wall with an ice-cold squirt until the traducer dropped to the floor, squealing and laughing like a six-year-old, the cuckold roaring curse words in polyglot Russian, Turkish, Anglo-Saxon and Yiddish.

Then they dressed and Irving fried them half-a-dozen English kippers. It was Irving's English year. Ibn Khaldoun: Anglophile. Loved the English so much he cultivated an Oxford *a*—with a Ukrainian drawl. A few months before, Zeke had played a dirty trick on him. For his birthday—a big party—he bought Irving a veddy nice umbrella.

"Made in London," Zeke said in front of everyone.

"Could tell imme-jitly," Irving said very loudly, showing it off to the guests.

"Yes," Zeke continued, playing the crowd. "*New* London, Connecticut."

Irving didn't talk to his friend for a month. Just sent anonymous letters—drawings they were. A scimitar dripping blood.

That morning Irving fried English kippers and Zeke made hot coffee in a pan, not forgetting the egg shells to give it that wonderful Sunday morning flavor. They ate English kippers, a dozen Jewish rolls and two-and-a-half cups of Brazilian coffee apiece. As Zeke prepared Jennitl's bottle, Irving hard-boiled two eggs, grabbed a sweetcorn out of the vegetable bin, put the hard eggs and the cob on a plate, wrote a note, "Enjoy yourself, Temple Drake," and placed the plate and note on the bed table for Volya to chuckle over when she awoke.

They left the house and walked across the west Bronx

[56]

to the New York University campus not saying a word all the way. Though they did stop once at a candy store for Zeke to buy a piece of halvah. Irving grinned, the fool.

Once at the rotunda with its bronze busts of famous men, they examined carefully the wrought image of each and decided none of them could have had the fun they'd had that morning. By acclamation they elected each other to the Hall of Fame.

A week later, they threw up their jobs, and the three of them—and Jennitl—went to the Newday Co-operative Farm, a utopian refuge from the Depression of the 'Thirties.

VI

With hope.

Zeke Gurevich and Irving Green and family went to Newday with hope that if they worked they would eat, which is usually so on a farm. But that was not the sole reason they went to Newday. They went because they had ideals. If there is enough to eat, then greed can be eliminated. Eliminate greed and soon selfishness, dishonesty, injustice, arrogance, dominion of the weak by the strong, will also be eliminated. Jennitl and her future brothers and sisters will live in a beautiful, serene world. Zeke will find a wife, have children, they also will live in a new and beautiful world.

In the beginning it *was* beautiful. Newday was an excellent farm, so with work, one did eat. It owned ten thousand acres of fertile soil, many miles of irrigation canals, powerful pumps, enough water, its own electricity, sturdy, well-kept barns, a stable full of huge, splendid, tawny, Belgian dray horses, enough cows, chickens, hogs and sheep to feed the entire community. The soil was black muck—"Just like the Ukraine," drooled Irving—and there were trees for timber and for shade; the air was fresh, so fresh a city punk like Zeke Gurevich became drunk just breathing. There were also tractors, four-wheel and track, and Zeke soon learned to love the feel of power under a tin seat. The farm cost a quarter of a million at Depression prices and the co-op organizers had gotten five hundred families to buy in a share at five hundred dollars apiece. Most of the families believed in an anarchism derived from Prince Kropotkin, gentle and communal, though there were Bakunin anarchists, too, gentle and fierce (two of whom were known to have been on the firing squad which had executed the Czar and his family at the outbreak of the Russian Revolution)—with all the idealism necessary for running a true collective. They called Newday a co-operative; technically, it was a kibbutz, since there was no private property, everything being owned collectively. The Newday members were erstwhile auto workers off idle assemblylines, masons, house painters, needletrade workers, carpenters, small shopkeepers, union officials, Irving Green, engineer, and one universally recognized bum, though he preferred to call himself a maverick: Zeke Gurevich.

Zeke's first job on the farm was one he found to his particular liking. He himself called it "the ramming." He was assigned to assist the professional shepherd, a slouch-backed, tiny-nosed man who spoke in one-word sentences. Each sentence was comprised only of a verb, and between each verb were spread ten minutes of sodden time. First Zeke helped the shepherd build a large pen into which were run forty-some-odd ewes. Then as he held the ram, a scrawny, tough little mucker, the shepherd painted the animal's underside with red marking dye bought from a firm in Casper, Wyoming, mentioned because the shepherd happened to come from that city. The ram, duly painted, was placed in the pen with the forty ewes. The horny, woolly beast went to work.

As soon as the shepherd and Zeke saw a ewe with a red behind, they grunted, "Ha," and lifted her out of the pen before she went back for more. The ram and they worked round the clock. In less than twenty-four hours, the rammer had rammed all forty ewes. When Zeke lifted the last of the lady sheep out of the pen, the ram came after him. As he hurdled the fence, Zeke remembered Lamiel Forté (he blushed violently) and thought what a wonderful time the ram could have had with him. The ram, crestfallen, galloped about the empty-ewed pen, and Zeke eyed him with awesome respect. What a superior rammer.

Zeke worked with the shepherd a few weeks, during which he learned, and stashed away the knowledge for some future use, that rams with ewes in heat will mate up to forty-eight times in twenty-four hours, with an average rate of twenty-six matings every twenty-four hours over a three-day period. With ewes *not in heat* the average is cut in two. An extremely significant statistic.

Zeke's second job at Newday was less exhilarating but just as basic. The colonists, as they called themselves, lived in a row of houses which had once been inhabited by Mexican and Indian farm workers employed by the sugar beet company which had owned the farm before Newday. These houses had no inside toilets, of course, and the co-op decided to build what Irving Green, engineer, called a wet tank sewage system, since who but a barbarian could enjoy the use of an outhouse which served hundreds of people. It piled quickly. A hot day, the wind wrong, everyone's thoughts turned to city living. Irving Green, engineer, Zeke Gurevich, assistant, and a crew of needletrade ditchdiggers dug sewer trenches, laid tile pipe, built a huge wet tank from which emanated underground leaching ditches into the fields, installed plumbing in the houses; and life, more full, became less fulsome. Amazing how quickly everyone's constipation dissolved.

The first time Zeke pulled the chain he visualized a piece of himself floating through the pipe installed by Brother Masiello, around an elbow sweated by Brother

Grant, along tile laid by Brother Borowitz, stop a moment to examine the cement work of Brother Slutsky, empty into the tank designed by Brother Irving Green. Who knows, a year later he would bite into this piece of himself in a scallion picked at random from the fertile truck garden dug above those beautifully executed leaching ditches.

Fine. But one day something or other got plugged in the wet tank and it overflowed. In the middle of August.

Now the colonists' idealism was put to the test. Unfairly.

"Of course, I'll go," Irving Green, engineer, mule, and honest man, said quietly, heroically perhaps. "I need another man."

Silence in the meeting hall.

Then someone suggested outside help be sought.

Exploiter! Capitalist! Landholder!

All right, you go, then.

Silence.

Zeke had a strong intuitive sense which quietly and firmly instructed him to depart. He searched for an open exit. But, of course, the great engineer, the honest man, had to call out, "Well, I suppose Brother Gurevich should go down with me since he was assistant engineer on the job."

Immediate and unanimous assent from the colonists, most of whom quickly disappeared. Unanimity is a symptom of authoritarianism, but one should not be too rigid or principle becomes dogma, and dogma is the angina pectoris of libertarianism.

The sun shone hot yellow, the peppermint smelled, the rising corn stalks swayed ever so slightly in a gentle summer breeze. Brother Lubow's battalions weeded the long rows of asparagus; Sister Slavin's layers in the chicken house ate, shat and popped eggs on the hour; the tractors roared; the horses sweated as they pawed the ground before the harvester blowing golden straw.

And Green & Gurevich, engineers, dressed in rubber boots, rubber pants, rubber shirts, rubber gloves, rubber hats, descended the iron ladders, Zeke boiling and breaking out in hives, since he was allergic to honey—down into the liquid hell which Dante, lacking imagination, neglected to invent for evil humanity. The great engineer, scientist and honest man could not comprehend the anger of his aide, and for that very reason what followed came as a complete surprise. As Irving turned to explore with a hook the plugged leaching hole, Zeke, holding on tightly with both hands and one foot, not breathing, lifted his free foot, placed it jarringly on the shoulder of his friend and superior and shoved. Once, twice, three times the scientist went down into the greenish ambrosia, ingesting a mouthful of such cubic volume it squirted from his ears for weeks.

Zeke lived off berries for a few days, then hungry and lean, issued forth from the woods to take his licking like a man.

Everyone worked hard; there was an absence of greed; ergo, no one was selfish, unjust, dishonest. Not that an amateur observer like Zeke Gurevich could notice. The theory was that all would work and all would eat. There's just so much a man could eat. If he had his fill, there was nothing else he would covet. He had a bed, shelter, some work clothes, a clean shirt for the evenings, all the food he could put away. Yes, what else would a man covet?

One morning at breakfast in the big messhall, Brother Masiello, a sweet, gentle Kropotkin anarchist from Boston, Massachusetts, left the side of his wife Lois, a Yankee from Portland, Maine, shuffled quietly on his handcrafted

[62]

leather sandals to where Roots Slutsky—*ski* or *sky* means *son of* in Polish—a violent Bakunin anarchist, ate his vegetarian breakfast of roots, nuts, and fruit with his young wife, a sumptuous blueblooded Russian girl (whispered by her enemies to be the mythic Anastasia, though the two colonists who'd helped execute the Czar *et famille* said, "Impossible!"). When Brother Masiello reached them, he raised a stiffened palm and rabbit-punched Roots Slutsky so hard the entire community heard his spinal disks crunch.

Anarchy ensued.

Irving and Zeke, Trotskyite and Stalinist, respectively, began to fling anarchists in all directions, and shortly brought order out of chaos.

The entire collective, men, women, and children, assembled that evening to try Brother Masiello as democratically as possible consistent with the principles of the noble *Magna Carta* for his seemingly purposeless attack on Brother Roots Slutsky.

After a long, harrowing evening of shouting, interspersed with quiet, the testimony adduced proved that Roots Slutsky had not only been cheating on his vegetarian comrades by eating hawg at a farmer's house up a ways, but had been partaking of Masiello's frugal Yankee wife in a haystack every second afternoon when Masiello was at the other end of the farm gathering sunflower seeds.

"Why, that dirty sneak," Zeke sneered in an aside to Irving, "laying a comrade's wife."

"Ought to be castrated," Irving replied in a whisper, his scimitar turned menacingly in Zeke's direction.

Brother Masiello was acquitted since his had been a crime of passion and it was Roots who had violated the canon of vegetarian ethics and himself been proven beyond a reasonable doubt to be guilty of moral turpitude: had poorly concealed his affair with a comrade's wife and thus injured the comrade's feelings and dignity.

It was voted by a majority that public censure was punishment enough.

Years later, when Zeke Gurevich was a more serious man, he told Mike Berg (a man who when he was born drew two lines, one for himself and one for life—in between lay a battlefield) that it was said by many of the colonists this incident marked the beginning of Newday's end. "Probably nonsense. I think it truer to say when utopia is the goal, disaster is the result. The utopian spirit is only a sprinter in a marathon race, soon brought to exhaustion; then the real runners take over—greed, selfishness, dishonesty, and injustice. Before a man starts running marathons, he'd better be in condition to run the middle distances. I hate to admit it, I'm a pusher myself, but a man has to pace himself, otherwise he'll die the violent and painful death of a burst heart."

"Gurevich, you're incorrigible," laughed Mike Berg, a tough-edged man. "Thinking it's possible for man to pace himself is in itself utopian and romantic. Man is a swine who on occasion acts like a man. That's the most you can hope for."

Rachel, present at the converstaion, chimed in, "You're both way out of line. Newday failed," she knew many of the organizers, "for a simple reason. Jobs became more plentiful in the cities from which a majority of its members came. These were city people, their jobs opened up, so it was to the city they returned."

It took some three or four years.

Zeke remained not quite a year, though Irving and Volya, pregnant again, stuck it out to the end. Zeke worked like a jackass, kept his stomach filled, and left one day to see the country, having made a swift decision that he was bored. But not before spending a week with the ewes during lambing season.

The ram does his yeoman service and then is sent off to eat, sleep, and reinvest his virility. The red-assed ewes must carry their burden for one hundred forty-eight days, having pleasured with the ram's ramrod for but a speedy second, unlike a sow which can pleasure with a boar for twenty-four solid hours not once parting, and then has to carry for only one hundred thirteen days. Incidentally, Zeke learned, the gestation period for an ass carrying an ass is three hundred sixty-five days, though an ass carrying a hinny does so for only three hundred fifty-five days.

When the lambing season began there was snow on the ground and the ewes were herded into a tremendous barn lit by a few yellow bulbs hung high in the rafters. It was Zeke's job—he did the night trick—to keep an eye open for the birth, since most ewes after dropping their lambs, being bad mothers, tended to lose themselves in the flock, and then there was a motherless lamb to be bottle-fed. He had to move very quickly. Lamb born, dip mother's umbilical in iodine solution, dip lamb in mother's afterbirth, dip mother's nose in own afterbirth, place lamb near mother's nose, keep after lamb to get at mother's teat. Soon happy family. Often a few lambs would be born at the same time and they were placed with wrong mother, but it hardly mattered since ewe and lamb go by smell of afterbirth, and blood be damned. Zeke was certain there was a profound meaning to all this. After spending a week of nights with ewes and lambs, he began to love the beasts, and came to understand the professional shepherd's innuendoes in one word sentences about them. Lambs do gambol and ewes are endearing, though he did on occasion lose his temper and curse some of them out for being lousy mothers, let alone lovers.

After leaving the world of animals and returning to the routine life of the colony, he found himself ravening; he couldn't sleep for thinking about himself as a ramming ramrod of a rammer.

There were three sisters among the colonists with whom he fell in love simultaneously, since one was never seen without the other two. They were called Ona, Mona and Sue.

The three voluptuaries had come from Kansas without their parents, whose name was Stuhldreyer, and were big, cornfed libertarians, probably the only anarchists left in that state of the union since John Brown was hung. Infatuated, famished, and horny, he proceeded one evening without fanfare or subtlety to their warm pen, a big one-room affair near the tractor barn across the large dike from the community post office. Ona, a huge smiling libertarian female, could find no reason to say no. The challenge quietly met, the red dye symbolically impressed, he turned to Mona who, equally large, equally libertarian, met him more than half way. Ram slam dam. Now Sue, as large, as libertarian, but not quite as smiling, in fact grim, and he wondered why. He rammed, but to no avail. Ona and Mona, an exceedingly interested audience, had difficulty repressing their laughter. Sue shed copious tears. Zeke panted, raged, the image of Mr. Ram in the barn up a ways galling. Was man inferior to beast? He paused; Ona and Mona, their large cornfed heads resting on equally large cornfed hands, bemusedly waited in the semi-darkness; Sue bit her nails. Energy renewed, enthusiasm revived, Zeke leaped to the attack. The enemy was willing, but there was no giving. Soon Sue and he were both

[66]

bruised and bawling, Ona and Mona squealing with repressed laughter. Merely a man, some sense still gleaming in his young pig head, he gasped, "I quit."

Tired, they pushed the single bed against the double, and slept crosswise, arms, legs, breasts, appurtenances intermingling.

At five, the sun an inflamed hoop, the community bell woke them. As they dressed, he asked about it. It turned out that Sue, poor wretch, had a pelvic misplacement. A bolted vault. No man—and it seemed hundreds had tried—had ever succeeded. It would take an operation.

"I'll be darned," he said. "Until then, what you need is a guy with an undersized rammer."

"That's why we picked you," Ona laughed, joined by her two sisters.

He fled.

Helped cut timber, did fall plowing and disking, shot the breeze around the pot-belly stove in the messhall. He hated to write letters but under Irving's urging he forced himself to write to his mother, to Abe, to Rachel and Simon in Phoenix. In return he received a sentimental letter from his sister full of weepy protestations of love now that he was gone, but also informing him that they were managing to eat and that they were well; Viola wrote about Abe and the children, gossip about friends; Rachel and Simon wrote not at all. It was from Viola he learned that Simon was holding on, that perhaps Arizona weather was doing him some good.

Winter began to close in, it snowed endlessly and the community, it seemed to Zeke, would soon be locked in. People were beginning to find enough time to be nasty and nagging with each other, which he and Irving managed to ignore. Volya, who was becoming the community gossip, loved it and her big voice could be heard all over the messhall tearing someone or other down. Zeke became bored with the life—bored and uneasy. Everyone knew when he peed, shat, changed his drawers, slept with a girl, caught the crabs and from whom. He began to daydream of Rachel, his eternal love, became obsessed with the thought of her. A day didn't slip past that he didn't think of her, envision her beauty in his arms, bite his lips to suppress the cry that asked to be let loose from his heart. Then there was Simon, gaunt, skull and bones, haunting and dying. Guilt smote Zeke in two.

Besides, he wanted to see, to touch, to smell the large world—to begin living that life that eighteen-year-olds dream of—nothing concrete, even less than vague, something shining brilliantly in that unconscious mist out there. When he became older he realized most people go through life busily preparing for the time when they will reach that brilliant something, only to find themselves lifting their head from a sleepless bed some nasty night and coming to the understanding that the preparation was over, there they were—ready for that stinking narrow box. Then he remembered Chava Green, yes, she'd been right, everyone ought to make of each day a joyous feast. But how?

Now he was eighteen years old and impatient. He wanted out from this collective living, he wanted to be his own man. Besides, he wanted some damn privacy. He woke one morning, dressed, went to Irving and said, "I'm going."

"Where?"

"Don't know. Whichever direction the road leads."

"You're going to Phoenix. For God's sake, she has a dying husband, why don't you leave her alone?"

"I'm not going to Phoenix. I'm just going."

"You're crazy, Red."

"I know. I'm going."

Irving looked at him sharply. He knew this boy. Nothing would stop him from going now that his mind was made up. "Just to remind you, because you tend on occasion to forget, while you're on the road remember you're not an animal."

"Okay, Pop, I'll remember."

"I haven't got a dime to give you."

"I'll manage a job here and there."

Volya took him to her big, pregnant belly, her bosoms already smelling of milk, the halvah long ago eaten. "Here is ten dollars," she said in her loud voice, "that's all we have."

"Thanks. That ought to get me to Los Angeles."

"You'll be lucky if it will get you to Detroit," Irving said, wondering where Volya had gotten the ten dollars, "and that's only ninety miles away."

"Okay, okay." Zeke kissed Jennitl full on her young hot mouth and hit the road, carrying nothing but what he had on his back.

It was as cold as hell.

He thumbed a ride to Detroit, then headed cross-state toward Lake Michigan. A big brawny closemouthed farmer gave him a lift, one of America's strong, silent hemen. My goodness, if the old bastard doesn't slip his horny fist down Zeke's thigh. Zeke, ticklish, dribbled laughter, which the agricultural nance took for encouragement. Zeke had to jam his foot down on the brake and jump out of the car while it was still moving. Mr. Hayseed Queen hit his accelerator hard and disappeared into the asphalt. Christ, had Lamiel Forté left a stigma on him? He'd once discussed it with Abe who had laughed and told him what had happened with Forté was not unusual;

not to worry, he was a Gurevich, not one faggot going all the way back to antiquity. He forgot about it. The night was young. A car whooshed out of the dark, squealed to a stop, the right front and rear doors opened and out flopped two bags of rags, followed by a booze bottle which smashed on the road. The car sped away. Two bimbos, age indeterminate in the darkness, stood raggedly before him, weeping, their tears cutting ditches through the dirt on their faces.

He asked them what had happened and they told him they'd been picked up by two farmboys who promised food for a tumble. The idiots had tumbled first, now they were hungry. He still had the ten bucks which Volya had given him, so he bought some sandwiches and a can of warm cow's milk from a farmer's wife up the road. Then he led the two bimbos behind a billboard whose slogan some smartaleck Hoboken hobo had altered to read, Reach for a Nucky instead of a Teet, and shared his wealth with them. They bolted the food and then offered to share *their* wealth with him which he declined with pious indignation, pious, since the fact they were dirty, smelly and over-all miserable had as much to do with his gallantry as his idealism. He told them the sandwiches and milk were for free and was certain by their shrugs and the way they looked at one another they thought him a sucker, but he didn't care because he thought he was eighteen years old and it was time he grew up. Still, they all slept on top of one another because the night was very cold. In the morning, they parted company, the women—even in daylight it was impossible to determine their age or find any distinguishable features so dirty, ragged and disheveled were they—heading due south (they said they were from Alabama) and Zeke northwest, or so he thought. On his own now, an adult, he advised them, "Remember. Eat first, tumble afterwards." They giggled and crossed over the road to the southbound shoulder.

He hitchhiked most everywhere he went, though once he connected up with a white-haired kid from Ohio named Cooke who showed him how to jump a freight, which they did outside Chicago and after three days saw daylight in Ogallala, Nebraska; jumped another freight and three days later saw daylight in Joliet, Illinois. In six days he'd advanced his travels about ninety miles. He didn't care for it; besides having to keep an eye out for yard bulls, he didn't like being cooped up in a dirty freight car. He liked the paved roads out under daylight or sitting on the high soft seat of a truck or sleeping on the pad in the back of the cab of a truckdriver who felt sorry for the kid that he was. He and Cooke separated amicably, though the Ohioan did look down his patrician nose at Zeke, for hitchhikers were *déclassé* among the elite of the road, those romantic heroes who rode the rails.

He managed in two weeks, the freight hopping interlude consuming a week of it, to go six hundred miles. He had two bits left, his clothes were frayed and dirty, his lumberjacket barely adequate against the cold of January, and his young red beard beginning to sprout. With angry pride he saw Jew written all over his face in an aquiline scrawl. From Wisconsin he came by local jalopy into Minnesota on U.S. 16, the sweetheart route, had two bits, so he stopped at a truckdrivers' diner. It was crowded, steamy and smelled of bacon fat. No sooner did he sit down at the counter when some wise guy yelled, "Hiyah, Ikey, what y'doin' in God's country?" Zeke ignored him, the guy was obviously among friends. He ordered coffee and a jelly cruller; the waitress, middle-aged and tired, slipped him a roll and butter, too.

He gobbled the roll down, started on the cruller.

"Hiyah, Ikey, where y'hidin' yer gold?"

Zeke finished the cruller, drank the coffee down, also a glass of water, paid the waitress a dime. She winked, whispered sotto voce, "Don't mind him, Red."

"Hey, Ikey—"

His papa had fought the Cossacks, what the hell kind of piss flowed in his veins. He spit in the cretin's leering face.

The truckdrivers stood in a circle behind the diner and let them fight it out. They were both crazy—young and crazy and wanting to take it out on somebody. Zeke was always afraid at the beginning of a fight—perhaps so was the other man—but after a while, when he realized he wasn't going to be killed, in the pain and the anger he stopped being scared. Then, obsessive, he could fight for hours and never give in. Obviously, his opponent was the same. It was the truckdrivers who finally put a stop to it because the fight had become a bore, the blood poured and they were arm weary. After they washed the blood off themselves, his adversary offered to buy him a sandwich and another cup of coffee. "Good fight, Red."

"Yeah, good fight." He accepted the offer of the sandwich and coffee. Fighting the guy had had a salutary effect on both of them.

To finish off the day grandly, he got a two-hundred-mile lift into South Dakota.

Winter, the snow covering endless miles in any direction, the soaring mountains, the plains and the black fir trees, all laden with snow, covering the poverty of a country on the balls of its ass. Minnesota, South Dakota, Wyoming, Idaho, a country of milk and honey, an awesome country of formidable beauty, divers and inspiring, ravished by hunger. Milk poured into rivers, honey was money and money was scarce.

[72]

Yet, somehow he managed to stay alive. A truckdriver, a farmer, even a hobo was willing on occasion to share a nickel or a crumb. He kept heading northwest, pulled by what he knew not, then abruptly one morning in February, the snow up to his ears, newspapers lining the rags to keep him from freezing to death, his shoes tied on to his feet, he swooped south on the tailgate of a broken down Model A pickup truck whose motor was a song and whose driver was a sour-faced, no-lipped, no-muscled, no-tongued cowboy on his way to Arizona.

Phoenix. Hell, that's where he'd been headed all the time.

Ninety-eight in the shade in February.

Five days too late.

The thin lady in a mother hubbard who had been the Farrells' landlady told him Simon had suffered an attack and almost died. As soon as he'd felt slightly better, Rachel had packed him and herself on the Santa Fe and headed east. No matter how hard Zeke tried he couldn't dissuade his inner voice, that nag, from its ugly bleat. Why don't you go back to New York, it said, and wait for him—him, he was afraid to say the name—to die? There hasn't been a day since you last saw her that you haven't thought of her. Sleeping with a hundred girls is like hiding behind your fingers. I love her, God, I love her. Yes, he loved her. Ever since that first time she'd taken his hand in her own in Abe's place in the Bronx. And he'd been wishing Simon dead for years. Zeke Gurevich: bum. His own mother thought he was a bum—and he'd set out to prove it.

No.

He searched out the nearest truck stopover and found one at the edge of town. A desert.

He caught a big International heading to San Berdo and Los Angeles, the driver, a tough-faced Italian from

Mamaroneck, New York, telling him he'd take him all the way. But Zeke left him at one of the water and gas stops in the Mojave desert seventy miles east of San Berdo. It was a crumbjoint with a big dilapidated sign: SAN WICH S & COK S. A tired peroxide blond in a skimpy, dirty white skirt and high heels worked the place. It seemed she was alone. She had a faded, peaked, white-skinned prettiness. Tired and hard-eyed. She had long veiny legs, a skinny behind and hard apple breasts under her blouse.

"Y' wanna job, Red—room and board, a buck a day?"

Without even thinking, he said, "You bet."

He worked there three months. Behind the shack from which she did business, there were two tiny bedrooms and a kitchen. The outhouse was a hundred feet behind that, in the middle of an auto dump. Most of the time, to pass water, he used the kitchen sink; she just spread her legs in the shade behind the shack. She hardly ever talked. Her husband had walked out on her a month or so before Zeke showed up. It was no place to live, a crummy desert, nothing to do, absolutely nothing. To see a movie or buy a pair of shoes they had to drive to San Berdo, seventy miles over the desert. You stepped on the accelerator and whoosh.

"But it's a livin', ainnit?" she sniffed through her sinuses. She had a habit of saying, "Better'n hustlin', ainnit?" Or stealin' or beggin'.

"Yeah," he'd say, "it's better'n hustlin'," or whatever, thinking that people have so little to be proud of.

Her name was Edna Nimienski and she came from Scranton, Pennsylvania.

There was something about her, the hard eyes or the tiredness or the jut of her jaw, he didn't know, which pricked him under his skin—pricked hard as if it wanted

[74]

to make him cry. Maybe it was that which made him answer "You bet" so quickly. He just didn't know.

The third night he simply walked into her room, got undressed and slipped into bed with her. Not a word between them until she was ready, then she said, "Go, Red, go," and began pinching his behind. Finished, she fitted her skinny ass into his washboard belly and went to sleep. That was it.

He was an eighteen-year-old kid. A kid doesn't see anything, except himself; he doesn't even feel anything except himself. He's a blotter, blotting it up. Capillary action. Only when he became a full-grown man and he thought about it, could he smell the place. In the winter the desert is unbelievably dry and sweet from the mesquite and the sage. He could remember that and the smell of the greasy fat used for frying the hamburgers; the dry purity of the desert nights; the cars slapping by on the two-laner as fast as they could go; could see the sticks of wood she called furniture, the cheap black squeaking fans; could hear the tinny spring of the bed; and then again smell the dried sweat under her arms. See the fear behind the pokerface. What the hell else did she have to hide behind? Her highfalutin' manners? She was a grub and naked to the world. Then he thought she was fearless. He could remember sitting in the kitchen behind the store, hearing her wait on some biff who had stopped for gas and a Coke. "I'll give yuh a buck for a fuck, honey. Let's go."

"Go blow it outer yer ass, buster," in a monotone, and he could see her in his mind's eye slipping her fist round the lead pipe she kept for that purpose.

Sitting in the kitchen, he could hear the guy laugh and leave. One time some bastard said, "There's nothin' on yuh to fuck anyway, baby, you're so skinny I c'n see through yuh," and then slammed out. He caught the guy

[75]

before he got back into his car and gave him a going over.

Years later he could see the man's face, too. Scared.

Then it was all one-dimensional. Dry. Pretending there was nothing more than he saw with his eyes, and his eyes were glass. Later, of course, it was all there, coming out of every cell, all that stuff he'd blotted up when he was a kid.

The place was open twenty-four hours a day. How can man and car be refused drink in the desert? When a customer opened the front door, it buzzed like a rasp scraping a tin nail, and he would jump out of bed quickly. Or she. She more than he. Young men need their sleep—specially after they've given their all to their girl. She herself said it once with a straight flat smile. She didn't care, there was plenty of time to sleep. What else was there to do?

It got so they hardly ever washed. When there's nothing to do, a person doesn't even want to do whatever there is to do.

Once he forced her to close up the place. They washed, put on clean clothes—he was a real dude when he put his mind to it—slid into her jalopy and went to San Berdo. They saw a movie, Greta Garbo in *Queen Christina*. Holding her hand and watching Garbo, he became transfixed and thought of Rachel Farrell. Rachel, Rachel. His heart ached, he felt weepy for himself, and he took her hand and kissed its palm, and his eyes filled with tears, and she said, "You're a softy, aintcha?" They ate in a restaurant with livid lavender tablecloths and he tried to hold a courtly conversation with her. He told her she was pretty and that he liked her awfully and they ought to go out more often. She just stared at him with those hard eyes in that pokerface and without her saying a word he knew exactly what she was thinking: Don't go cornholing me, buster. She was a tough broad, all right; more than that, she was right, he was cornholing her. So there was nothing more to say, not a word except about the place: how much money it was making. After eats for both of them and his buck a day, she broke even. He had no intention of taking the money when he left. What for? Who needed money? Sleep with a broad, and then take her money? He knew he would be leaving soon. Whether she thought of it, he didn't know. The best way to hide is to go live in the desert and live behind a frozen face. Yet there was enough there to not want to hustle, beg or steal. Enough anger, really. And to say, "Go, Red, go," and pinch his behind to spur him on when they had their pleasure, the tangy dry sweat under her arms not unpleasant.

One morning, about five, the buzzer made its tinny rasp and she jumped out of bed to take it, though he was already awake. Whoever it was came straight in and walked into the bedroom.

"Steve," she said coldly, and Zeke knew it was her husband.

He slipped out of bed, naked, and began dressing, wondering if he were going to have a fight on his hands.

All the guy said was, "Keereist, he's a Jewboy." But there was no malice in his voice. He was a long skeleton with a towhead and pale blue eyes with pink lids. His face was as flat as hers. Edna and her husband went into the kitchen and Zeke finished dressing.

She made Zeke a breakfast of juice, upside-down eggs, coffee and a cruller, which he ate, a word from none of them. Zeke made up a blanket roll, took a tenner out of the cigar box in which he'd kept the money she diligently had paid him and then hitched a ride with the trucker who delivered the groceries. When he said goodbye to her, Edna shrugged her skinny white shoulders and just said, "Y' know how it is."

He nodded to her and then to her husband and left them both hiding behind their flat pokerfaces.

VII

In three days he was in Los Angeles. In the spring a sprawl of hotness. He wasn't downtown ten minutes before the town lived up to its reputation. Some jello-mouthed old geezer in a loose flapping straw hat and overlarge flapping white pants, dirty, tried to sell him God, Griffith Park, and an old Graham-Paige in that order.

"No. But if you got some human beef—"

"Jest wait a few minutes, mebbe I c'n rustle some up fer yuh."

"Beat it, bum."

He stayed at Josh Abramson's, Abe's kid brother, who'd become so thin from the sun and, incidentally, lack of food, that his entire face was now a mere extension to his huge nose. Josh lived in a garage behind a house on Van Ness near Western and Wilshire. The place still smelled of crankcase oil and gasoline. It had a dirty sisal rug over the concrete, a shaky army cot and olive drab blanket for linen, a torn beach chair and a four-legged table with three legs. It was strewn with old newspapers and books, thousands of books, because Josh preferred reading to eating. It was the year Josh ran away from college and the protection of his family. He was the youngest of nine children, both the most protected and loved. It was a burden which oppressed him. When Zeke, who had his address from Viola, found him, Josh was on the shaky army cot contemplating the ceiling. He raised his head as Zeke marched in, asked, "What do *you* want?" Didn't wait for an answer, proceeded to make a Roman oration. "A first class mooching son of a bitch, my cousin Zeke Gurevich. What's the matter, got tired trying to steal my family's love from me, now coming to steal my peace? Look at him, a first class bum, thinks he's king shit. Keeping track of all the girls you've screwed? Bet he's got a double entry ledger—assets: nine blonds, seven redheads, thirteen brunettes; liabilities: one dose. You can sleep in the corner with the mice, just let me alone. A man has the right to be let alone. Most revolutionary slogan of all time. Everyone laughs at Garbo's 'I vahnt to be alone.' She should be admired and respected for it." He resumed examining the garage ceiling.

Zeke placed his *bindle*, which consisted of a blanket roll, two pairs of socks, two pairs of underwear shorts, one white shirt, in the corner with the mice and left. In a half hour he returned from the Pig 'N the Poke drive-in on the corner with hamburgers and coffee. Josh ate with him, staring penetratingly at him with his deep-socketed brown eyes, slightly mad. Zeke said not a word. Then Josh told him he'd heard from Abe that Simon Farrell had died that past week in New York. "St. Simon, the pacifist apostle of communal living, collective masturbation, every room with a peephole, toilets like barracks, love on a mass scale, your St. Simon is dead."

"You make him sound like a monster and he was a gentle guy who left you alone."

"He didn't leave anybody alone. He was a poseur and so's his wife, Rachel, the phoney nymph. He composed his features, grew his beard, and wore his clothes in a fashion to make you look at him and remember that he was dying—all for the purpose of making you feel guilty for his death. El Greco Jesus. Balls. I refuse to accept guilt for what is not my doing. My own guilt is enough—I don't need the burden of his or anyone else's. Here," he snarled, throwing Abe's letter so it hit Zeke in the chest, "read about the funeral."

There had been a service held before Simon's cremation which had ended in a brawl among all his anarchist, communist and socialist friends who'd come to the funeral chapel to claim him as their own. Simon had been one of those men who always seemed to agree with whomever was at the moment talking to him and then proceeded to go his own way. Perhaps he didn't have the guts to disagree openly; it could have been he was too gentle, didn't like to hurt anyone's feelings; it could have been he couldn't bear to think someone would turn away from him with hatred; or it could have been that he was too tired—in the years they had known him they had never seen him when he wasn't tired. He lived a short life, but it took him a long time to die. Dead, his family, friends, acquaintances in the hundreds had stormed into the chapel, each demanding equal time before his corpse was thrown to the flames to speak not about him but to sell the validity of their respective causes at the top of a screech. First someone read from Shelley—"I weep for Adonais—he is dead!"—and then spokesmen for the various groupings tried to take over the public address mike. A melée resulted and the capitalistic cossacks had to break it up.

And Zeke? He gave Simon a moment's silence, wiped away a tear, wished him Godspeed, and turned his thoughts to Rachel. Rachel, Rachel. His phantom love. Oh, how he would love to bury himself in her. Simply had to head east. Had to stake out his claim. Eighteen years old and had loved her for nearly six. And he had an intuition about her—she wouldn't wait long, it was impossible for her to live without a man—always had to have a man at her side and at least one trailing after her. He knew her all right; too well. She would weep, tear her hair, and simultaneously be aware of every male stare. He hated her. He loved her. She was that very brilliance in the mist to which he aspired. He chewed his nails to the quick.

The ten dollars were gone, Joshua was literally starving, ecstatically awaiting death and the landlord of this hovel to arrive at the very same moment, one to claim him and the other his grand possessions (that would show his family, damn them). Hitchhiking would take weeks and Zeke didn't trust himself on freight trains; he would probably end up in the clink. He saw Rachel in his mind's eye every moment of the night and the day. In her loose-bodiced dress lying on the couch, Empress Theodora or Isadora Duncan, what matter, surrounded by hundreds of men with hungry eyes and hands. He couldn't sleep. Josh of course was in that hallucinatory state which comes about after days of hunger and a self-imposed regimen of ceiling contemplation, seeking to discern how close he could come to death without dying, ecstatic in his aloneness. Zeke himself wouldn't have been able to eat even if there had been anything to eat. He was burning for Rachel. Love. Absolutely burning. He could smell her. She had a habit of bathing every day at about four o'clock in the afternoon. Then she would come out in her robe, her black hair long to her buttocks, her breasts showing through the open robe, the free woman, smelling of fresh, clean, good soap, smiling her white intimate smile. He was obsessed with a vision of her in someone else's arms and it made life impossible. "What shall I do?" he cried out in the night, his voice ringing clearly about the garage, the mice scurrying.

Josh, roused from his hallucinatory sleep, his apartness disturbed by this fellow suffering, this not quite mad cousin from his quite mad family, called out in exas-

peration, "Rob the Bank of America, but let me alone."
To hell with everything. Who cared?

On Friday, at noon, he slunk down crowded South
Spring Street to a branch of the Bank of America. Leaned
against a telephone pole and waited. A sleepwalker. Saw a
guy leave the bank with a little canvas bag. He edged
towards him, with a lightning move yanked the bag clean
out of the man's hand and ran. Whistles blew, men yelled,
women screamed, someone shouted, "Run, Red, run," a
shot sang out, but he ran—his obsession ran like a man on
fire running in panic. "Go, Red, go." He got to Olivera,
ducked into a flyspecked restaurant and hid in the dread-
fully stinking toilet of a Mexican chili joint. Somehow
they're extra bad. He opened the canvas bag while sitting
on the pot, counted out six hundred bucks distributed
among the thirty pay envelopes. He counted out $150.00
for himself, which he put in one pocket and placed the
remainder in another. Some poor bastards might not get
paid today. Well, they'll get it tomorrow. He hid the canvas bag in the toilet tank, one of those high up near the
ceiling, pulled the chain, and left. A sleepwalker, he was
cold as ice. Obsession can do these little things to people.
When he got back to Joshua, now lying on his belly on the
dirty sisal rug reading *Interpretation of Dreams*, he
reached down and pulled his nutty cousin to his feet.
Folded him over a knee and paddled his bony ass until
Josh began to cry; the harder he cried, the harder Zeke
paddled him. Josh's face became flushed and he began to
look alive—almost happy. "Here's money, get yourself
some food and return to college. You're going to be the
greatest psychiatrist that ever lived. Raskolnikov you'll
never be, that's more in my style." Josh kissed him—for a
moment there was a duel of noses—and said he was a
good cousin.

Then Zeke wrapped all the emptied pay envelopes in

brown wrapping paper, picked up his *bindle* and departed, stopping in the post office to mail the package to the company from which he'd stolen the money. The afternoon papers made a howl of it as he caught one of those circa 1930 planes in Burbank for New York.

It took three days, what with stopping every couple of hours, repairs, transferring to another plane and what have you. He literally voided green lentil soup everytime he saw a cop. The obsession had burned itself out. Jail he wasn't afraid of. Could blot that up too. It was the family. The family would cry, one of their own, a thief—well, to hell with them, they cried at everything, it became a bore. Friends would say, it figured—he couldn't take the discipline of the movement, running around like a bum, he's just no damn good. A thief.

Zeke Gurevich was a crook. He hadn't thought of it before. After all, it wasn't like stealing potatoes from the grocery man to make hot mickies under a fire in the street. A crook. For seventy-two hours he thought of nothing else. For an honest man to become a thief is something special. Those who say it's a form of rebellion against society don't know what they're talking about. They give society too much credit, make it too big. It's a personal matter. He couldn't say he'd done it to assuage his hunger— he'd done it because he had become obsessed, lost control of what and who he was. No one to blame but himself. He'd stolen, committed an atrocity on himself. He promised himself he would never steal again. Of course, he didn't go so far as to turn himself in.

As he approached New York, he realized he hadn't thought about his mother for months, not once. Why he hadn't he did not ask himself, not once. But now that he approached his native heath, she appeared in his mind:

[84]

stubborn, squat and sullen, a short square-shouldered gray-haired woman who had worked hard all her life to feed her children. Her husband, Zeke's father, had died five years before. She worked hard before he died and she worked hard after he died. And never let anyone forget it. Specially Zeke. But of course she had a right. Ever since his father had died from his fall from the ladies' hairnet billboard, Zeke had stayed away from home as much as he could; there had been nights he had slept in the park rather than go home. Everyone who came within reach of her voice she wanted to rule. Everyone, everything she tried to draw into orbit about her—to burn with her hatred, to freeze with her contempt, to overshadow and belittle. Thinking for those seventy-two hours about having become a thief, crapping green about being caught, wondering why he had yielded to his obsession, querying himself about his passion for Rachel Farrell, asking himself if he was going to become a bum or going to remain a bum already being one, he realized he had been running from her, his matriarch, and became contrite and sentimental about his poor hard-working mama who really loved him.

So when the plane finally touched down in Newark on a belly-scaring mist approach, the first thing he did was grab a bus to New York and then a subway to the east side, to Hester Street, his native heath, his very own slum. The creaking dirty stairs stunk of boiled red cabbage soup and rat turds as he ran up the five flights as swiftly as a hind.

He snatched open the door and ran into her clutching briny arms. "Vae is me," she cried in Yiddish English, "my kentser is here."

VIII

Simon was dead and Rachel was bereft. Her eyes were sunk deep into her exquisite skull, her soft underlip constantly gnawed by her large teeth, her black hair longer and wilder than ever. She acted as if life were impossible without Simon, her great depthless blue eyes stared into some Cretan labyrinth, as her scarlet diaphanous scarf fluttered listlessly behind her. Abe consoled. Viola consoled. Hundreds of friends consoled. Matthew Cahn, a handsome Arab of a man Zeke had never met before, consoled. Zeke consoled. She wept, inconsolable.

When Matt Cahn was not consoling Rachel, he was out with the beautiful Elaine Robinson who lived on Perry Street. He tried very hard with the beautiful Elaine; too hard, and she found him a bore. Finally, one afternoon, after a stroll in Washington Square Park, as they reached the threshold of her basement flat, she conceded to his persistence, but asked did he have a rubber, because, as she said it, "I have the clap." The beautiful Elaine had read him well. He begged off, remembered he had to meet mother at Rogers Peet to buy a winter overcoat at a June sale. As Matt hurried away he thought he could hear her laughing.

Matt Cahn began to devote full time to consoling Rachel. She responded to consolation by making a stab at suicide—slashed her wrists with one of Simon's sharp sculpting chisels a few minutes before Abe and Viola were to appear for an appointment with her. They found her slowly bleeding to death and moaning, "I want to join Simon."

Six weeks later Matt Cahn half-moved into her flat on Charles Street. Only half, because he still lived with mother and dad on West End Avenue and 86th.

"You're too young," she told Zeke, smiling sadly. Zeke took it badly, cursing her and wishing her misfortune, so that she wept and closed herself in her room until he became frightened and knocked the door down. She forgave him and he left. To himself he said what she meant was that he'd been too late; Matt had been the first to come to her after Simon's death, that's all it was. A month after Matt moved in with her, she gave her son Sean to her mother to keep for a short time. It was to be ten years. Matt, it seemed, wanted to be alone with his half-bride.

Matt Cahn was a tall, handsome man, so fastidious he wore rubbers, raincoat, rainhat and umbrella at the merest threat of clouds; he argued over pennies with shopkeepers and beggars; he was considered by those in the know to be one of the shrewdest, most intuitive and daring crapshooters in the city and had such large and quick hands he could have played shortstop for almost any major league ball club; an honor graduate at MIT, where he had majored in math and been a demon in logic, he worked as a political analyst for a major news service part time; Abe, who disliked him, had to admit, "His political sense is uncanny—he has the ability to see the truth even when it's obvious and to remember what happened the day before yesterday, a talent unheard of among modern journalists. Odd man, Matt. If someone needs money, Matt will scrape together his last dollar, he'll share his food, and yet can drive you crazy waiting for him to check

[87]

every last cent on a restaurant tab after lunch. Then he'll overtip the waiter."

From the start, Matt had a lot of trouble with Rachel—and for the rest of their life together—because he took her too seriously. Simon had known she was a pretender, had shrugged at her affectations, and gotten along fine with her. Simon, though living with death a constant, harrowing neighbor, had known how to wink. Matt Cahn never winked in his life, yet he did have a beautiful, white-toothed smile. Though he saw immediately behind Rachel's pretense at intellectuality (she was really a very common-sense *gal*) and learned even to live without being constantly offended by her pretensions—his search for truth was always confined to a very straight, very narrow catwalk—he couldn't live with her pose of earth goddess, Ishtar and Emma Goldman all commingled with Pegeen into that tasty baggage whom everyone knew as Rachel Farrell.

Matt finally moved in wholly, though his parents opposed his marriage to Rachel. She was a year older than he and offered him nothing—not even an incentive to be other than who he was. His parents—father, lawyer; mother, obstetrician—had hoped because of his extraordinarily high IQ, his superior scholastic record, and his rhetorical brilliance that their son would ascend heights which they as professional people could never attain. Be a creative writer, or achieve greatness in the theatre as playwright or director. Rachel couldn't care less. (When she became older, years after the war, she did care, admitting with a gleaming white smile, "There's a little of the philistine in all of us; one gets tired fighting off the hounds of success.") She pretended at first that she loved Matt and soon did and that was enough for her. Status? She would sneer. About money she didn't care; it was so bourgeois. In those days when jobs, money and food were scarce, a disaster, she paraded their poverty proudly, a distinction. Of course, if Matt's parents wished to supply their son with cash, why should she refuse it? That would be phoney bohemianism. And if Abe and Viola, both of whom worked very hard, didn't object to feeding them (and half the Village), why not? They had it and she and Matt didn't. If or when Matt and she would have it, they would share their bread with everyone too. About that there was no pretense. They never once in their lives turned anyone away, even if there was only a half-pound of cottage cheese in the icebox for all of them. It never occurred to them that self-preservation came first. One had: one shared.

Rachel, the fifth of eleven children, a child who grew up believing the four elder had left her nothing of their parents' time or love, and then believed the six younger had taken the rest of the nothing, ran off at sixteen to live with Simon Farrell. There was no pose about her sensuousness and sensuality. At an early age it had been apparent she loved nothing more than to be caressed, touched, made love to by a man's eyes, his hands, his hair, his shoulders, his voice, him. Her father, a former Dubliner, a Jesuit scholar, in anger (later he suffered the pangs of conscience) once called her "Jewess" because of this sensuality. She told Abe at that moment she became a Jew. Simon confirmed it by telling Abe when he first met Rachel—she was sent by a friend to model at an art class he conducted—she had pretended to him her family was Jewish. Once she left her family, she had very little to do with them, though when she needed her mother to take Sean she didn't hesitate to ask. A strong need for physical love seemed to motivate her dress, her movements, her every act, and very few virile men could resist offering her

[89]

what she so obviously desired. Zeke Gurevich, terribly wounded by her rejection of him, pondered often the mystery of her love for Matthew Cahn. There was nothing about Matt, except his dark Arab handsomeness, which Zeke—or Abe or Viola or anyone else who knew them—could see as touching Rachel in any way. He was exactly what Rachel was not. She detested the details of living; Matt could never get beyond the details even of himself. There was nothing the man could enjoy. Not music, because he was too taken with each individual note and marking—to the end that even Bach became absurd to him. Not painting, since he became too concerned with the pigment used, the price of it, the brush used, the knife, the canvas, the frame—every detail but the painting itself. He read books incessantly, would never discuss one character or scene, but would discuss every typographical error or ungrammatical sentence. He was a man who never saw the whole of anything—a man so taken with the details of living, he neglected to live. Rachel, a true-blue wife, pretended after a short time to be like him—a nitpicker. But with her it was a fake. Practically colorblind, ignorant of form and structure, she could jabber on about paintings like an expert. What had begun as an affectation had vanquished ignorance and even colorblindness, and soon she learned to appreciate what was good and what was bad, and that *great* was to be reserved for the very, very few. Rachel Conyngham Farrell Cahn grabbed at life and held it tightly—perhaps too tightly, and the details be damned.

Of course Zeke never asked her why she loved Matt, or lived with him, for that matter, because he knew even at that time it was an absurd question. As one or another of those who used to sit at Abe's dinner table would say to terminate one discussion or another, "Thank God, no one's gone full ahead yet in an attempt to make love into a rational science," and everyone else, utopian or scientific, would yell a rousing "Amen!"

But though Zeke never asked her, he couldn't help but wonder—bitterly, angrily, obsessively—how she could sleep with Matt Cahn. He was positive when Matt made love he saw the knish as a piece of molded dough filled with mashed potatoes, which is not the way of a knish at all. Matt himself in Zeke's presence once blurted out to a roomful of friends that he'd never enjoyed sex as much as when he was a kid masturbating.

When Matt moved wholly into Rachel's apartment, Zeke conceded defeat and thought seriously of wearing ashes on his head. He saw them often at Abe's place a few blocks away. When he did he merely stared into space, baleful. Rachel saw he'd become a brooding, sensitive youth, less *gauche,* though still *farouche* as Simon had called him. She tried to rouse him from his despair with gentleness, a hug, but he would turn angrily away from her, telling her to keep her hands to herself. A few times he shouted obscenities at her; at first she turned away, unhappy for him; then once she slapped his face, telling him obscenities were for fun, not for hatred. He blushed and ran out into the street. Friends asked him to come to meetings or demonstrations and he refused, saying, "The revolution'll have to get along without me." He was immured in his misery—the rest of the world walled out. Though once he did go *break heads* at an outdoor meeting of Lovestoneites at Hunts Point, and went a few times to a secret party school where he learned to make stink bombs out of valeric acid and oil for the revolution.

He brooded and planned revenge and daydreamed of Rachel's coming to him, throwing herself at his feet, begging for his love. Go away, he would say, you're a whore.

Free love is honest, beautiful love. It is pure love. You don't love Matt, it's me you love.

He took to visiting her street and walking past her house, a self-inflicted wound, knowing if she were to catch him haunting her neighborhood he would die of shame.

No other women existed, and at night, whether sleeping at Abe's or on the rare occasion at his mother's, he wept. He loved her; she was the sun, his entire life, without whom he was doomed to perpetual darkness. Ah, me. Poor me. One morning he awoke with the conviction that unless he touched her with love he would that very day die. He hurriedly dressed and ran, speedily—a man afraid of the dark.

IX

Outside it snowed, the sun cold, white-yellow through the hoar.

He found her sleeping on the low, wide studio bed which rested on red bricks, four bricks to a corner. The door to the one-room flat as usual was unlatched and he walked straight in. Her slender supple body was curved in on itself almost like a snail, her head buried under arm and shoulder, her long black hair spread wildly about her back. She slept deeply and didn't hear him as he entered, locked the door behind him, and came to stare down at her in the room which was lit by daylight reflecting off the courtyard concrete and brick. The cold sun looked gray through the sooted window. The room was lined with rickety bookshelves, long shelving also on bricks, laden with thousands of books—all the Russians, the French, the Greeks, the German philosophers and all the anarchist philosophers from Proudhon through Ferrer and Rocker, hundreds of magazines, the literature of revolution and nihilism, Marx and Sorel side by side and both flanked by Bakunin and Lenin. From one cracked wall glared an old, blackened metal bas-relief of Robespierre, and on one of the bookshelves stood a glued-together plaster replica in miniature of Rodin's *The Kiss*. On the floor near the head of the bed on which she slept lay an old edition of *Sanine*, a turn-of-the-century novel by an anarchist writer, one Artsybashev. Over the long side of the bed hung a print of

Delacroix's *Liberty Leading the People*, and over the head Goya's *The Executions of May 3, 1808*.

Zeke stood gazing down at her as she slept, clenching his teeth and unbeknownst to himself holding his right hand in a fist under his heart. He had become nineteen that very month, tall, strongly built, a large aquiline nose, his head a mass of tight red curls. There was strength and violence in his face, indecisive yet as to which would conquer.

He stared down at her with great sadness in his young eyes, almost self-pity, yet again indecision, because he was so young, between the sadness and the self-pity.

Tensely, he stared down at her, trying to come to a decision—almost like a young predator struggling to decide whether to plunge or soar. He couldn't see her face which was hidden by her shoulder and the crown of wild black hair. With a stifled sigh he lowered himself on the bed, and curled himself gently about her, to enfold her in himself.

She didn't wake and he didn't sleep—merely kept a strict guard on himself under closed eyes, his ears at the stairs outside the locked door, though he knew for a fact Cahn wouldn't be back for hours.

Slowly he relaxed about her, smelling her sleepwarm sweetness. He'd touched her so many times in his life that she was as familiar as a wife to him and he was certain she would know it was he before she opened her eyes. She would know that no one on the entire earth could love her as he loved her. To love her just for her. To want to give her love without asking anything in return but her presence.

And it was so. She slept deeply, without remembered dream, just that everpresent gnawing at the center of herself. Gnawing, consuming, corroding, eroding at the cen-

[94]

ter of herself. It had been there for years. Forever, perhaps. And it would be there to the end of her life. She knew it without giving too much thought to it. That half-conscious knowledge that she would never do whatever it was necessary to do to satisfy a need she could never understand—a need once satisfied which would pacify, satisfy, ameliorate, mitigate that gnawing, that dissatisfaction at the center of herself.

She waked quietly without opening her eyes, aware of her body encircled by his young self and knowing immediately and contiguously with her waking that it was he. He knew I'd be alone, that the door would be open, as it always is. I know his body as I know my own. How often he has touched me—it's always been impossible for him to be within fifty feet of me without touching me. Bursting to give his love. He wants to give it, envelop me with it, imprison me with it. Giving love is too important to him. He's so young, but changing, becoming a man.

She pretended still to sleep, her body completely relaxed, curled and curved inside the shell of his. Then as in sleep she took his hand, as she had once done when he was a boy, only now she led it to her breast. Quietly he rested his hand there, holding his breath for a moment fearful of waking her, then slowly, gently, he began to caress her, feeling her heart underneath beating slowly, then swiftly, half-knowing she was awake, pretending sleep, both pretending she was asleep, both knowing the other knew she wasn't.

He gave her love, a boy giving a woman his adolescent love until its warmth covered her completely and she relaxed into it, into the rhythm of his loving, her heart beating quickly, and his, until with the depthless sweetness of his love and caressing she was overcome and reached alone the full sweet contract.

They both lay quietly until he whispered his love into her ear. And she answered, terribly ashamed that she had taken his love this young way without having given him any love in return, "I'm very selfish, you know. But another time—"

"Ssh, I'm happy having given you pleasure. I've been wanting to so long—"

She turned and stretched loose from his encircling body and lay alongside him the length of the bed. "You're very sweet and very wild, but I'm a woman and you're still too young. Still too young, and Simon said I would hurt you and I wasn't to."

"Simon's dead. Stop talking about him as if he's somewhere around. Besides, I know you better than Simon did."

How arrogant he was. "You'll find someone to love—someone as young and as needing of love as you are to give it." She kissed him full on his lips, gently, without passion.

He began to tremble and she knew it was from desire too long restrained. Why didn't she just take him into her arms, into herself, give him what he'd wanted so long? She wanted to and if he had moved aggressively she would have acceeded, but something in him felt he must wait until she herself said he should, perhaps a young pride or stubbornness or still perhaps a fear of at last bringing to fruition the want of many years. And with her it was a willful restraint, a fear too perhaps that once yielded up to him she would lose this young lover, this youth, forever.

His trembling controlled, he stood, and looking up at him from the low bed, he seemed to her extremely elongated, reaching to the ceiling almost, someone who had grown out of her side, a son or a brother, and it frightened her. He said, "I'm going away again."

And before she could utter a word, he left, closing the door behind him forcefully, as in anger.

She closed her eyes and slept fitfully the remainder of the morning, the gnawing, the dissatisfaction more conscious now. Later, when Matt Cahn returned, fastidious yet restless, tight yet impatient, and she awoke, Zeke's presence earlier in the day seemed but a fitful yet very sweet dream.

X

At home food was scarce that winter. Zeke was made to feel, or himself felt since he could find little work, that every piece of food he ate was a piece less for his mother and Rebecca. Hell, he was a man. Tired of mooching off Abe and Viola, he decided to take off for the South. Besides, he had to get away from Rachel. He loved her obsessively, but still a carping doubt nibbled at him; it seemed to him she acquired some sort of strength from having both a husband and a young lover who hung around. He didn't understand, wouldn't even talk to Abe or Viola about it, it was too private—he was being foolish, Christ, what thoughts go through a man's mind, what impossible, insoluble thoughts. Anyway, he wanted to see the South, it was a goddam cold winter, he heard one could find work in Miami Beach waiting on tables. So again he put shoe leather—thin—to asphalt or macadam.

On U.S. Route 1 in Jersey, he met a young man headed for Florida too and joined up with him. They had fair luck, considering the paucity of cars.

When he saw the famous road sign between South Carolina and Georgia, he wanted to turn back. Most states had big welcome signs. So did Georgia, but in addition, "Conviction in this state means the chain gang." His new friend, Harold Clemens, Methodist—small, extremely thin, Andy Gump face—convinced him to ignore the sign;

they had a few dollars in their pockets and couldn't be held on a vagrancy charge.

"There must be *some* law and order down here; after all, they're Anglo-Saxons," urged Harold.

They were fortunate and were given a lift by a very nice middle-aged lady about thirty years old who was going to Miami to marry a hotel clerk. One never thinks of hotel clerks as marrying, but it seemed they did. The lady needed someone to help her drive because she wanted to get to Miami swiftly, she could hardly wait. She was in fact so impatient she stopped at a motel in Jacksonville and took two rooms, one for her and Harold—"I find you very sympathetic"—and one for Zeke. Then, no less than now, motel rooms had paper walls. All night Zeke could hear their bed flying. He found it disturbing and had to go and sleep in the car, but not before arriving at a firm conclusion that women were much brighter than men. A woman didn't care if a man was ugly—Harold was even uglier than he—and they didn't give a damn how big or little he was either: if they found something sympathetic in a man, that was enough.

When their lady dropped them off in Miami, she and Harold promised one another lifelong fealty. Because she was a lady of good breeding, she married her intended but every Wednesday afternoon for twenty-five years Hal dropped in on her for what he once told Zeke was the hottest bang in these here United States. One day about twenty-five years later, Zeke saw what looked like a familiar chinless face covering the entire front page of a tabloid. Harold Clemens. He'd emptied his gun into her. Married though both were, each with their own home and children, he discovered she was cuckolding him with a third man. At the trial Harold played it cunning: pleaded *momentary* insanity. He was remanded to the state hospital to which every week Zeke sent him cigarettes and secondhand copies of *Life*.

Immediately upon their arrival in Miami Beach, Florida Hal found a job as shill for a couple of small-time gamblers who operated out of the rhinestone brilliance of the lobby of an old, worn velvet and lace hotel in which both Hal and Zeke had found lodging—they slept in a back laundry room lined with old-fashioned wash tubs and busy with mosquitoes and cockroaches. Every night the gamblers found what Hal inelegantly but accurately called a *fish*, whom they proceeded to bait, hook and fry. For his help, Hal received a small stipend from the gamblers, both of whom wore dark, pin-striped winter suits, pointed black shoes, loud bizarre ties, tiny mustaches, and looked exactly like movie gamblers. Zeke ate off that fishy money for a month and then picked up a job as busboy in a big kosher hotel on Biscayne Bay. Eats and tips. The food was overcooked, but the tips were lavish. One old gent, a dead ringer for Calvin Coolidge, tipped Zeke very generously because he admired Zeke's big nose. Banana nose, said the old gent, like that of a young jockey at Hialeah on whom the old gent had begun to bet and to make himself a young fortune. Zeke was so pleased, he sent Arcaro, the jockey's name, a note. "Every time you win, I get a big tip. Thank you. By the way, my nose is bigger than yours—do you think I'd make a good jockey?" Arcaro, a very serious young man, didn't answer.

Besides eating enough and having money in his jeans, even after sending most of it to his mother, Zeke, as would be expected of a young man, picked up a girl friend on the beach—a white Southern lady from Alabama who lived with her cross-eyed, foolish mother in an apartment on swank Lincoln near Collins while her father was on the road earning money as a shirt salesman. He specialized in

[100]

white shirts. Her name was Atalanta Morgan Swift and she was very tiny and very shapely, sort of a dwarfish Mae West—cinched in with a broad leather belt so that she burgeoned out top and bottom. Tiny as she was, in a bathing suit—or without—it was apparent she had the largest, longest bosoms on the beach and was a sin for sore eyes. Zeke had a lot of trouble with her. She just adored doing it on the flo'—she on top. "Ah feel lak a ribroast on the butcher's block," he complained to Hal, simulating as best he could her mode of speech, having complained first to Atalanta and gotten for answer an idiotic giggle. Besides he had to get her to keep her girdle on when they made love—chop chop—because she was so capacious he didn't know whether he had entered and she had to inform him by kicking his loins with her heels, which he found very debilitating to an already scarred ego.

He decided to give her up, but didn't know how to go about it, so clinging was she. Finally, he told her his tight curly hair, though red, was derived from a Negro grandfather. To his astonishment, she reversed the order of things, she lay on the floor before him and pleaded, "Whup me, boy, whup me."

Convinced she belonged with Krafft-Ebing, he departed.

After deserting Atalanta, Zeke enjoyed his stay in Miami Beach. His hours of work weren't too long, the work itself not too strenuous (after Newday, no work was ever to be again), food plentiful, a couple dollars in his shoe, the beach populated with more girls than boys—always a delightful statistic—and Rachel Farrell far away, not forgotten, an undefined sadness hidden deep behind his ribs. In all, an easy life.

Too easy.

One afternoon, strolling through downtown Miami, he

witnessed a small Negro boy accidentally drop a milk bottle on the sidewalk and be the immediate victim of a quick and harsh policeman's boot in the behind. High and hard. The boy befouled his pants and ran crying from the scene of his crime. The cop laughed. Zeke faced him, the cop grinned, Zeke thought better of it, turned his back and walked away.

Shame.

He had to take it out on somebody. The following afternoon, serving tea at the hotel with one of the waitresses, he found that the woman, a middle-aged harpie, with a face like boiled cabbage, had stolen ten cents from the glass in which they pooled their tips. Overwhelmed by righteous anger that one worker would steal even a dime from another, he left early, proceeded to the parking lot across from the hotel and deflated one of her car tires. Abruptly sorry, he ran away.

Shame compounded.

The following afternoon he was astonished to find the devil in the face and form of Charles Evans Flagg waiting for him. Charles Evans Flagg would have called it the forces of history, the class struggle, the revolution, the ubiquitous, the ineluctable, the remorseless clash between the modes of production and the modes of distribution and exchange.

Charlie Flagg was an immense fullback with an easygoing style, a very handsome face, clefted chin, strong short nose, charming smile, cynical blue eyes, a riot of wavy blond hair. A real devil of a fellow. Cleancut. Zeke had met him quite a number of times in his cousin Abe's house. Charlie would come for supper whenever the party neglected to pay him his ten dollars a week, which was often since the party leaders were playing the stock market with its so-called Moscow gold. Flagg was a party organizer, a very good one, a professional's professional, as they say, a man who stabbed with exclamation points. Theory! Practice! Stalin! Action! But a nice guy. Once, seeing Charlie in serious conversation with Zeke, Dr. Abramson, using his immense belly like a bulldozer before him, pushed Charlie against the wall. "You can come here to eat all you want—food's for everybody. But stay away from my kid cousin, do you hear! I don't want him ground up." Charlie had grinned, cynically of course, and replied, "Don't worry, Abe, he's a tough bastard who'll end up in the party without any pushing. So will you." It was inevitable.

There was no coincidence to Charlie's waiting for Zeke. Charlie had been to New York about a week before, had eaten one night at Dr. Abramson's—even had gotten into political argument with Matt Cahn and Rachel whom he'd met there. Matt had joined a committee headed by Professor Dewey to investigate the charges made by Stalin against Trotsky. Matt joined this committee not, as he said, "because I am a follower of Trotsky or even a Marxist—I am if anything a liberal democrat—but because I believe in the decadent idea that every man deserves an opportunity to be heard in his own defense." Charlie said the investigation could only help the fascists, and Rachel retorted that truth was the strongest weapon against "the enemies of man." Charlie laughed contemptuously. "Pure romanticism," he said, "which can lead only to a concentration camp." To which Matt replied, dryly, "Or a slave camp in Siberia." Charlie shrugged and began discussing the necessity for organizing in the South and someone said that Zeke, Abe's wild cousin, was working in a hotel on Biscayne Bay, the beach side. Charlie found him.

"Listen, kid!" he said, hardly waiting to shake hands. "I need your help!"

"Go away, Charlie. I'm down here to earn a few dollars. I'm eating good and want to have a little fun before the war breaks out and I'm sent to die for democracy and against fascism."

"Not for a few years yet, Zeke!" Charlie snapped, making what turned out to be an accurate prophesy. "You've been running away! It's time we caught up with you! You're one of us and you know it! Doesn't being in the South get you mad?"

"It sure does, Charlie. The way they treat Negroes—"

"Stop talking and start doing! Action! We have a chance to organize some Negroes! You going to run away from it?!"

No, no, he wasn't going to run away. He was no coward. Cowardice makes one do shameful things. Yes, perhaps it was time to do something. Eating good was making him fat and forgetful. There were things to do, so many things, and it was time he started. So he said, "Okay, Charlie," and was led by Comrade Flagg, who let not even a flicker of victory light his charming face, to his room in a dinky hotel on Washington, near Fifth. There Charlie locked the door and pulled two chairs to the exact center of the room where they would be least likely overheard by neighboring roomers and possible snoops. Charlie spoke in a whisper so that Zeke had to cup his ears and lip-read. Charles Evans Flagg, a handsome young man, tough and cynical though he was, took his job—and role—very seriously. Men like Charlie were drawn to the party because they could play at conspiracy and revolution, a game they loved, and they played it so sincerely it became to them the living truth.

One evening two weeks later, having made arrangements to have his tables in the hotel dining room covered by other busboys, Zeke met Charlie Flagg in a quiet Miami street. Comrade Flagg drove a brand-new black Ford.

"The party's doing okay by you, I see," Zeke joked lamely, really too serious and scared to make a healthy attempt at humor.

"It's a beaut, isn't it? Conned old Bird on the ninth floor—you think I like this, Zeke—driving a new car when men are starving in the street? I do it because it's necessary! I'm not sentimental about it!"

Zeke laughed at Charlie's swift switch, and then Charlie was hurt, his face reddening in the darkness, the cleft in his otherwise square chin throbbing. Charlie had meant what he said, perhaps unaware of his personal conflict between cynicism and idealism. It was a conflict which was to demolish him. Eighteen months later he couldn't make the switch fast enough. Carl Vlanoc, short, squat, and just as schizophrenic, head of Stalin's secret police in Loyal Spain, had a party *pistolero* put a bullet into Charlie Flagg's very handsome head. When Samuel Zeke Gurevich, an itinerant soldier with an itinerant Spanish battalion, heard of Charlie Flagg's execution, he took a deep swig of very bad Spanish brandy which an English novelist, first apologizing for its inferiority, had given him in the trenches dug near the Jarama River, and laughed to himself. Serves Charlie Flagg right. Justice has its own circuitous route. Excepting this time, justice made a bad bargain.

It was a bad bargain for Rafer Madison when Charlie Flagg and Zeke Gurevich stuck their noses into his life. Because Rafe Madison was an innocent. All he wanted was to speak up against his plight. He wanted to say: Look, for God's sake, I didn't ask to come into this world. Now I'm here I don't want to be a footstool, that's all. I want a chance to earn a dollar and I want a chance to be left alone. I don't want to cry about it, I don't want even to have to talk about it. I just want to be left alone to make my dollar and to have my peace.

Mr. Madison was a cotton sharecropper outside Savannah. He was a scrawny muscle of a man with a round head and black skin. He was no hero. During the day he was a yassuh man; during the night he wondered why he had to be. That's all. Wondered. Perhaps he would have let it go at that, but the man whose land he sharecropped decided to put the squeeze on a bit tighter, he too was being squeezed, and Rafe had to go over and scrape his feet, look down at his shoes and yassuh when he wanted to say no suh. And he wondered why out loud one night, perhaps he'd had a drink, though he wasn't much of a drinking man—corn mash was too strong for his stringy belly; he was a cranky, skinny man.

So he wondered out loud among his fellow sharecroppers one night, and one of them—perhaps no longer innocent since he'd heard a speech once at a meeting—passed the word along to a Negro schoolteacher by the name of Ella Johnson. Years before Ella Johnson had been to junior college in Atlanta where she'd met Susan Reynolds who knew Ronald Avis who was now a friend of Charlie Flagg, the party organizer in the South.

Ella Johnson wrote a letter to Susan Reynolds in which she said there was talk among the sharecroppers (exaggerating a bit because she was so anxious) that something ought to be done among them to lighten their load, soften their plight, to help them earn a few cents more. It's time, said Susan Reynolds to herself, it's time someone did something. She remembered Ronnie Avis had told her one night that he'd met this white man who was like an old-time abolitionist, a man who lived and worked to help people, black and white, make a better life.

Susan Reynolds, a tush of a girl, contacted Ronnie Avis who worked as a porter in a Savannah hotel and told him what Ellafat, their school name for Ella Johnson, who lived and taught Negro school in one of the small towns outside Savannah, had written her. Avis read the letter, also said, it's time, and thought, this is something for Charlie Flagg. Flagg had left with Ronnie an address in Miami Beach, the home of a rich dame who lived on Palm Island, and who was one of a circle of rich who gave money to Charlie's party which, Charlie said laughingly, meaning it was a joke, was dedicated to liquidating the rich by lopping off their heads.

When Flagg read Ronnie's letter, his heart beat faster, his feet wanted to dance—this was the break he'd been waiting for. While the iron is hot, strike. Call a meeting. But his orders were never to reveal or expose himself to more than one contact at a time. Party organizers were finely cut diamonds, they were not to be wasted. He must find a fearless innocent to do the work. Zeke Gurevich was perfect: a young man emotionally tied to the movement who'd been evading his responsibility and could be easily made to feel the knife of guilt. That the knife was already dripping with Zeke's blood was a bonus which Comrade Flagg hadn't expected.

The plan was for Zeke to meet Ella Johnson who would arrange a meeting between him and Rafer Madison and his sharecropper friends. Charlie, an excellent organizer, instructed Zeke on what he was to say. Charlie also seemed to know what Rafer would do and say: he and his friends would listen because they were innocent and wanted to believe the words and to do something. They would believe Zeke because he would speak with authority—a white man who risked the chain gang and tar and feathering, or worse, to speak words of truth and justice.

Those words clanged like a bell from Charlie's mouth. "They will be suspicious but impressed," Charlie told Zeke. "In the end, if you do and say as I instruct you, they'll act!"

Yes, Charlie Flagg was a pro, so first he spent many hours with Ronnie Avis instructing him how to speak to Ella Johnson and on what to instruct her to do, and to impress her with the importance of her job and of Zeke whom she would soon meet. Then Ella would speak to Rafe Madison and convince him how important he was and how important his work was to be in the liberation of the Negro. Charlie Flagg spent many days in Savannah devoting his time to this. And because he was a pro, and very sincere, and obsessed, he invested Ronald Avis with the importance of his work. And Ronnie, who for the first time in his life thought there was a chance at changing their lives, became excited and enthralled. It was a contagion he passed on to Ellafat Johnson, who in turn passed it on to Rafe Madison who, less cranky but with severer stomach cramps, convinced his friends to meet one night in his glued and tied-together shack with this important, courageous man from the No'th, a man who lived to help them, and who would teach them how to come by an extra few cents for their crop.

Everyone except Charlie Flagg was scared, yet it went as he predicted.

On the evening of the day that Zeke Gurevich again saw the sign he so detested—Conviction in this state means the chain gang—he showed up in Ellafat's shack on what the white farmers euphoniously called Coon Road. Zeke, who never felt so white in his life or so scared, acted very seriously, spoke sparingly, created an image of himself as a strong, quiet-spoken man, just as he'd been instructed by Comrade Flagg. "You have to give them the impression of self-confidence and inner strength, which is after all what a man has when he belongs to a party which already has power over one-sixth of the earth's surface!"

Ella Johnson, no fool, was taken aback at his youth. But Zeke, sweating profusely and holding his stomach intact by his newborn bolshevik iron will, followed Charlie's instructions to a nicety, and acted his part. The pre-cut stones had been well-laid and Ellafat yielded to the inner strength which was revealed in the white man's calm, slow movements, his firm but quiet-spoken words. She led Zeke through a sweet and peaceful Southern night to Rafer Madison's shack which contained a terrible smell of old sweaty clothes and poverty. He knew the smell well. There weren't enough chairs and most of those present, ten Negro men, sat on the floor. They all looked at Zeke through very serious, suspicious eyes. Though he was nervous, could feel sweat dripping down his back, and the roots of his hair hurt—so stiff were they from fright—he spoke quietly as he had been told to, playing on their wants, their poverty, their humiliation at the hands of the anonymous and specific white farmers for whom they sharecropped. As he spoke, he was captured by his own words, via Charlie Flagg, and by his own heroism and goodness at what he was doing for these poor, black people, all of which gave his voice a tone of inner strength and passion. Then he spoke of the party to which he belonged and which he represented, its adherents which numbered millions throughout the world, its conquest over the most vicious landholder the world had known, its sovereignty over one-sixth of the earth. The Negroes stared at him coldly, red-eyed from fatigue and sun, suspicious. But he continued in a slow, remorseless cadence.

They must organize, alone they were the individual fingers of a hand, easily broken; organized they were the fist of a hand. They must organize.

He was silent. They examined him from head to toe, took their time, for with them it was a life and death matter that they make an absolutely correct decision. As he stood before them he felt there was something wrong here, there were forces at play he couldn't understand, he was over his head, yet his pride and arrogance forced him to do as he had been instructed, to stand silently, pretending to be at ease in the face of their examination of him. Charlie Flagg better know what he's doing.

After they had stared at him for a few moments, they looked at one another, an embarrassed silence, then at Rafe Madison, whose face was creased and grimacing as if he were suffering from cramps. Then Rafer asked in a quiet, halting voice what they were to do, for Ellafat had done her job well, and had coached him that that was what he was to ask.

Zeke told them that they must first organize themselves into a committee, the Sharecroppers and Fieldworkers Organizing Committee; they must speak among their friends and get as many as possible to join. Then, very quickly, they must have a meeting, an open meeting held at night to which their members and friends must be invited to discuss a program for going forward. "A man can't do it himself. When there are enough friends, a man has the courage and strength to go forward."

He was silent again. He could see they wouldn't speak in his presence. Charlie Flagg had known and instructed him to excuse himself so they could speak freely among themselves. They would inform Ella Johnson and she would relay the message to him.

He offered his hand for shaking to Rafer Madison and

Rafer looked at him with a pained expression in his eyes—no white man had ever offered to shake hands with him before and he didn't know if he should. Zeke stood there with his hand out, embarrassed, too late now to draw it back. Now all the others in the kerosene lighted shack stared at them and Zeke wished he had never come. But Rafe saved it by abruptly touching fingers to his and they both smiled, then Zeke left with Ellafat.

At her shack, a one-roomer with an old table and chairs in the center, and against the wall a huge tarnished brass bed with a sagging mattress, they had chicory coffee and cookies. She told him, her round brown face bittered by disappointment, that she had expected a more enthusiastic response. "Why should they talk in front of me?" he asked her. "I'm a stranger so far as they're concerned. Don't worry about it, Rafer'll convince them, you'll see. Man, but he's got a sour face; is he always like that?"

She laughed. "He's been colicky since the first day he was born."

As they finished their chicory, Benjamin Calhoun appeared, half-drunk, foul-mouthed and nasty. A thin black pipe of a man. Then his eyes focused and saw Zeke, saw he was a white man, and he went into his act, the jig jigger, the jazzy jazzman, the smiling spook. Disgusted, Zeke told him to knock it off. "I'm leaving, mister."

Zeke and Ella concluded their business, and he left to meet Charlie Flagg at a predetermined place.

"Get yo' big black ass ovah here and let's go to bed," said Ben Calhoun to Ellafat. "Get yo' hustlin' ass ovah here. Ah got to get to the sto' in four quick tired owahs."

"Go to sleep, Ben," she said softly. "I'll come when I come."

"Yo' long past comin', Ellafat. Long past comin'."

"It wasn't what you think, Ben. He's a friend of Susan Reynolds, a girl I knew in school," she repeated for the third time since Zeke had left. She must not tell him more.

"What yo' talk about?"

She couldn't tell him, he talked too much, so she ignored him.

"Yo' gettin' yo' fat black ass ovah here or does ah come and get you? What's ailin' you tonight? You dyin' a grief fo' that white boy, or is it Rafe Madison? 'A man gotta wash, Ben,'" he screwed up his face and mimicked Rafer to a T, "'iffen a man wawnts to be clean' as iffen a man wawnts to be clean. What fo'? Not even Pete Kane"—he spoke the name as if throwing a knife and she cringed—"bathe every day—an' he a white man. Don't you all like ma smell tonight, Ellafat? Yo' like it good fo' ten fat yeahs. Every brown gal in the county like it good—and plenty white gals too," he lied and laughed his hoarse-voiced laugh. "C'mon ovah here, Ellafat, ah gonna plumb ma black pipe tonight," he laughed again to hide the hurt.

She didn't answer, now barely heard the words—the same words and boasts she'd heard for ten years. Soon he would tire of his own jabber and turn towards the wall and fall asleep. And snore. And talk in his sleep. And dream. And whimper, scared. Then turn to curl up and hide in her soft weary body.

Yet tonight was not like other nights. They'd lived their lives on this back dirt road in their faded stinking shacks, stealing crumbs from the stale broken bread of white town, barely richer, a goodly number just as poor. They were all caught in some tangled twine, and the harder they fought to break loose, the tighter the tangle. Well, perhaps something would change now. They were doing something. As they'd sat in Rafe's shack, a guard at the door, the white boy had said, "Man is what he makes himself. It's in his own two hands man has the ability to change his life." The boy had spoken with passion. She had guessed he was scared, but had to admire the way he concealed it. Well, he was no more scared than she or any of them.

Ben snored, and she looked up. Once he whimpered. She raised her two hands before her eyes to examine them. Could these two hands help change her life and the lives of the children she tried so hard to teach to read and write? There were some things these two hands could never do—they could never teach her whom to love or not to love. She loved Ben Calhoun, understood and loved him. And every other day despised herself and him. He was a rotten apple. Not even that. Even a rotten apple has a core, shriveled, worm-eaten, but a core. Ben had nothing. Sap, but no core. He loved nothing. Nothing? A thirst, yes; a thirst, like a sponge, a thousand thirsty cells, thirsty for whisky, for food, for a woman's body. When the sponge cells became overladen, he spread out in the white fields to dry. A day, a week, a month. Dried out, he'd scramble to his feet, a thin black man, and again begin to sponge. Some day, like a sponge, he would dry up, harden, turn gray, curl, and die. And Ellafat Johnson would waste away, because she couldn't live for more than two weeks without him. Tell me why, two hands? Tell me why?

They over there had destroyed Ben Calhoun and all his mirror images past and present. But still, because she was an honest lady, she must ask herself why are there some not destroyed? And she saw Rafe Madison, a scrawny, skinny muscle of a man. Even when Rafe yassuhed to his white man or the sheriff or the general store man, Pete Kane, that dirty, filthy, no-good white bastard, it was with an unhurried unashamed smile which they must know and understand was a smile of complete and utter contempt. He moved his slight weight to a rhythm of his own making. He had not been destroyed. Why?

An unanswerable question—or a question for another time. Now Ellafat looked at her dollar watch. She yawned—it was late. Ben was, for him, fast asleep. His head and body were pressed hard against the polished gray wood which was the inner skin of this crumbling ancient shack on what white town with a quaint smile called Coon Road.

Ellafat picked up a brown paper bag, blew out the kerosene wick and stealthily slipped into the Georgia night.

In the darkness Zachariah walked through and among the pines which flourished along the bank of a sluggish muddy brook. He walked to the rhythm of a song of his own making.

Kill.

Kill.

Kill the white man.

Kill the bastards.

Kill and kill.

Kill the stupid bastard white man.

You want to know what a white man's made of?

Get a white man—a thirteen-year-old or a sixty.

Pick him up—hard.

Set him down—hard.

Under a tulip tree, any tulip tree on a dirt road bounding any cotton field.

Set him down rough and hard.

All alone.

Then get a Nee-gro girl—yaller, tush, or brown-black.

Eight or eighty.

Set her down on that dirt road bounding a cotton field.

No other man around.

Give her a little shove to start her towards that tulip tree.

Now you watch that white man.

His face.

His blue blue eyes.

The hound-dog point of his skinny nose.

His white-pink ears.

His breathing chest.

His pants where they catch at the crotch.

YOU WATCH HIM.

You know that Nee-gro girl's moving.

She's getting closer.

She's close to him.

YOU KNOW.

Because his skinny pointy nose is twitching, because his blue, blue eyes are blurring, his white-pink ears are swinging, his chest is wheezing, that little bone at his crotch is growing, his lips are dry, his tongue is mumbling:

"Y' dirty little niggah gal. Y' ruttin' dirty niggah gal. C'mon heah—watchuh runnin' fo'? Oh, goddam tuh hell yuh ruttin' fuckin' dirty niggah gal."

This time that Nee-gro girl—eight or eighty—has got clean away. She's got clean away because you're doing the picking up and the setting down. This is *your* ex-per-i-ment.

You're showing what a white man's made of.

Next time you're not there. That stupid bastard white man grab that girl and put that white bone right to her. Nine months later *we* got another tush child to worry about.

Kill the white man.
Kill and kill.
Kill.

Zachariah heard a door open and close and he smiled. She's coming. The sweet lady who never forgot him was coming. Closing his eyes, he could see her by the light which shone night and day inside his very bone-white Negro skull. She would be close to him, would touch him with her soft hands, and he would open his eyes and see her. The sweet lady.

His eyes closed, hearing her footsteps, light and sure, approaching closer, he sat down on the earth and leaned with his back against a tulip tree.

The sweet lady's footsteps were close by now and he was filled with a sweetness greater than the sweetness of all the tulip trees in all the south, because the sweetness did not cloy, did not overwhelm, did not make one grow dizzy with nostalgia; it was the sweetness of a quiet love, bittered by sadness, and now the sadness overwhelmed the sweetness and he wanted to cry. To cry large tears. To be overwhelmed by tears. To be drowned in them—go down deep into a sea of tears, deep, deep. Now he wanted to kill her too. Kill. And hate. And sweetness. Sadness. And tears. Overwhelmed with tears.

He could feel her standing near him. He could smell her presence. There was no other smell quite like it in the entire world. Hers. That's all.

Both her hands were on his cheeks and he turned his head first to kiss one and then the other, then stood up, a good head taller than she.

She looked up at him, the son of her youth. He'd become a night man. Lived only in the night. In the day he hid in his shack a few hundred yards behind hers, under the trees and near the brown muddy brook among the bull frogs. In the day he hid behind windows covered with old burlap, under the blankets of his bed and slept. She hoped and prayed he slept. At night he came out to play-act and talk to himself. He wasn't mad, she thought, it was a phase, growing up. He was nineteen years old, though she herself was barely thirty-three. The son of her youth. Her childhood.

"I've brought you something to eat, Zach. When are you going to outgrow this nonsense? You can't hide from the world forever. After all, there's nothing wrong with you—is there?" she asked plaintively.

"No, Ellafat, there's nothing wrong with me. Thanks for the eats. Goodnight, ma, it's late for you."

"Yes. Goodnight, Zach. And try to come out of it—it's been long enough. Will you, Zach?"

"Yes, ma."

She pulled his head down towards her and kissed his cheek. He had a sudden urge to strike her, to beat her, because she once had walked all alone on a dirt road bounding a cotton field; instead he smiled.

The lanterns were quickly out, there was cursing, shouting, several shots and Zeke Gurevich was running—running, frightened, belly-scared, sweatless scared, his skin drawn taut, crying scared, running in the darkness, through the trees, heedless to the clutching boughs, a thousand fingers grabbing at him, whipping his face, his neck, his legs, hating the occasional light of the moon when it broke through into an opening, hating the shadows it made. Running scared, fighting back the panic and hysteria and tears, still conscious of where he ran because he'd been over the way with Charlie Flagg ten times till it had impressed itself on his reflexes, and glad now that

Charlie Flagg was a pro—but was he? This fiasco. This terror. It had been too hurriedly done. "Hurry them! Strike while the iron is hot! Don't give them time to get cautious!" Charlie Flagg. And they—Rafe Madison, Ella Johnson, Zachariah Johnson, and the others, their friends who had come out to a meeting to sign petitions, a night meeting—why?—to make a show of strength—to whom? Betrayed. Somewhere a betrayal. Who talked? Talked too much? Sung. Sweet canary sung to the cops—sung to white town: the niggers are organizing. Fifty Negro men and women had shown up in the yellow pine grove far back off Coon Road, not too distant from the muddy brook near which Zach Johnson lived his night life. Fifty men and women, an army of spooks, an unheard of army, joining in battle against the white landowners. What now would be the end? How dare they organize? If he didn't hurry, the end would be him.

He heard footsteps behind him, racing footsteps and he stopped thinking as he ran, his feet driven by controlled hysteria and uninhibited fear.

The footsteps behind him were faster still, closing in, and he wanted to scream, to hide, hot tar and feathers, the chain gang, but Charlie Flagg had said don't stop ever, come all the way, and he ran, broke out into the open of a dirt road, and the footsteps were closer, friend or vigilante or cop, who knew? Who cared? Run, run, and then a bullet past his ear drained his blood, and another cut his breath in two; then there was the new Ford, the door open, and he fell in and the pro was gassing her, shifting gears like a race driver, and they sped down the dirt road and he was sick out the window and sick again, and yet again.

"There's a bottle of hootch in the glove compartment."

Charlie Flagg, a pro ready for every contingency. He took a long slug and hated it, but the fire of it burned its way down and he took another slug and it helped him to put a stop to his shivering and trembling.

"You knew this was going to happen. How?"

"Because someone always talks."

"Then why did we do it? Leading them to slaughter. Those fascist bastards were all over the place. We'll get away—but they live here."

"It has to begin some place."

"This will set them back thirty years."

"This will only make them hate the enemy even more."

"No, it'll make them hate us even more."

"For a short time only."

"Why'd we do it?"

"We have a reason."

"What's the reason?"

"To educate them in the methodology of organization; to make them aware of our presence."

"Suppose someone got killed back there? Someone who came not even because he wanted to—just not to hurt a friend's feelings?"

"The innocent die every day. At least this time it would be for a good reason—to let the enemy know it'll not be his way forever."

"Oh, go to hell."

"People die stupidly every day, Zeke, because they want to take a swim, go for a ride in the country, lay a woman while the husband's away—step on a rusty nail. So for once someone can die for what's worthwhile."

"There's something wrong in what you say—what, I don't know. But somehow your logic's all wrong."

"It's the logic of the revolution."

Rafer Madison's head was blasted open by a shotgun burst at five feet. Two days after Rafe was buried, Zachariah Johnson slit Ben Calhoun's throat with a razor, because it was Zachariah's belief, founded in fact, that Ben Calhoun had followed Ella to a meeting and had heard their plans and talked to his boss Pete Kane, the owner of the general store in white town. Pete Kane and his white gentlemen friends came after Zachariah Johnson, but he evaded them and lived in the woods of south Georgia for three weeks. One morning Zachariah couldn't hold it back any longer and showed up in white town and ran amok. With a razor he killed three white men, one being Pete Kane, his natural father. One of the men Zachariah killed was completely innocent. Zachariah was shot dead as he ran like a wild dog through the town square, a charming place overgrown with ivy and magnolia trees, his razor flashing red in the white Southern sun.

Ella Johnson somehow managed to stay alive and went to live in Chicago where she became a disciple of Marcus Garvey who advocated a Negro exodus to Liberia and Islam. When Garvey was sent up on mail fraud, Ellafat joined the Black Muslim movement. Ella Johnson is a big fat brown lady who believes white people are sprung from the devil. When she stands on a speaking dais she can enumerate several long standing facts to prove it.

XI

Charles Evans Flagg drove him clean out of Georgia, past the Conviction in this state means the chain gang sign, straight to New York. Zeke didn't even say goodbye, in fact he said not a word to Charlie in the last twenty-four hours he spent in the car. Every time he began to articulate his larynx and tongue to speak he tasted blood.

They parted. Where Charlie Flagg went Zeke didn't know and he heard no more about him until both were in Spain, when he was told Charlie had been executed by a party commissar for having broken revolutionary discipline. Perhaps Charlie had learned something down in Savannah. He intervened for a friend who had been condemned to stand at the wall for questioning the party line in Loyal Spain. For this subjective behavior, Carl Vlanoc ordered him shot too, and buried without ceremony, refused to have his corpse draped in a red flag even though it rained that day, always a happy occasion for Spaniards since Spain is an arid country. But that was a year or so later.

Zeke had a couple hundred dollars saved from the tips made in Florida and couldn't speak for dread of the taste of blood. He did what was customary for him to do in his low moments: he hid behind dumbness. He rented a room from an elderly couple who sold buttons and ribbons from a pushcart on Orchard Street. Their son had run off with a gentile girl and they'd worn ashes on their heads as for the dead. Now they had a spare room. They were busy at their pushcart from early morning to sundown, so he had the tenement to himself all day. He slept during the day, his room dark because it opened into one of those dismal New York courtyards. When the old pair, like two worn shoes, sagged into their flat at sundown—it was spring, sundown later every night—he ventured out into the streets. He didn't go near Hester Street where his mother, the pickle lady, and his sister Rebecca still lived; neither did he go near Abe's place or Rachel's. Once he saw Irving Green's sister Bosporus wheeling a baby carriage on Allen Street—her second child—but he ducked into a side street.

He remained alone. Two hundred dollars went a long way in those days, especially on Orchard Street where he could live off pushcarts and dirty basement restaurants. When, a month later, he read about Zachariah's running amok and his death, he practically stopped eating entirely—his stomach wouldn't take food. Inside he was just bleeding throats. Zachariah's razor had been very long and straight. Zeke Gurevich thought of killing himself. Without dramatics—quietly and intensely. He was nineteen years old, a strong boy with lots of juice, and it occurred to him that killing himself would be cowardly. Ducking out. What was he—a piece of scum? Hiding for a while was enough. He didn't even dream of that meaty almond, that graceful leaf curled in at the edges, of that sweet full-lipped mouth. An excess of violence had stilled the juices. Perhaps he was arid—no, inside he was full of wetness, red and sticky.

Remained dumb as punishment. How quickly he'd become a golden-voiced orator, captivated by his own vanity. Fork-tongued. Charlie Flagg had pressed the button and he'd talked. And they had listened, Rafe Madison and Ella Johnson. What innocent fools.

One afternoon in May, weeks later, as he lay abed staring at a cockroach make tracks along a desolate ravine sunk into the wretched ceiling, he heard a heavy rap on the outside door which he ignored. Then he heard Abe's loud voice. "Zeke!" He closed his eyes. Abe's voice became insistent. He wrote a few words on a slip of paper, "Please, Abe, let me alone," and slid it under the door. But Abe wouldn't go away, kept hollering and soon had an army of brats out there helping him. Zeke became embarrassed—even when you want to die, he thought, you can be embarrassed because you don't want the whole world peeking into your grave. Finally he opened the door, and when Abe barged in, big, fat and bouncing, his cousin Abe whom he loved, his brother, his father, his blood, Zeke, in keeping with the family tradition, began to cry. Abe merely led him back into his room, opened the window wide, "It stinks in here," and sat down on the bed with him and let him cry. Abe was the exception in the family, never did Zeke see him cry. Not even at family funerals. He once told Zeke, "If I begin to cry, I'll never stop, so I just don't begin." Abe was rarely if ever sentimental and rarely if ever cruel. Tough, but never cruel. Now he was wearing a beard, something new, and he just let Zeke cry.

Then Zeke told Abe what had happened exactly as he remembered it and his cousin listened. When Zeke concluded his gory story, Abe stood and put his big fat fist through the door; a thin-paneled affair, it is true. He began to pace heavily through the tenement, back and forth, the dark hall, the dismal kitchen, the old couple's damp bedroom smelling of camphor balls, the hall again, Zeke's room, out again, back and forth, heavily, angrily, his nose white. Zeke, sitting on the sagging bed, became scared because he had never seen Abe so mad. This time Abe was going to give it to him—and Zeke sort of hoped he would.

But Abe knew better, he wasn't going to give this boy any satisfaction. He stopped at last, stood before Zeke, an infuriated prophet, wet his thick lips with a red tongue under the brownish red mustache, pulled sharply on his beard, stared icy cold into his young cousin's despairing yellow eyes. "Charlie will get his, and from one of his own, I hope." A curse which came true. "He manipulated them and you helped him, you vomit." He stuck his thick finger under Zeke's nose and for a moment the boy thought he was going to jam it through his head. "One thing's certain, you didn't do it for them. Only for yourself. To give yourself a squeeze in the right place. Wasn't that it, you little bastard? To make yourself a big man. Next time you want to squeeze yourself, do it in private. Now you're hiding in shame, are you? That's not—" He saw tears in Zeke's eyes and became infuriated.

"If you cry, I'll beat you. You're not a child, grab hold of yourself." Then quietly he said, "Those people down there allowed themselves to be victimized just one more time. How long will they continue this way, just how long? Some day soon it's to be hoped they won't allow themselves to be victims, and then they'll change their lives and do more for themselves in one day than men like Charlie Flagg will be able to do for them in ten years. You want to help people, then have the decency to stop to think about what you're doing. And you! You're a big boy now, a man, and the one who can hurt you most is—stop crying, I say. All you're doing is relieving yourself, like taking a piss. It won't help them any. The dead, I mean. Now stop your bawling and come on."

Abe took him to his place and told him to take a bath. "You smell like a rotting tooth." Afterwards he gave Zeke a physical. "Your heart's like iron."

"And the murmur?"

"What murmur? It beats a tattoo like an iron drum. You'll live."

"You've told me that before."

They ate a hot pastrami sandwich, pickles, and drank cream sodas. "Go down and see your mother. She won't eat you up—neither will Rebecca. Will you ever learn when your mother says my kentser she means my angel? Give her her due, her life was harder than yours, and besides she gave you life—that's worth something, isn't it?"

"Yes, but what?"

"A three-cent piece," Abe said, and they laughed.

Zeke visited her, ate one of her burnt meals, talked about the pickle business—it was controlled by racketeers, they should all croak from a mixture of leprosy and diarrhea—and then she began to eat him up. "Muf beck to der house. Live duh. Sell pickles. I vill make you partner in pushcart."

Her eyes pleaded and he sensed she needed him, but he smiled, shrugged, parried, evaded, lied, hardened his heart. All proof he had become a man. They made a deal: he would come once a week for supper and she wouldn't bother him with questions and demands.

Zeke lived in Abe's house (washed the car, read to the children, ran errands) and almost every night, as always, he became dizzy tuning in on the Ites, the Ists, and the Isms. On frequent occasions an Ist became an Ite and got himself a new Ism. Though there was one thing none of them seemed to lack and that was a lot of Jism. If one did, he got Abe to give him an injection. They all came to Abe's to eat, to talk, to receive an injection of one sort or another, for hormone deficiencies, asthma, allergies, a dose, narcotic addiction, too much booze. Abe experimented with everything, looking to cure the world. Many who came to dinner called him a quack and blowhard. Joshua, home for vacation, beginning his respectable stage, stared down, over and beyond his nose (mustache, filled-out face, and suddenly the big nose took on grand aristocratic dimensions) at his brother and the surrounding mob. "They all need a deep analysis—and Abe most of all. They're not rebelling against the economic system, they're rebelling against their toilet training. Want to make the world sterile and shitless. My brother wants to do it with innocuous inoculations; this phoney mob (in which Abe seeks to conceal his loneliness) hopes to do it with blasts of hot air." Abe laughed, his belly bigger and fatter than ever. Ignoring Joshua, he said, "I may not cure you, but neither will I kill you. Can any of you Washington Square revolutionists say the same?"

Viola, as thin as ever, sallow, two eyes like targets, as silent as ever (Zeke was visited by a startling thought one morning, watching them at breakfast, that perhaps Abe was overpowering her), had the maid prepare food for everyone, and returned to her room to read her pupils' homework or mark test papers. Abe was in and out, satisfying a busy practice, as were the children who never lacked for company, for love, for someone to read or tell them a story.

It was Rachel who ruled their living room, still wearing her flowing dresses, colors clashing, her diaphanous scarves, her black hair wild, her ankles superb, her girdleless rump solid and round, her breasts blatant and bold under the loose bodice, hemmed in by ten revolutionists, vintage '36, a truly fine year for sour grapes. And not too far away stood Matt, his rectum tight, his diction exact, a bottle of Scotch at hand, his sharp voice cutting through the crap like Drano. He and Abe despised one another (Matt: Abe's a man who helps everyone hang out his dirty linen; Abe: Matt's all Narcissus), but made alliance against the lot of them. One night they emptied the Abramson living room in forty-five minutes of thirty men and women—hardy street corner speakers, agitators, organizers, conspirators, and sundry heretics—by daring everyone who opened his mouth to prove it. After the mob left, Matt and Abe sat down to play pinochle, a quarter and a half, while Zeke dozed with his head on Rachel's lap as she reclined on the couch, her fingers playing with his fiery red curls. In a corner of the room, Helen, Abe's sister, the one who gave Zeke a quarter every time she saw him—he never refused it—was quietly weeping as she read the afternoon newspaper report about the bombs dropped that very day on the Puerta del Sol in Madrid, Spain.

Zeke dozed off and on, sort of euphoric from the close, clean smell of Rachel's thighs. He was in love with her again—still, yet. She was all of twenty-four years old—would that October, two months off, be twenty-five—and in full blossom.

And more schizophrenic by the day. She wanted to tear loose, to embrace the entire world—she was parturient with the world, and she was married to a man whose poor lot it was to possess simultaneously and oppositely a tight fastidious ass and the insolence and genius of a big-time gambler. Fastidious always won out, the fruit of victory more and more fermented. Perhaps she was too much for him. He was beginning then, living only a year with Rachel, to tear her apart with his caustic tongue. Her ignorance could no longer be concealed behind pretense and he never let her forget it either in private or in public, so she began to parrot him. One didn't quite believe it. But it drove her to the reading of books instead of merely talking about them. Her talk was always interesting since she had the opportunity to brain-pick, and she did so with fine accuracy, those gentlemen of letters whose names bestrode the mastheads of the literary magazines of the time. Matt was certain she slept with every one of them. Years later, Zeke realized that in those days she hadn't learned yet to respect or at least recognize her own central virtue: her ability to invest even ennui with life. He loved her and was certain her sweet almond would soon become dry and bitter living with a man who looked back on his onanistic puberty with such sad nostalgia. Like every man who met her, Zeke believed only he could change her life and give her the greatest glory.

Rachel, because she'd known Zeke when he was a young boy and she already a woman of experience and tragedy, felt uneasy facing him and incidentally herself about the silly love affair they'd been having all those years. And since love is nothing if not a harsh discipline, Zeke came to understand that if frontal attack was out of the question he must then turn a flank. He'd waited long enough. So one morning after Matt had left for work, Zeke ventured to their apartment on Charles Street and found Rachel in a short, translucent nightgown bending keenly over the kitchen sink washing the breakfast dishes. The oval beauty thus revealed to him shook him to the bone. He came to swift decision and quickly moved upon it.

Flank turned; victory won.

All rumors to the contrary, all whining, sighing, tears to the contrary, for a few months life was shaped like an almond, and her name was Rachel. She taught him the beauty of a measured moment, the breathtaking flight which is tenderness, the absurd seriousness of laughter, and then, at the end, he cried.

"I'm not a toy," he wailed.

"No, you're not a toy," she said softly, "and I'm not a

flower, and life gives least to those who expect most."

"That's a lie," he cried.

"No, no," she said, wiping his tears with her hair. "Laugh at it, ignore it, even ridicule it, it'll come seeking you out to give you riches. But go at it with a gun and you'll find only a fog. I warn you—in fact, I've been warning you for years." He tried to burrow his head into her heavy breasts, his leg already buried in her thighs, but holding a clutch of his hair firmly she yanked him back. "Let's pretend what we have is only a small thing so then we'll find the rewards are greater."

"No," he cried again. "You're mocking me. You're mocking everything."

"Me is everything to you," she said in exasperation, reaching for her robe with which to cover herself. She rose from the couch and sat on the straightbacked chair nearby as he hid his head in the pillow and cried.

The apartment was dead quiet. Matt had left for work without even a goodbye earlier that morning. He was becoming catatonic. He might have guessed about Zeke, but no, he'd been engrossed in some misery of his own for months. Never had she known anyone who so detested himself as Matthew Cahn. She had again married someone less than whole. Matt kept reaching into the mirror for what was missing in himself. One day he would forget it was a mirror and attempt to enter through it to the other him. Narcissus: Abe was right. Smash would go the mirror and he would remain empty-handed, but bleeding. There was no other he but the one he knew and detested, the one who wanted to swing loose, go loping through endless plains. Really, he envisioned himself a buccaneer, unafraid of the horizons or of storm clouds, impatient for the sight of booty-laden sails, a lusty brawl, busty damsels, Captain Crossbones on the high seas. Silly man. But he was afraid and concealed himself in the dark corners of himself. When he stepped into the light his fear hampered his movements, he minced, he held on to his bowels for dear life from fear he'd let loose and befoul himself. It colored his life: color obvious. Poor man. Her female vitality he took as a challenge; he treated her as though he believed she were female merely to show her contempt for him—if she truly loved him she would shrivel her breasts, thin her thighs and conceal her center. Zeke, this romantic maniac of a lover, called it a knish, an almond, licked his chops and went right to it. Ram! She laughed. Matt approached it as though it had teeth. But he wasn't a coward, he fought it in himself and for a few days in every month he conquered himself, for a few hours he became a buccaneer. Then his intelligence and imagination carried them to heretofore unknown lands, two pirates pillaging the culture, mores, and sex habits of two second-generation aborigines.

Simon had tried to hide from reality by reaching for the impossible every moment, had tried to teach her that every second must be made exquisite with excitement and adventure and joy; Matt tried to teach her that every moment must be examined so closely one could hear the seconds tick by, lost in the coils of the horological spring. Simon had wanted to cheat death by challenging the impossible; Matt wanted to cheat death by challenging the second hand.

Zeke had once said she lived with Matt Cahn because she couldn't live without a man and Matt was the first to present himself after Simon's death. Half true. Zeke was still too young to discern the other half—or was he? There were times she had a feeling he knew. It went together with her previously perceived pattern of marrying men less than whole. She knew what it was but refused to admit it. Secret, she smiled to herself. As soon as I approach what I know will hurt, since *I* can't, *it* vanishes. She was no less a coward than anyone else. Well, what is it? No, it was gone. Vanished. Unsolved riddle.

Zeke Gurevich, five years her junior, what did he hide behind? His energy. He challenged even his own fears. He was a racer. Fast. Joshua Abramson, a very bright boy, said that the fastest runners were those with the greatest fears. He was probably just talking, but Zeke could certainly run a fast race. She had to admit she loved him— had loved him even when he was a boy: a strong, big-nosed, ugly-faced, red-haired challenging boy who couldn't keep his hands to himself. Clutching at breasts, a motherlover. Was it that which made him roam? An itinerant traveler? Challengers are always wanderers and rebels, looking for new worlds, better worlds, more exciting worlds—so long as it isn't this world. Poor world. She loved Matt, too. But this boy had forced his way in. He frightened a woman because he expected too much. Who the hell could give him everything?

"You're still in love with the idea of loving," she said to him. "You still think loving is sucking a sweet tit, mortar and pestle. Your love for me is the common everyday variety of love of a young man for a goodlooking woman who is willing. Why, you still stare wide-eyed at my triangle—as if you've just that moment come upon a miracle."

"Isn't it a miracle, Rachel?"

"For how long?"

"Forever," he said seriously.

She smiled sadly. She felt twice his age. "Go finish seeing the world, Zeke."

"Are you sending me away?" He sat up, his face white. He had come that very day to tell her he was leaving, going to Spain, and here she was sending him away. Damn her. She saw the whiteness of his face and misread it. She hated to hurt him, his love had been constant, ardent, strong. With all his clutching, he was no cripple. Yet the secrecy of their affair had become demeaning to her; she was beginning to feel like a fallen woman. All their beliefs kept proving out half-baked. Free love. Not so simple. Being against tradition didn't mean being free of.

She saw he was clenching his teeth so hard the veins at his temples were swollen. Despite the facility with which he could be driven to tears, he was tough and had the ability to take it. "Yes, I'm sending you away, Zeke."

"Go to hell, Rachel Farrell," he cried, and hit the wall so hard with his fists the print of Goya's remarkable *The Executions of May 3, 1808* trembled on its nail. "Go live with your Matthew Cahn, Esquire." He leaped from the couch and began hurriedly to dress, ripping his shirt in his anger. She wanted to say something to soften his hurt but knew it was best for him that he leave angry. Anger's fire cauterizes wound.

Clothes awry, disheveled red hair like an unruly coxcomb, he rushed past her, elbows flung out like pointed wings so that the nearest bruised her shoulder, and threw himself out the door.

She waited, knowing.

He came running back in, took her in his arms and kissed her passionately. "I hate you, Rachel. I'm going to Spain. I hope I die."

"Oh, no, Zeke," she now wailed, but he was gone, and she heard him, a bignosed Icarus, flying down the stairs. It was November 1936. She wept. He didn't stop until he fell to his frightened, quivering belly on the ancient cobbles of the courtyard of an old Moorish *palacio,* not far from the Puerta del Sol, in Madrid, Spain.

The sun was very high and very white, hot, a compact white molten iron ball, and from his position under a romanesque arch of a low running wall of gray stone, he shielded his eyes for fear he would be blinded. Not that it mattered much, since he had no gun. The only man with a gun in his group was at the south corner of the wall, and he shot it only when an enemy soldier presented a perfect target, for in addition to the gun he possessed a mere dozen cartridges. Between Zeke and the man with the gun, along the protected side of the wall, lay three dead and two live men. Before Zeke could get the gun, the two plus the man who held it would have to be either wounded or killed. There was another man with a gun at the north corner of the wall, and four or five men who waited for him to be hit.

Across the paved street, to the west, behind a neatly erected sandbag barrier was a very busy squad of ten enemy soldiers. They possessed a machine gun and rifles and ample ammunition which they used incessantly, squandering it on the gray stone wall behind which were Zeke and his comrades.

Zeke hated the enemy and envied them their wealth. He had been lying under the arch for three days and nights now, bread, water and a pilfered can of sweetened condensed milk his only sustenance. The nights were terribly cold; the days, between ten and three, terribly hot. But hot or cold, he quivered. Such fright as held him prisoner he had never been able to imagine. He could barely think. And after three days his only thoughts were for the remaining three men, his comrades, to hurry up and get hit. He wanted that gun. If the enemy had charged—and he wondered at their reticence—all he had to protect himself with were some round, fist-sized stones which someone before him had gathered and piled near the wall. He also had a knife.

The enemy in this particular sector of Madrid's outskirts had gotten to this street and been stopped. To his dying day, Zeke would wonder how and why. But of course a battle such as the siege of Madrid encompassed tens of thousands of men over a large area, and a soldier could never know the whole of it until he read about it in a history book. And even then it would be some historian's conjecture. So still he would be left to wonder. The enemy proved no less courageous, were infinitely better equipped and armed, could not have been more poorly led than he and his comrades—chaos was chief, confusion his lieutenant. Matt Cahn, who covered the Spanish civil war for an international news service, wrote that the enemy was overawed by an opponent who dared fight a shooting war without guns and ammunition, and that the enemy must in fact have been cowed by his opponent's will.

Zeke, of course, had an obsessive will. He had decided only death would remove him from this position under the arch of the wall, where he cowered and cringed at every shot, and there were thousands of rounds—all, he thought, aimed at him. For three days and nights his skin crawled, his scalp ached, his throat hurt, his heart jumped and turned and fled, seeking cover from every one of those thousands of enemy bullets.

"Die, you son of a bitch," he on occasion called out to give himself courage. "Die." And he just didn't care if it meant one of his own, so long as it brought him closer to the gun. And if he got the gun—then what? He'd never shot a gun in his life. Wouldn't even know how to load it. He would worry then. But at least he would hold in his hands the weight of its deadliness.

The sun, at its zenith, white and hot, began to descend to the west, and as it descended, less compact, less white, less hot and molten, soon a huge diffused orange flame, the cold from the Guadarramas made its first infiltration of the day, soon it would become freezing cold, and the

wall's shadows would scowl across the quadrangle behind him. Then darkness, and perhaps the enemy, wised
up, would attack under its cover.

He would wait for the enemy. He wouldn't flee. He had
made up his mind. Flee from an enemy whose greatest
boast was his contempt for intelligence? Never. He had
decided. He would wait in the darkness and grapple with
him, kill him with his knife or with a stone, take his gun
and bullets. If the enemy didn't come, he would steal
across the street to where the enemy lay in hiding behind
his sandbag wall and with a stone or with his knife—he
shuddered at the thought of the knife entering flesh—he
would kill one of them and steal his gun. He needed a
gun.

The sun descended swiftly now, the cold began to filter
through his heavy lumberjacket, his trembling increased
to the point where he thought of using his belt to bind his
jerking, jittery knees. He recognized this as the worst part
of the day for him. He sipped from his can of sweetened
condensed milk, the sweetness giving him a moment of
peace and pleasure. He allowed himself two sips a day,
one at dawn and one at twilight, when he seemed to need
it most.

It was dark.

All along the street it was quiet. Cold. He supposed the
enemy except for his guards was sleeping or being relieved.

The sky was black mesh. In the distance there was can-
nonading. It was said the enemy soldiers never went into
attack without the aid of artillery.

"Ezekiel. Ezekiel." It was the German comrade, the
closest to him without a gun.

"Yah, Kurt, what do you want?" he whispered in Yiddish German.

"*Schlafe*, Ezekiel. I and Czeslaw will stand guard."

"Thank you, Kurt."

He slept.

An enemy patrol of three men ventured to the wall two hours later and Kurt was killed. But Zeke (he couldn't use his knife, not yet) and Czeslaw and the man with the gun managed to turn the patrol back, killing one of them.

Now they had two guns for three men, and a belt of cartridges.

XII

It was never to be quite enough.

He fought for two years at Madrid, Toledo, Cordova, Teruel once, Teruel twice, the Ebro River, the final retreat to France. A passionate war. "The African sun burning up the asshole of Europe," a crude Russian colonel, a brigade adviser, said. Zeke hated the colonel. He hated the Russians. They and the Nazis had made a deal to exchange captured Germans and Russian officers. Most everybody else was killed. Zeke not only hated the Russians, he hated the Nazis, the Falangists, the party commissars—he hated all the manipulators, all those who thought of themselves as molders of human destiny. Though Zeke was a volunteer, his Interbrigade commissar refused his request to join a Spanish battalion. He went AWOL, found a Spanish unit to his liking, a maverick crew from every section of Spain, and soon was accepted as one of them. They even gave him the privilege of naming their battalion, as was the style of the war. He suggested The Third of May, after Goya's painting, and the Spanish captain, a former professor of literature at Salamanca, a little, narrow-shouldered man with a large drooping mustache as black as tar, embraced him in the European manner. "Why?" the captain asked him, and Zeke likened Spain to the vulnerable white figure of the painting, on his knees yet defiant before Murat's firing squad on the Puerta del Sol. "Sí," the

Spanish captain said. "And you know what it is he is saying to his murderers? *Por el honor de la vida.*"

They embraced and fought side by side for two years. His Spanish comrades gave him a picturesque name, because that too was the style of the war. One man was The Cat, another Mr. Shit, Aguilar the Segovian was *el Enano,* the Dwarf. Zeke they named *el Loco.* A man must be *loco,* they said, to remain in Spain, fighting in a losing war, when he could return to his homeland, eat beefsteak and screw Jean Harlow, already dead, yet the most desired woman in all Spain, loyal or fascist. Aiee, they dreamed, *me pinga en su boca.*

Zeke was certain they were right, he *was* crazy. Nuts. Obsessed. "If those lousy fascists win, the world'll stop," he said. "Better be dead," he said another time. "They don't know the meaning of honor and they don't know the meaning of life," he said still a third time. *"Pobre España,"* he said bitterly at the end in his terrible Spanish accent.

"Pobre España," the few who remained alive at the end echoed.

As the months screeched by, he became emaciated, and he couldn't even say what day of what month it was. Who could count the months? There were too many dead faces intervening. Besides he was too tired to count. Too hungry. Too crazy. But never too much of anything to forget his love, his Rachel, whom he always remembered with a lip-biting stab of pain.

In the early fall of 1938, he and his battalion lay sprawled and embittered in the Ebro valley, the fighting centered on the river, which they crossed on attack and in retreat four times. Zeke was bushed, beat, tired, his cheeks hollow, his head shaven, his yellow eyes afire, twin reflections of the sun. He hid behind a rock and some corpses in a sparse cypress and chestnut wood. He was hungry. The battle beginning just north of his sector sounded like an endless freight clanking over an eternity of iron rail. It was early dawn, the sun naked in a purple-blue sky. Knowing the battle would soon reach his sector, he hurriedly dismantled the bolt of his carbine, cleaned and polished it. Yesterday the battle had been extra fierce and his gun overheated so that he had to urinate on it to cool it off. He felt out of sorts. Extra bad that day. Observing the enemy from behind his barrier of rock and corpses—almost as good as sandbags, though they were beginning to stink sweet—he thought the air thin that morning, the fascists up ahead looked too close. Everything appeared enlarged to him—his eyes were like magnifying glasses. He observed an ant on the ground, two ants. He could see the miniscule hairs on their bodies. Monstrous. His tongue seemed large in his mouth. He ran his fingers along the barrel of his carbine and he could feel every scratch, the gunsight sharp under his suddenly oversensitive thumb. A red bird flew past in slow motion and he thought he could see the bird's eyes—innocent and terrified. His own body seemed as sensitive, as vibrant as a flower stem, stretching to reach closer to the sun. He saw an enemy soldier's head, the man's eyes like two black holes, his nostrils flaring, his lips full and red and moist, his black beard like coiled wires. He raised his carbine and put a bullet through the man's forehead. He was filled with hatred, terrifying hatred, making his head throb, his tongue grow fat in his mouth. Rather kill him with my bare hands, he thought to himself. Best way to kill an enemy. Bare hands. He lay flat on his back, clutching his gun, staring into the rising, naked sun in the blue-purple sky. No longer hungry. Forgotten. He was lightheaded. The sun was beautiful and gentle on his hollow cheeks and shaven head. His body, controlled by some magician's hands, felt as if it were in a state of levitation. The red bird among the cypress green twittered, a sweet shrillness. Ten feet away Aguilar the dwarf, *el Enano*, sat curled in on himself, his brown saurian eyes intent on the enemy line. "Throw your gun away, *el Enano*," Zeke called out. "Today we fight tooth, knee and claw."

Aguilar grunted, "*el Loco*," never taking his eyes from the enemy line.

Zeke closed his eyes. Slept—rather—hallucinated. Saw a naked Rachel on the couch over which hung *el Sordo's* painting of *pobre España*. She held her hands out to him in mute appeal, yet defiantly, her breasts fruc-tif-er-ous, he said the word slowly to himself, wondering how he had come upon such a word, and he found himself sitting up from behind his rock, wishing to respond to her appealing arms, she was so beautiful, and his mouth was open, his lips curled over his teeth, and it was a black hole from which no words issued, only his throat contracted and expanded to utter the harsh gutterals of a mute. He raised his arms to Rachel and he could see they were emaciated and without strength and his response to her was meaningless. Half words. He could see in her huge eyes anger that he had failed her, anger but not contempt because she understood. I have no strength except for the enemy, he said. She nodded and he kissed her and beheld a giant flower growing among the cypress and chestnut trees. It stood alone above all others, easily the most beautiful flower he had ever seen. He approached through a mist which hung about him like a liquified stained glass window, the flower's hugeness overwhelming. Since it was a flower, its hugeness seemed a paradox, and without knowing why, he became frightened. He had expected to be through the mist quickly but now he learned its depth was hidden by

[140]

itself. The discovery disturbed him and intensified his fear of a flower so gigantic that from its stamen he could observe the curve of the earth. Ah, there's the end of the mist! No. It was merely a light, a klieg, shining powerfully on a man sitting straight up on a makeshift handmade wooden chair which he felt certain would give way before he reached it. When he did he discovered its makeshiftness to be a camouflage, that its parts were bound by shining steel bands. The man's scalp was missing, and from his head steam spiraled upward. Ah, he thought to himself, the source of the mist. Now he knew why he'd been smelling a familiar oversweet odor. Putrefied brain. The man, incidentally, was dead. It was *el Alvarez,* his Spanish captain, killed by a fascist explosive bullet in the head, except *el Alvarez* no longer smiled gently. Death had given a bitter turn to his lips. Sullen. *El Alvarez* kept telling him something with his eyes, and just as he thought he was going to understand, a little gust of wind swirled some of the mist before the captain's dead eyes, thus concealing their meaning. He couldn't wait, he had to go to the flower, for he wanted to see the curve of the earth from its tilted stamen. Quickly he kissed the bitter cheek of his dead comrade and resumed his journey.

He emerged from the mist. A yellow sun illuminated a garbage heap confined by barbed wire; from the center of the garbage heap rose the huge purple flower. He tripped over a banana stalk. Picked it up to throw aside and saw it was a rib cage. A mound of discarded dead bodies was revealed to him, but his eyes were permitted to see only one dead body at a time, since in mass, corpses tend to become unreal. Each dead man touched him personally and he began to feel the weight of each too burdensome. He recognized many of his comrades at the front, but among them were also dead enemy soldiers, turbaned

Moors, Nazis, commissars as red as drops of blood. He became angry with himself because the burden of all the dead was equal, whether friend, comrade, or enemy. As his sympathy for each increased, however, he became less frightened. The significance was a revelation and he became bemused, his mind wandering to a shack in the desert, Edna Nimienski married to Josh Abramson. He forgot the dead completely and fear returned with all its strength. He remembered the purple flower, stepped back the better to see it. Its roots seemed to be dug into the open center of each corpse. The green stem was ancient and gnarled and as his eyes followed it upwards he saw it was no flower at all: a tree trunk carved from stone, such as they had placed at the grave of his father. His father stared at him from his immurement. Challenging. Stern. He became frightened, began to call for his mother, turned and fled wildly back into the mist. As he passed the chair bound by steel bands on which *el Alvarez* sat— no, it was the Dwarf, the white kneeling figure in Goya's painting, arms outflung, challenging the phalanx of executioners. He called out, *"el Enano,* tell me what it all means?"* And Aguilar the Segovian, called back, *"el Loco! el Loco!"* And he shook himself loose from his hallucination, for the enemy was attacking.

He shot bullet after bullet, but only at targets. Aguilar, as he shot his gun, counted those who were falling. *Una, dos, tres, cuatro, cinco.* . . . Zeke heard himself laughing. The battle lasted an hour and at least in their sector the enemy made no advance. During the entire battle Zeke had to fight with himself not to throw his gun aside and go after the enemy with his hands. He found himself in love with the roar of battle, the smell of powder, ecstatic every time an enemy soldier fell dead or screaming in pain.

[142]

When the battle ended he felt depleted, an empty sack. Slightly nauseous and scared. There was something wrong. He must go speak to the captain—no, the captain was not dead, what had happened before had been a dream, a seizure of some sort. All day he lay behind his barrier of rock and corpses, ten feet away from Aguilar, whose brown saurian eyes never left the enemy line. He damned the hot sun, wondering about himself, had he gone mad. In early evening, cool now, the sky red purple, the sun robed in gray blue silk, the enemy quiet in the day's defeat, victory so close, so elusive, Zeke dragged tail from his position behind the rock to battalion h.q. He told his captain, the very same, a cultured, learned man, he must have a word with him. They sat under a tall, graceful cypress still somehow untouched, bullets sawing about them. The captain, littler, narrower, black mustache droopier, listened as Zeke told of his recent seizure, as he himself called it, his hallucination and his irruptive passion for war and death. When he finished, the captain looked at him, saw the gauntness, the obsessive madness in the pupils of his comrade's yellow eyes, what a mad stubbornness, what a ragged, demented, defeated soldier. "When our dreams are too beautiful and too great for us, we tend to go mad, Ezekiel. Aie, you're on the verge of collapse and madness," el Alvarez said softly. "Leave before it is too late. I'll give you a pass to Barcelona. You've had too much, far too much."

"I'll never leave this battlefield. Never. I hate those bastards more than I love life."

"No. You're not in love with war, you're in love with hate now. We won't win now, we'll only die here. All we have left is honor, and you haven't even got that anymore, Ezekiel. All you want to do is kill. You've even forgotten why we fight. You look like a wild animal. I also, I suppose. What would you do if you caught one of them in your bare hands?"

Grabbing at levity as at a lifeline, Zeke said with a tired smile, "Eat him, probably. Because as much as anything I'm hungry. *Mucho* hungry and tired, *el Alvarez*."

The captain cast down his eyes, he was tired too, and hungry, and perhaps also a little mad. Wondered what to do with this man; so many had died, gone mad, now Ezekiel. Truly, *loco*. Perhaps it's only that you've had no sex for so long a time and death and violence have taken you prisoner. Filled the vacuum, so to speak. We should have camp followers as in the olden days, for this is still an old-fashioned war, despite the planes and the bombs. The last of the old-fashioned wars. In fact, my dear comrade, this is the end of the nineteenth century, some forty years late. When this war ends, the historians will write their books and then will die, because history books will never again adequately describe the events of the time. Only the poems. Aie, Ezekiel, there's little I can do for you. Take the next *camión* to the rear, go to a bordello and satisfy that hunger anyhow. Return with the *camión* in the early morning. We'll wait for you," the captain smiled.

As if he hadn't heard the last, Ezekiel said, "I've never slept with a whore." Said almost with a sullen boastfulness.

"How fortunate for you," said the captain dryly, perhaps a little angrily. How obsessively righteous can a man be? "I can't give you the time it will take to find a woman to love."

On his way to the *camión* to do as the captain suggested, all he thought of was that the expression *aie* sounded the same in all languages. In the rear, he caroused with a whore in a big Moorish *palacio* for five hours. With little emotion, just straight banging. Oddly

[144]

enough, his malaise left him and he returned to The Third of May battalion to fight on and on, defeat after defeat, but somehow his honor returned.

He fought on without sentimentality and without tears. He'd lost the ability to cry.

In the following few months, as in the previous two years, those in his battalion died and were replaced, died and were replaced. Only he continued to live, and that was a new guilt he had to bear—why was he spared? That too passed. The captain was killed a few days before the final fascist breakthrough to Barcelona and its subsequent capture. Still Zeke lived and fought, a scarecrow of a man, the only thing alive about him the growing flame of his shaven head and the bitterness in his eyes. Before the captain died, he passed among The Third of May battalion a leaflet, a yellowed, badly mimeographed, cheap piece of paper with words, a quotation from a Spanish philosopher, an official of the republic. Zeke memorized the words, often repeating them to himself, as a student does to keep fresh in his mind the Gettysburg Address, intoning it, almost like a well-worn prayer:

. . . The political doctrine which has represented the loftiest endeavor towards common life is liberal democracy. It carries to the extreme the determination to have consideration for one's neighbor and is the prototype of indirect action. Liberalism is that principle of political rights, according to which the public authority, in spite of being all-powerful, limits itself and attempts, even at its own expense, to leave room in the state over which it rules for those to live who neither think nor feel as it does, that is to say, as do the stronger, the majority. Liberalism—it is well to recall this today—is the supreme form of generosity; it is the right which the majority concedes to minorities and hence it is the noblest cry that has ever resounded on this planet. It announces the determination to share existence with the enemy; more than that, with an enemy which is weak. It was incredible that the human species should have arrived at so noble an attitude, so paradoxical, so refined, so acrobatic, so anti-natural. Hence, it is not to be wondered at that this same humanity should soon appear anxious to be rid of it. It is a discipline too difficult and complex to take firm root on earth.

Share our existence with the enemy! Govern with the opposition! Is not such a form of tenderness beginning to seem incomprehensible? Nothing indicates more clearly the characteristics of the day than the fact that—

at which point the leaflet had been torn, the remainder lost.

The soldiers of his battalion had been, and were, most of them rebels who had always thought they wanted more than even that. Oh, they had wanted to besiege heaven and return with it captive to earth. But was heaven only sacked Troy, and the captive, Helen, everyman's whore? Faced with an atrocious enemy in front and a treacherous ally in the rear, each equally possessed of a megalomania so devouring neither could abide the most insignificant digression, they came to realize that what Ortega y Gasset spoke of was the most rebellious demand ever made: the sacred right of every man to his private feelings and beliefs.

That's all.

They fought and died for it, the last romantics of their

time, only Zeke Gurevich and a few others coming out alive.

They fought until the enemy drove them into France. Some socialist group saw to it that Zeke Gurevich received passage money home. With despair he left his remaining Spanish comrades in a French internment camp. He boarded the vessel without even bothering to change his clothes. He felt the world, at least his world, had come to an end.

He returned to his country and his city more dead than alive, having promised to honor life till death, and he knew there was only one place he could go to begin replenishing himself.

He scurried on a biting February day in his torn Spanish sandals and faded blue beret through the dirty streets of Manhattan to his mother's place on Hester Street. Morning, there was no one home. It was in its customary state of disorder and stink, his true beginnings. To kill time, a restful change from killing men, he set about cleaning the place. He was going to live here for a while—make peace with his beginnings the easier to come to terms with his future—and all of a sudden he yearned for cleanliness and order after two years of filth and riot. He wanted to live in a house as clean as a hospital delivery room.

He worked for eight solid hours—it hadn't had a thorough cleaning in years—and filled six large cardboard cartons with dirt from the closets, from under the beds, from behind the sink, range, and icebox; then he scrubbed every floor until it shone, washed the walls, the woodwork, the bathroom, straightened out the closets, washed all the odd assortment of movie give-away dishes which had lain on their shelves for years without once having been washed, covered with city soot and grime; then he polished the old European silver, breaking his nails to get into the scroll-work and the beautifully elegant large G. He cleaned that goddamn house so that human beings could begin life anew in it.

At sundown, the door opened and his mother entered. She wore the same old dirty overcoat belted by a dirty old piece of string, the same old faded kerchief tied about her dry frizzed gray hair, the same old brown bunion-de-formed high shoes, one laced and hooked with a black shoelace, the other with a brown; her hands protruding from the torn, worn sleeves were angry red, swollen and misshapen and scarred; her face beaten by decades of New York weather, sullen and gruff. Her little eyes, two blue steel agates, stared round and cold first at him, then about the clean kitchen which the outside door opened into, then back at him again. No less coldly, he stood in the center of the room under the light and returned her stare.

Slowly she shuffled to the battered kitchen table, pulled out a chair, turned it towards him and lowered her tired aching body, and stared. Finally, she said, speaking in her own tongue, "A soldier? A Gurevich should be a soldier? Remove your clothes, please."

"No," he retorted, stepping backwards and thinking of escape.

"Remove your clothes, every stitch, you're my son."

She was his mother. Slowly, he removed every stitch, just as she'd ordered.

"Come here, my child."

He stood before her, naked, as he'd been born. And she examined every inch of him.

"No wounds, my son?"

"Nothing."

"You're very thin," she said.

"There wasn't much to eat."

"Well, to you it wasn't news to go hungry, was it?"

"No, mama, it wasn't."

"Or that our side always loses?"

He didn't answer, merely shrugged.

She stood up, groaning. "All right," she said in Yiddish English, "get dressed before you ketch ammonia."

XIII

Empty and defeated though he was, his mother, seen perhaps for the first time in his life, astonished him. She was perpetual motion, an internal combustion machine. She was E equals MC squared. She was the archetypal source of all power. She walked on those bunion-deformed feet, a squat, square powerhouse, sullen, tough, challenging the very airspace about her.

She hawked her wares in all weather, never begging customers to buy, daring them. "I sell these pickles three for a dime; are you good enough to eat them? You don't want my pickles? A plague overtake you. Look at her, my son, look at the way she squeezes a pickle—so elegantly. Lady, you squeeze your husband's piece like that, you can be sure he keeps a tart for his pleasures."

"Is that the way to sell pickles?" her son would ask. "You have to speak nicely to them."

"Why? You think they'll say a blessing for you? To the devil with them; they want a pickle, they'll buy one. Here, mister, sour tomatoes, two for a nickel. Smell. As succulent as your wife's thing. Ah, mister, you are a fine gentleman, an expert."

She challenged, she fought, she cursed—she smiled with a fine irony. Held on to life with tenacity.

An icy winter, she held on to it hard enough so he could get a grip on it too.

He lived with her, worked with her at the pushcart, and

kept her house clean. No matter how loudly she nagged or complained about his worthlessness—"Vot you going do mit yourself?"—he kept his mouth shut; only on occasion, when she carelessly thwarted his newfound fastidiousness, did he shout at her. The fact was he'd become so fastidious he kept his mother's flat cleaner than she could endure. It hampered her free and easy contemptuous style. She had a lifelong habit of dropping her dirty wet shoes on the floor precisely where she happened to sink her weary bones into a chair—the spotless kitchen floor, the just swept parlor. He would yell so loud, the neighbors would run and the mice evacuate the walls.

"Are you certain you weren't wounded in the head? There's never been one case of insanity in either your father's family or mine—though I had a cousin, four removed from my grandfather Wolf's side, Molke was her name, who it was said consorted with a Ukrainian *mujik*, so she must have been slightly mad."

To please her son, an eloquent concession to maternal love, she wiped her shoes on the door mat he bought and even stopped her nonsense with handkerchiefs. They could be found stuffed under pillows, under her mattress, under the table, under the bathtub (an old-fashioned, tin thing)—closets, drawers, the flat itself overflowed with handkerchiefs obtained by barter with soft-voiced, back-stooped, double-horned, timid Jacob Wasserman who had a dry goods pushcart three removed fom hers and with whom Zeke became certain she'd been having an affair for years, since she ragged the poor man unceasingly.

Zeke worried more about the handkerchiefs. You had a headache, she doused one with vinegar and tied it round your head. You began to sneeze, she stuffed six into your pocket. Done with a handkerchief, she dropped it where she stood, place-kicked it under whatever. Zeke supposed out loud that she had suffered a dearth of handkerchiefs as a child. She denied it, but how else account for it?

"And how long has this affair been going on with Wasserman?"

"Not your dem bizniss. I'm a woman. I have a right to live, your father dead now ten years."

"Live, Ma."

"Hawkay."

She was an independent woman. However, in order to avoid sending him off on a wild tear, she stopped dropping wet shoes and stuffing handkerchiefs. He soon realized he held a dominant position over her, and began to take mean advantage of it. Made a mental note to himself: signs of reviving life first indicated by extreme selfishness and meanness; *goodness* comes later, when it can be easily afforded.

On bleak, ice-cold Sundays (so they all seemed that winter and early spring), his mother would dress in new black high shoes, a black satin dress with lace collar, underneath an old-fashioned bone corset, pulled till bulging, a woolen black scarf and heavy black cloth coat with brown cat fur collar and a brown woolen babushka. Then she and he would take the Jerome Avenue subway to the Bronx to visit his sister Rebecca, a ripe olive-skinned beauty, for whom one Roger Temple had acquired a taste and then married. Temple was thirtyish, plumpish, English, a man who had converted from the Anglican church to Judaism and was teaching Rebecca, a heathen, against her will, how to keep the Sabbath and bring up their children, three and a fourth on the way, as orthodox Jews. Roger also had big ears, a slender, sensitive nose, buck teeth, brown-blond hair, thinning, and who, disliking this world, lived in the world of antiquity and beyond. He at this time earned eighteen dollars a week as a member of a research team at Columbia University delving into the origins of fertility symbols in the Euphrates valley. Two years after its publication, the study was torn asunder by a huge fallacy, and Roger thought of suicide. Judaism saved him; Rebecca nagged him in her ripe-olivy way. Grateful for the attention, Roger began to study the origins of the Adam and Eve story.

After the heavy Sunday meal—for dessert, a heaping portion of scorched heart—Rebecca would wash the dishes, Zeke's mother would scold, cuff, and in sundry ways demonstrate her affection for her grandchildren, as her son sat mutely by, daydreaming, staring into itinerant space—a new type of wandering for him—and Roger pored over parchment, a wanderer into the dry itinerant past.

After the aging lady had enough, she would kiss them all goodbye—"A decent, human custom," said Roger Temple—and she and Zeke would return to Hester Street. He would go to their flat and lie in his bed and stare at the ceiling. On occasion, twenty years ahead of his time, he would strike the wall with the ball of his fist. His mother would drink tea with her old cronies, then wander off to Jacob Wasserman's two room bachelor railroad flat on Essex Street where she and he would barter sour tomatoes and dry goods for sin and love.

All his life he had run around blotting it up for himself. If someone had asked him what he'd done, he would have shrugged tiredly and said, "Nothing." Pausing, he would have reconsidered, then said, "I've been reacting to events, to life. I'm being manipulated. But in good measure it's my own fault. I've always had the feeling that somewheres up ahead was utopia. Oh, no, not in the political sense, nothing as vulgar as that. That when you grew up and could fight yourself clear of the childhood diseases, there would be a coming out into the clearing and life would be space and beauty and happiness and joy. Oh, shit, now I'm lost," he would've said if he'd been asked, embarrassed at his romantic turn of phrase.

But he nurtured strength from his mother, from his sister's children, from Abe whom he saw on rare occasion— not too often because he didn't want this substitute father to carry him any longer. Besides Abe reminded him of Rachel—and he was afraid of Rachel, what she could do to him. Somehow Rachel and that coming out into the clearing were interchangeable and he had already learned enough to suspect that only disappointment waited for him in that direction.

After saving up a little strength, he decided to use the accrued interest in a migratory venture he'd ignored for many years now. His education. As was his custom, once set upon a course, he traveled it obsessively. Jaw jutted, yellow eyes slitted, he hurried to the public library on Second Avenue near Eighth Street, a library set among the poor, so one would expect it to be a poor library. It was rich. Started with A and went straight through Z.

He decided in his compulsive fastidiousness to read the entire library. Fortunately for him, the high walls of obsessiveness had, after years of siege by reason, begun to show stress and strain. Now reason found a wide crack and made a swift entry. Before beginning his onslaught on the blottings-up of others, he decided to count the fiction and non-fiction under A. In this little neighborhood library for the exploited, disinherited poor—some idiot ya-hoo from the Middle West would in the early 1950's infer that it was *education* which was the opiate of the peo-ple—there were exactly two thousand three hundred seventy-six books, averaging three hundred pages per volume, about seven hundred thousand pages of *A*. At two hundred pages a day (heavy reading even for someone who had nothing else to do but sell sour pickles and tomatoes), it would take him approximately thirty-five hundred days or ten years to read all the books under the first letter of the alphabet. He quickly scanned the rest of the shelves and was relieved to see the paucity of volumes under *I, J, Q, X, V, Y*, though Zola alone seemed to make up for all of them.

He realized he was going at it all wrong. This time he'd better move with caution. Books were dynamite. Better go to Abe and explain the problem.

Reason celebrated a great victory—defiant Zeke Gurevich was finally coming round.

He sneaked in between patients—the waiting room overflowed into the corridor, the corridor into the vestibule, the vestibule out onto the stone stoop—and spoke to a fatter, older, yet intenser Abe Abramson who was beginning to find there wouldn't be enough years and knowledge to cure the world's populace of all its diseases.

"Hurry up, Zeke," he smiled bitterly.

As quickly and concisely as possible, Zeke defined his symptoms. Not laughing, Abe explained that one has to be selective, even he had to, and he was an exceptionally swift reader, could read a book a night since he disliked sleeping and went to the toilet regularly. Hesitantly, looking for a moment through his window off into the distant horizons where hope sulked and despair beamed, he said, "Simon left a most lower case *c* catholic library. If you read all his books you won't become a learned man, you won't become a wise man, but you'll certainly become a well-read man."

"Are you sneering?" the redhead asked, temper flaring.

"No," Abe smiled, happy to see the blood boiling again in this most beloved of cousins. Then he wiped the sweat which always dripped from his fat, full, face with one of a dozen handkerchiefs Zeke had given him from his mother's cache, the trade of her lover. "You're not the kind to become a learned man—not enough meat on your behind, too much get up and go, as they say in the business community; though a wise man you may some day become—if you live long enough. The essence of genius is the ability to work obsessively within the limits of one's talent—you have the talent of a hobo, so don't waste it on scholarship. Go up to Rachel's, Simon left her a library suitable to your talent." Again he wiped his face, now sadly he said, "Your limits are the world and your obsession life: go grab it." He looked at Zeke with profound paternal love, and something more which Zeke discerned but didn't understand until years later. Abe loved Rachel.

Now Zeke said, "I don't care for Matt Cahn."

Abe laughed, his little blue agate eyes—just like Zeke's mother's—losing themselves in the fat of his face, his enormous belly as sprightly as ever. Zeke observed him coldly. Is this fat bastard laughing at me? At last Abe stopped heaving and hawhawing. "You never asked, so I haven't told you. Matt's in Europe. He's writing a series for an English periodical. He's just gone out on a limb with the bold statement that Russia and Germany are negotiating an agreement to carve up eastern Europe between them."

"If it's true," Zeke said bitterly, "then it's a plague the world's earned by its sheer stupidity and inertia." Then grudgingly, "Matt's a great political analyst. His stuff on Spain was almost as good as Orwell's." Matt Cahn had eyes to see with—an utterly amazing man who could see through the chicanery of politicians, political movements, historical events, could see the ghastly truth of an entire epoch, yet had such colossal difficulty seeing himself.

"What's so amazing?" Abe asked. "It's a daily phenomenon. How many of us can see ourselves? Perhaps a few—but how many of the few can do it without turning away?"

"I'll die trying."

"Don't boast and don't die. Go up to Rachel's, she'll be happy to see you. She hasn't stopped asking about you since you've returned."

"She knows where I live. And she never even wrote me a letter."

"Don't you know her yet? She doesn't go after anyone—they have to come to her."

"What's she afraid of—being turned down? That's a chance we all have to take once in a while."

"Maybe. But she won't hurt you any more than you let her." He saw that Zeke hesitated, so he added, "She and Matt broke up shortly after you left for Spain. I understand she told him the truth about you two." With a pang of terrible envy, he saw his young cousin's eyes light up; the boy would go and feast off Rachel. True, Rachel took little chance of being turned down, but when she gave, it was a banquet. What the hell did the kid have to complain about? Then Zeke was embracing him, and they kissed each other's bristly cheek, smelling the tobacco on one another's breath, and then Zeke ran out as Abe asked the nurse to call the next patient, who was complaining that here it was April and she was freezing.

April showers. A slate blue sky with a crazy patch of yellow.

Rain dripping from him, stopping to leave his soaking shoes at the door, Zeke loped into that same room, with the same bookshelves, same Rodin, same paintings and prints on the walls—no, one new one, to Zeke at any rate, a green nude of Rachel which Simon had done when she was a girl—the same couch and as far as he could see the same Rachel. Purple. Blue. Green. Wearing glasses, she was farsighted, she was reading when he flew in the thrown-open door. He stopped in the middle of the room.

Without even looking up—it could only be Zeke, no one ever entered a room quite like him—she put the book down on the sooty window sill, the glasses on top, and then stood slowly to face him. His wet red hair was plastered to his head. His face was clenched tight, compact. He's a strong attractive, ugly man, she thought. Still wants all or nothing. Her own heart beat in excitement and she had to fight to keep from panting like an overwrought, oversexed school girl. Despite what everybody said or thought, she'd lived without a man for two years, longer than she'd been without a man since she first went to bed with Simon Farrell at age sixteen. Still, it had been sort of pleasant living an austere life—she'd even contemplated entering a convent, perhaps the ways of her Jesuit father gave the greatest peace, and somehow she'd needed peace, needed time for contemplation, giving herself to the Lord of Hosts. Her Jewish radical friends had laughed, not wanting to understand, except Viola Abramson, who had said quietly, "That might in the end be the best life for you—the happiest and perhaps the least painful. You took on the burden of adulthood at too young an age, Rachel, with too little understanding." Perhaps. Perhaps. But she hadn't time to think now because Zeke stopped staring at her and took a step towards her and for a moment as she moved to meet him she thought her legs would fail her. She wanted his stubborn, ferocious weight on her, that's all. He was thrusting himself at her before she even had a chance to say a word and they made love

[158]

furiously, anxiously, and it was over too soon. Bodies unsatisfied, emotions too suddenly spent, but, since she was Rachel, immediately an arm's-length negotiation.

Before he even had a chance to say an impatient, Oh, my God, she was saying that they must never consider themselves married and they must never lie to one another. "Permanency murders love," she said in his ear when he fought against conditions. "And lies are its bullets," and she kissed his temple.

"Conditions murder love," he answered angrily, trapped again, his fingers pressing into her exquisite thigh. "Love has to be free of conditions. Let our love be boundless, then it'll be true without having to sign agreements—the parties hereto agree never to lie to one another—and there it is, the first lie," and he grabbed her black furry muff and gave it a yank.

She broke loose and stood before him, marvelously made, proud of her beauty, vain; there was barely any change after all the years—yes, at the eyes, the tiniest of creases at the inner corners and a bitter sagacity which came from having become a mature woman in her adolescence. "Promise," she urged, "no lies. No lies and no *marriage!*" The word peeled as if it were a snake.

"All right," he said, conceding too quickly, catching hold of her outflung hand and drawing her down again to his side. All he wanted was her love, the plain, every day variety, nothing more. "I promise," he snapped, already unhappy for having conceded, and as she began to embrace him, their bodies anxious to fill the vacuum their depleted emotions had left, he saw the old Goya print, *por el honor de la vida,* so he gave her her truth. "Incidentally, I notice there are wrinkles around your eyes. Getting old, Rachel?"

Her face disintegrated, as if hit by an explosive bullet.

Horrified at his own cruelty, still he looked to see where the blood would splash, ready to call for the grave detail. *Aquí, compañeros, aquí!* She went slack in his arms, and said, "You cruel bastard. You—"

Unhappily he held his ground. "No lies," he said.

She said dramatically, "It'll be bitter. It always is. Truth comes in all guises, but mostly in those little frosted vials one sees in Abe's laboratory labeled with a death's head and crossbones. But then there is immense space and that makes up for everything." She kissed him tenderly under his chin.

He realized with her there would always be these little dramas—or were they melodramas? To hell with it. "I love you," he said quietly, without any nonsense, his hand clutching her breast. She smiled her very personal, white, intimate smile, and they again made love, anxious but generous, full. As they lay quietly, she began *à propos* of nothing to speak of Simon Farrell. He listened for a few moments, then, since he had recently developed an on-off device in his head, he switched her off and began to daydream.

Neither was happy, neither was satisfied, neither said a word about it. No sooner did she settle down to a steady existence with Zeke Gurevich than she began to think of Matt Cahn, a man who made love difficult, who made living difficult. She daydreamed of a *ménage à trois*; retreated. How trite. And no sooner did Zeke begin to comprehend this, begin to try to cope with it, to overpower her with his love, to give her so much love she would be surfeit, than the earth shook. Matt Cahn's outrageous prophesy came true. Hitler secured his eastern flank by dealing with the man he most respected, and then made his move on Poland. As *der Führer* himself said, England

and France betrayed him—they had led him to believe they would retreat, instead they fought. So the war began.

Zeke waited. He wanted to be sure England and France meant it, they weren't after all easily trusted. He knew he would have to do no less than he had previously done. He told Rachel and she answered he must do what he believed necessary. As he began to make arrangements to join the Royal Canadian Army, he noticed in Rachel impatience alternating with distress. She wanted him out of the house, she wanted to be alone, still she didn't want him killed. It won't take ten days, he thought bitterly, before she'll have Matt back in. It hurt but he hid it, because he had to admit to himself he too felt impatient to be gone. It wasn't only that he felt the need to go fight the enemy again, the same enemy (odd how he began to smell the mesquite, the sage, the close smell of the earth, the dreadful fear, the sweet stink of corpses), but that he knew their life together was elusive, he could grab hold only of parts of her, never the whole of her. Capricious reality. Why was it, he asked himself, when one looked so hard at reality it pierced the eyes—a chimera with a lance? Reality was across the sea—the silence between gun bursts. Fear. Death. Agony. Hope.

They kissed before he left, said little, held one another tightly, her hands trembling at the small of his back. There were tears in her eyes, and in his, but then her hands couldn't shove him out the door fast enough, and he had a very controlled, a very vicious desire to strangle her. Yet as he descended the creaking, wooden stairs, with the hatred and the tears, he restrained a desire to whistle.

Off again to fight the fiery dragons. Not chimera—reality.

And this time there was a plenitude of guns and bullets.

An overflowing horn of plenty, stamped Detroit, Pittsburgh, Birmingham, Fontana. In the end, that did it, of course.

He fought in Africa with a tank unit; when the United States entered the war, he transferred to the First Army and fought in France and Germany as an infantryman. In almost six years, forty million people died from violence, Zeke Gurevich personally accounting for some small fraction. Which led him to a blank page—correction: not blank, merely wordless.

Many years after the war's end, when Rachel was dying, cell by proliferating cell, they corresponded when he was in the South on an organizing job for a Negro association and in answer to some remark of hers in a letter about the war years, he wrote, "Each of us, Rachel, has the pitiful and perhaps obscene habit of frolicking in his guilt and grief about what happened in Europe. He either beats his breast a little too flamboyantly, watching his audience out of the corner of his eye, or turns on the tears a little too gushingly, at times doing both simultaneously. His breast beat black and blue, his eyes teary red, he goes off catty-corner, uneasy but forgetful. That's life, he says, hoping he sounds profound but uncomfortably aware he's blurted out a shallow cliché. I've beat my breast and cried my tears with the best of them. I know how easy it is to cry. In Spain I lost the ability to cry. In the stench of the burning flesh I refound it. Now I feel I must impose an aridity on my eyes and silence on my tongue. *El Alvarez,* about whom I've told you, once prophesied that what would come after Spain could not be encompassed by historians, only by poets. Where he received this prevision, I don't know, but it was accurate. For the rest of us the tears can only fragment our vision and words destroy its truth. No, no, we talk and we weep; we blame and we avenge. Too easy. It must be with us forever—silent, heavy, intrusive, unexorcized, unavenged, unwept for. Unforgotten. So why should I give you the unholy pleasure of frolicking in your own filth and mendacity? I won't do it for myself—and not for you. Or anyone, even my children. The page is wordless, its vision motley, the multitude of voices mute."

* * *

Samuel Ezekiel Gurevich received his ruptured duck in Atlantic City, stuck it into his army trousers (lost it the next day when he pulled out a wad of discharge dollars), forgot it, and stole into New York. A month before, in Dresden, just as his division entrained for the port of Cherbourg where it was to board the ocean transport for the States, he'd written his mother and sister, "I won't be home for six months yet. Am well, no wounds. Lucky me." It can be said he entered New York surreptitiously. It was noon of the second day of the third week of November 1945. A steel, blue, crisp, November day. He'd been in the Canadian and American armies exactly five years, six months, eleven days. He wore khaki underwear, khaki socks, khaki shirt, khaki trousers, khaki slipover sweater, khaki overseas jacket, khaki army shoes, no tie and no hat since he was now a free man. In his pockets he had a wad of exactly eighteen hundred seventy-six dollars, thirty-nine cents and six francs (ten years later he would remember it as some twenty-eight hundred dollars; ten after that as thirty-eight hundred), a khaki handkerchief and two neatly rolled and powdered khaki condoms, all in addition to a khaki wallet which contained his discharge papers, completely and one hundred per cent honorable, and a cracked, torn-at-the-edges, yellowed, nude photograph of Rachel Farrell taken by Simon Farrell when she had been eighteen and possessed of the furriest black Irish muff on the eastern seaboard. In demolished Dresden he'd had a German *fräulein,* a Jewish waif with numbers on her wrist and startling images in her Teutonic blue eyes. She was an extremely poor sleeper and he loved her for five months, loved her even to the exclusion of Rachel from his memory. He *could* love someone else. She was missing from his bed when he awoke one beautiful orange-purple dawn. He found her bleeding to death out in the yard, his bayonet self-stuck through her stomach.

Mr. Gurevich was six feet one-half inch tall (he grew a half inch in the army), weighed one eighty-five stripped, had moderately hairy (red) legs and chest, wore a close army haircut (red) and had two moles, one under his right scapula and one just beneath the crown of his penis, which the fellows in the army had enviously called his French tickler. The penis was not overly large as he'd once been urgently reminded by Ona Stuhldreyer of Kansas many years ago at the Newday Co-operative Farm. A large nose, which more than made up for the size of his penis, grew erratically from the not quite center of a lean, wistful face in ambiguous conspiracy against a square, mean jaw. He had thirty teeth, two having been knocked out in a kilkenny on Piccadilly Circus one dark night before the Normandy invasion. He had two full, generous lips and two small, mean eyes, yellow-green, sort of off-khaki so that he stood out in parade. The stubble on his cheeks and chin was reddish blond, a boon, since he could, when lazy, get along shaving just every other day. He was a neat man.

As he took a position on a bench behind a tree in Washington Square Park, facing north so that he could observe without being seen the goings and comings of Dr. Abraham Abramson's brown sandstone house, a beggar who had contemplated asking him for a handout decided intuitively not to, muttering in disappointment to himself, "That bastard's had it."

No doubt.

The returned veteran sat and observed Dr. Abramson's patients arrive and depart. An old lady who wore tight pants so that her behind looked like the backside of a double-humped whale, a brash red sweater which enunciated her huge paps, and a scarlet babushka about her head, skipped delightedly round the corner to the doctor's stone stoop, skidded to a halt, looked in either direction, put her right hand on her hip, screwed up her lips in simulated agony and, bent almost double, mounted the stone steps, never progressing to the next until both feet were solidly planted on the one below. As she proceeded upward, she groaned so that the veteran across the street could hear her. He sneered. She'll moan and groan, Abe'll tell her she's a big faker, wink, pat her hands, she'll smile naughtily. "How much, doctorel?" "For you, *mamele*, half." She would pay Abe $2.oo and limp out.

A pale, pimply, blimp of a girl waddled up the stoop steps, her buttocks dancing to a slow sad tuba. The veteran smiled. Abe'll tell her to stop eating ice cream sundaes, to find a fellow and get laid. "It's good for you, Alma, better than pills."

A lovely young woman sat down on a bench nearby; she was pale and biting a ripe, nervous lower lip. She crossed her long, delicately turned, exquisite legs, lit a cigarette and ignored his obvious staring. He shrugged and turned again to Dr. Abramson's stone porch. An exotic Negro woman, simply dressed in muted tans, alighted from a cab and sauntered easily up the steps, her hard butts mocking. He recognized her as someone he'd met in Abe's house years before; she was a famous blues singer, a junkie, whom Abe had been trying to cure for years. Zeke knew she would cry, plead for help—she wouldn't ask for a shot because she could get all she wanted elsewhere and she knew he wouldn't give it to her if she did ask. She would plead with Abe that he cure her; he would tell her he had cured her ten times, the rest was up to her. "But I need my kicks, how can I live without my kicks?" "Then stop your crying and go get your kicks, what do you want from me?" "But *they* drive me crazy with their eyes, plastered with eyes, screwing, humping, goosing eyes, as if I'm a fucking machine." "So stop being an entertainer and go hide in the cellar." "I want my kicks, got to have my kicks, Abe." "Stop that whining and grow up." She would cry. Abe would speak quietly to her, hold her slender hands between his thick ones, tell her how great a blues singer she was, the greatest perhaps, then he would give her an injection of his latest concoction, a recent experiment, and ask her to come by for dinner that evening, Matt Cahn, the famous foreign correspondent, would be there with his wife Rachel. "That cold bastard," she would say. Matt had once flirted with her and when she gave him the come-on had turned yellow and vanished. She would now wipe her tears on Abe's fat shoulder, smile softly as he pinched her snazzy, hard behind, and leave, sauntering down the steps to the street, proud possessor of at least one fat parcel of the world, since Abe had been her lover on and off for close to fifteen years.

Zeke looked at the beautiful long legs of the young woman sitting at the nearby bench. She still bit her lower lip, chainsmoking, staring at some harrowing movie which her mind projected onto an invisible screen. A little girl holding the hand of a stalwart woman came into view. The woman, wearing the white low-heeled shoes of a nurse, her white uniform showing beneath the hem of her trenchcoat, stopped and began to scream at the child for having soiled her dress, slapping and pulling at her. "Look what you've done, you moron. I can't leave you alone for ten minutes, you idiot." The little girl had both lips sucked into her mouth so it looked like a war wound, and her eyes were red from tears which wouldn't flow. The woman's voice spiraled wildly, her proficient hands cuffing the child; pushing; slapping. The veteran wanted to say something, but didn't have the guts, too taken with my own wounds, he thought, too tired. He merely stared at the woman, hoping she would become ashamed and stop her terrible scolding of her daughter. The nurse was oblivious, if she cared at all. "You stupid toad. Dirty child. You're just like your father, you moron." The brave veteran stared, sitting glued to his seat. The long-legged beauty on the next bench merely kept biting her lower lip, chainsmoking, noticing nothing but what the projector threw on the screen. A young swish stopped near them to observe the scene for a moment, then, a brave man, stepped close to the woman and said, "Can't you leave the child alone?" The woman cast him a nasty, hooked glance. "Mind your damn mincing business. *Daisy.*" The swish, his voice trembling, said, "Look at her. One monster making another." He fluttered a hand, squared his narrow shoulders, walked away. The nurse yanked venomously at her child. "Does that satisfy you? Is that what you wanted?" She slapped the little girl again. The child, still not crying, both lips sucked deep into her mouth, kept her red eyes intently on her mother. Suddenly they left, pulled, yanked, hurried off the street.

I'm a brave man, the veteran muttered to himself, and resumed his observation of Dr. Abramson's stoop. The very first lady, the old one in tight pants, limped out the door and down the steps. At the very bottom, she looked in either direction, saw no friend whose sympathy she might solicit, then danced off like a happy whale, her huge paps sighing and soughing under the tight scarlet sweater.

Looked again at the bench on which the nervous young woman bit her lip and kept her lovely legs crossed. A sweet clout. Returned his eyes to the brown sandstone, saw a young man start to cross the street towards where he sat, sort of a hippy young man with a pock-scarred, muscleless face. As he approached, the young woman on the bench became agitated, little moans escaping from between her bitten lips. Zeke realized she'd been waiting for this young punk, her lover. Lucky little jerk, he started to say to himself, stopped short and sneered. The sweet clout rose from her bench, sighed deeply, took her approaching friend by a fat elbow, blushing furiously. If only you'd give me a try, Zeke wanted to call after her, but didn't because he knew that was exactly what every man thought at such a sight. Aaa, they would go to the dike's room, fall into each other's arms, ripping at one another. Later the sweet clout would feel ashamed and weep, and her dike would scream hysterical obscenities at her for being a stupid toad.

Across the street, the pale, pimply, blimp of a girl waddled down the steps and slowly duckwalked out of sight, her coat awry behind her, part of it pinched between sad, fat cheeks.

Soon after, the Negro blues singer left, cool and elegant. Patients came and went for a few hours, Abe had a busy practice. After all who'd entered had left, the ex-soldier stood. "My turn," he said aloud.

"Nothing I can do for you," Abe said despondently as

Zeke sat before him on the white stool in the very white examining room. "What can a doctor do for you? Maybe perform a lobotomy—kill the smell of burn—"

"Shut up!"

"We can't hide behind silence."

"I don't want to hide behind silence and I don't want to hide behind words. I want to ram it down their throats. I want to put up big signs all over their goddamn country. I want them to read it morning, noon, night. But I don't think that'll work. What is there to say on the signs? How the hell does one say it? You know what's eating me? I know it's possible for me to be the way they were—that it's completely possible. I know it. I can read it in myself and it sickens me."

"Cut it out," Abe snapped. "You don't have to prove to anybody—" He stopped, realizing Zeke wasn't looking for solace or pats on the back.

"I'm not saying I would do what they did. But I know it's possible for me to do what they did. Isn't it odd that they had to do it to nine, ten million people—who'll ever know how many?—to make me see it's possible? We all forget so easily, don't we? How long ago was it the Turks put away a million Armenians? The world stood aghast, didn't it? And promptly forgot about it. A legend. In 1936, when they were sending *kulaks* off in freight cars, I could say, they're only kulaks, send them off. *Only kulaks.* Send them off to where? Where did they go? That I was a kid, was that excuse enough? Now it's nine, ten years later and I know what the Nazis did I could do. It's in me to do it. It's in you, too; it's in every man. It makes me sick. It makes me want to die. I can say that now. As we fought across France and then Germany, before the truth of the rumor was confirmed, I wanted so much to live through the war, I'd have done anything, absolutely anything to get the war over with. I kept being afraid I would be killed the last minute before the war ended. After Dachau, I didn't care any more. I don't care any more.

"Everyone's talking about Hiroshima these days. They ought to see Dresden. Just plain TNT, too, no atom bomb. A hundred thirty-five thousand dead and the city destroyed. Twice as much as Hiroshima. When I saw Dresden, I was glad. I was ready to cheer. In fact, I did cheer. I wanted vengeance after Dachau, more than just defeating them, I wanted to wipe them off the earth.

"I asked a German about it. A thirty-year-old man who looked like sixty, stooped and ready for the grave. He answered honestly enough. What did you expect me to do, I have a family, should I have had my family killed or sent to a camp just to save yours? I hit him and ran away before I killed him. Went back to my barracks and couldn't sleep because I wondered what I would do to save my family. I wasn't sure. Who is sure? Anyone tells me he's sure is a liar. I began—" Oh, shit, what made him go on.

Abe broke the quiet first. "Josh wrote me."

"Josh? How is he? Where is he?" Both glad to change the subject.

"He's in the army still. A doctor, stationed in Vienna."

"A prophet. When I ran into him in L.A. years ago, remember, in his most hallucinatory stage," they both laughed, "he kept saying, the greatest revolutionary slogan of our time should be: each man has a right to be let alone."

"Why don't you live here?" Abe asked. "Viola will be happy to see you and have you here, so will the kids— they're big now, you know," he said with a smile.

"No, I want to live alone. Besides, I couldn't stand that wild mob in your house any more."

"No more mobs. Things changed during the war. No one has time for wild talk; older, married, wanting to make a good living and be under analysis. And now to forget the war, since eternal peace has arrived."

"Oh, yes, eternal peace. They should read Matt Cahn's stuff." Abruptly, Zeke asked, "Rachel, too?"

"Not quite. She's old-fashioned, still wearing the same Isadora Duncan dresses, scarves, talks the same, calls everyone who shines his shoes a bourgeois and is very much married to Matt. You had your chance," said bitterly, as if Zeke's having missed his chance had missed it for him as well. "You had better forget it. Incidentally, Sean's living with them, a moody kid. Matt's paying for his analysis and the analyst's bringing his hostility out into the open; one of these days exposed to too much oxygen it will explode and Sean'll buy an axe and do a Lizzie Borden on Matt and Rachel—all paid for by Matt Cahn. They have three more children, you know."

"Wanted to make sure he wasn't drafted?"

"Be fair. He was a foreign correspondent—wouldn't have been. What are you going to do?"

"What can I do? I know how to strip and reassemble a rifle and sell sour pickles and tomatoes. What else do I know?"

"There's the GI bill of rights. You can go to school."

"Become a schoolboy at my age?"

"Why not?"

"The first thirty years of your life you have all the time in the world, the next thirty there's absolutely no time at all. I'm bushed and feel like an old man."

"All you need is rest."

"For the remainder of my life. She's a damn bitch. All she likes is—"

"Stop it, later you'll be ashamed."

"I found out in Europe I could love someone else, but still, I've loved her a long time. As I got closer to the States—"

"It's a different world now and you can begin life anew," Abe said dryly. There was no prescription, and there was no cure.

"What?" Zeke smiled without opening his lips, a hopeless smile. "Again?"

Before he crawled from under his rock to start life anew, he decided he should make a short, painful stop on Charles Street.

Matthew Cahn was by then of course a world-famous journalist—one of those fortunate men who always managed to be at the exact location where history stopped to vacuate its bladder and bowels. Matt always had the toilet paper ready; in return for his service, history gave him a scoop. It really wasn't luck. When Matt Cahn read reports tripping off the ticker, his eyes became ice-cold, his brain went to work, and sentimentality was cast out the door, a mangy cat. Besides, he accumulated knowledge for the same reason a banker accumulates money—to put it to work.

Though his income had grown, Matt and Rachel still lived in a Charles Street fourth-floor walk-up. A generous man, Matt always managed to guard the buck; a real, two fisted trooper. Like the aristocratic rich, Rachel never thought of money except as some abstraction one used for barter to obtain something one really wanted like a strangely shaped urn or an old picture frame. Rachel's trouble was she had poor taste. The years had passed, radical bohemia had gone respectable, even the anarchists, but Rachel Cahn still sported furniture from a second hand store on lower Fourth Avenue—"Rill chip, lady, rill chip"—Chianti bottles made into lamps, a mattress on a spring on piers of bricks for a sofa or bed, the same home-made bookshelves on, again, bricks. She still wore her black hair long and wild—Pegeen, Pegeen—her frumpish or bizarre dresses chosen blindly, and elegant high-heeled shoes. Sean, a fourteen-year-old El Greco Jesus—so much like Simon, Zeke's heart stopped when he saw him—slept in one tiny bedroom with his half-brother, five years old; the two girls, three and four, slept in the other bedroom, while Matt and Rachel slept in the living room under the same old prints. The iron bas-relief of Robespierre was gone, but the glued plaster miniature of Rodin's *The Kiss* still stood where it had always stood, more chipped, dustier than ever.

Zeke came in the afternoon, when he knew Matt would be out. Sean remembered him and they talked a few seconds, My, how you've grown, and, how are you, Zeke, spoken in a very low hesitant voice. Rachel was in the kitchen and must have heard Zeke's voice, for she came out on the run and leaped into his arms—a certain sign she suffered no guilt. They kissed warmly—what has anger to do with kissing?—and then remembered they hadn't seen each other for well over five years.

Full, dead silence. They just stared.

Sean blushed—how could he help but be in love with his mother?—and then disappeared into the bedroom to keep the children busy and himself concealed.

Zeke examined her through his yellow-green eyes. Her breasts lay heavy against the cotton thinness of her loose blouse; her hips were broader and her belly looked softer; her forehead had a couple of worry lines and the wrinkles at the inner corners of her cavernous eyes were more numerous—but her skin around her throat was still smooth Irish. His heart beat wildly and he wanted to cry.

He had loved her all his life and knew then and there he would love her the rest of his life—not that he would die for love of her, nothing as romantic or silly as that, he'd already proved to himself with the *fräulein* that he could love someone else. That he loved her, that's all, and he wondered if it would show itself as obsessive still.

"You've changed," she said with a smile. "Heavier about the shoulders, more forehead, more jowl and more ass."

"Must be truthful at all times," he said. "No lies and no marriage. Permanency kills love and lies are its bullets."

"You yourself always said I couldn't live ten days without a man."

"Is that how long it took? By the age of the boy, it hardly seems you waited that long. Or is he mine?"

"Not yours."

"Mine you once aborted, didn't you?"

"You're being sentimental. It was a gob of blood." She could see by the look of him he was going to say something which would make them both unhappy. "Let's stop playing at theatre. I've got a husband, a fourteen-year-old son who calls me Retchel and despises my husband, and three small children who call me mama. My husband reads during meals, throws me a lay when he's in the mood or thinks I am, and I have this hovel to keep clean. On occasion I've thought of you with love and wished I had your weight on me. Now go away and please stay away. Ours had always been an incestuous sort of love." Jocasta, he thought; incestuous for you—for me it was really a special piece of ass, I suppose. She was talking, "There was always too much possession involved—and unease." Right, he thought. Correct. "You knew it before you went to Canada to join the army and you know it now." He shrugged admission, and she continued. "I love Matt, I suppose I have for a long time, in my half-assed way—the way it's been with everything for me: the revolution, free love, my artiness, my social consciousness. Matt, who doesn't know how to handle the simplest personal crisis, still chases truth. Oddly enough, despite himself—his constant cracking of nits with his fingernails—he's the only one who has even the vaguest acquaintance with truth." All right, then, we'll put up a statue to him on Sheridan Square. He barely listened, stared out the window, as sooted as ever, into the courtyard. She didn't seem to mind his inattention, continued, "But all on the outside. Inside he suffers, lost in some dark wilderness." He watched a man on a rooftop down the block, towards the river, opening his coops to give his pigeons their daily exercise, and he could hear that as she spoke she came to stand by him near the window. "He compensates by seeing the external world with extraordinarily clear eyes. Simon was a faker—found truth by pretending it didn't exist. You know, it's only recently I've stopped talking about him to Matt." He turned away from a tumbler pigeon doing its tricks to look at her. So she'd finally buried Simon. Thank God—the corpse had begun to smell. "Matt said Simon was my personal myth. True. Even after he died." She smiled wanly now, hoping to gather him in to her monologue, like an actress on a stage anxiously trying to hold her audience. He returned her smile, tiredly. He didn't want to hear this old crap any more. She guessed, waved her hand forlornly. "You've had lost years," she said, "the war and all—I don't expect you'll shed tears for those, but it's time you outgrew your obsession for the beautiful, tragic Rachel Farrell and went about making a life for yourself. Now go away. All we mean to one another is mortar and pestle, trying to crush some perfume out of dried rose leaves." She saw him shrug, begin to leave. A little wildly she called, "Here you, before you slam the door, give me one of your murderous kisses."

He turned back to her, angry, but saw her helpless smile and his anger left him. Poor Rachel. She kept a man standing on one leg; that way she always had half of him. She stood close to him, her hand on his elbow, and by the look of her he knew she recognized it now, and so did he. Half men are easier to live with than whole men. Simon somehow around in one form or another all these years had made three—thirds easier still than halves.

She saw the newfound knowledge on his face—so he'd finally learned her secret. Courageously she pulled herself together, smiled wisely, and with dignity asked him to sit down, they had much to talk about, she would make him a cup of coffee.

When he left her an hour later, his respect for her was intact, only his obsession was dead.

XIV

So he crawled from under his rock and started life anew. In a hurry.

Got himself a job with the textile union in Paterson, New Jersey, through a Spanish civil war comrade, Michael Berg. In the union office he met Ida Delson—plump, buxom, handsome in a hawkish sort of way, as quick and as explosive as he. One of him was enough; two, impossible. He wrote leaflets; she handed them out. In the office she kept throwing her huge eyes at him, and he was always a sucker for huge eyes. She had guts, too. Together they organized a new plant. To celebrate, they ran off to Atlantic City. She was wild and called him her ram. That did it. The next week they were married. In a hurry.

War from dawn to sundown.

The bed was their green table, diplomacy restricted to laying of semantic snares more dangerous than land mines. Every week they called a truce to battle and negotiations and separated; he went to live with his mother while she stayed on in the apartment in Stuyvesant Town, then spanking new, a towering barracks up near the East River. Set the architectural style for the future. Contemporary ugly. He commuted to Paterson every day. Every other week he would come running back to Ida, dying of boredom. At least she kept things hopping. Nothing he said was right and silence on his part was proof that he didn't appreciate her mind, all he wanted was her body.

She was a goddamn bourgeoise bitch. Flaubert's definition: a mean soul.

They managed to live without putting one another in an early grave. Jacob Wasserman had a late grave. Seventy-nine, his mother said, when she buried him. A kindly, timid man. His mama boasted once Jake was a fierce lover. The older she got the more she tried to invite his attention to her most intimate life. In her youth she'd been quite a *brenn*. Flame. After Jake died, he talked her into opening an appetizing store in the Bronx and giving up her Hester Street flat. She cried the day she moved, and he almost did himself. His very own slum. She'd lived there since the day papa led her off the boat in 1910. The store, fifteen by twenty, was on Burnside Avenue in the Bronx. Where she used to make twenty-seven dollars clear off the pushcart, now she made seventy-nine off the store. She moved in with Rebecca, a big, fat, ripe olive from Mount Carmel. Roger had lost his plumpish, English look, had become thin and wiry. Rebecca must've been like Zeke, wanting it all the time. Roger, a man of sensitivity, had decided single-handedly to replenish Jewry, bolster it with his fine Anglo-Saxon blood, and at that time he and Rebecca were already making their seventh child. Before they were through, they made thirteen, by God. By Roger. Roger knew more about Judaism than Maimonides, by Christ.

The store did so well, Roger entered the business with Zeke's mother, thus becoming the first Anglo-Judaic sauerkraut and halvah salesman in the world. Roger also wrote a fine paper for an anthropologists' journal on fertility symbolism found at the bottom of a brine barrel.

Wonder what he would have found at the bottom of Ida's barrel? Bitch. She filled their apartment with deli-

[178]

cate antique furniture which she refinished herself, exquisite napery, books from ceiling to floor (mostly Zeke's, half given to him by Rachel when she and Matt moved to their Westchester home, "Simon always wanted you to have them." "What about Sean? After all he's Simon's son." "I offered them to him. Refused them. Said he would burn them. Hardly ever see him." "Don't blame him." "Neither do I. And must we be so honest?" "No. Let's get laid." They did.). Ida also had a baby grand on which she played a weak left hand but a passable Schubert. She had received a fine education, even knew how to ride a horse. Bitch, could she ride. They lived a busy life, each at the top of his voice. After every fight, they decided calmly and reasonably to separate—yet neither was capable of it. Something called family tradition inhibited them. No divorces in the Gurevich and Ida Bitch family way back to the first Jerusalem.

He found an answer. Asked the union to send him to the South.

"They eat union organizers in the South," the International vice-president said.

"Yes, I know. But I have the old-fashioned idea that when a man becomes a union member he begins to be a little more human."

"Old-fashioned? Antiquarian. And false."

"Okay, I'm a utopian idealist. Let me try."

Six weeks in South Carolina, four weeks home to recuperate with Ida Bitch. It led to a semi-tranquil existence. After her the South was a blessing. She wasn't that bad, seen every other month or so. Until the day he returned home and caught her two-timing him with a wooden crate.

Her very own orgone box. Unlatched her orgasm, she

said. That's what had been wrong with their relationship. Orgasms too shallow. Left her dissatisfied. "Come to bed, damn you," she urged, laughing lasciviously, showing her teeth, wiggling her wig. "I'll demonstrate."

He wasn't able to walk for three days and passed blood with his urine. Exuberantly. A confirmed non-believer, he now conceded perhaps it would work. Look at Lourdes. "God knows, you need lots of curing," he told her. She didn't even fight—just smiled toothily. A loving, passionate shark.

Unlatched orgasm for a month.

Went South again. Should never have come back. Secured enough signed authorization cards to have an election ordered by the National Labor Relations Board. Had a rough time. Hard not to become barbaric when you live among barbarians, are ruled by barbarians, are cajoled by barbarians, have to eat with barbarians. Barbaric food, too.

The corporation, owned by a northern family noted for its works of charity and lack of bigotry, had a picture passed among its cracker employees showing Zeke dancing with a Negro girl at a union dance in New York. Then it began to dismantle one wing of its plant and got the rumor started it was prepared to move to another state if the union won certification. For freedom. He worked round the clock, wrote leaflets, made speeches, stayed in the South four months this time, lost his head once—to pick up a few more members he almost conceded to *antinigger* talk, caught himself in time, and to do penance actually fasted for three days and put thorns in his bed. In the end he saved himself but lost the election by a hundred votes. Defeated twice. Headed North. "Dirty crackers. Deserve the little they get."

Entered his apartment. There she stood, sleek, handsome, and very brash. "Sorry, lady. Wrong wife. Wrong flat."

No, it wasn't the wrong flat, just wrong wife. She wore a man's haircut, wore a mannish suit, shirt and tie. The orgone box was gone. In its stead had been installed a new, elegant wardrobe to hold his wife's girl friend's clothes. "Sorry, Zeke. That's what it was all the time. I really hate being a woman. That hole and that mess down there. I just hate it."

"Then die," he said. "Just die."

Oh, how he wanted to die. No surcease. Defeat was his name. Was the flaw his—or the world's? That was the question he kept asking himself. He was getting no younger, he wanted a wife and children. He'd run around enough. His own fault. The flaw was his and the luck was bad. That was too hard to take, so he began to blame the world. Everyone was nuts but Zeke Gurevich. Possible, but hardly likely. A hollow laugh.

He took a leave of absence from the union and ran up to Maine and bought a shack on the beach. Needed something to call his own, all his own, and he even overcame a lifetime's prejudice against the owning of private property, but it was really personal, wasn't it, like a pair of pants, his beach shack where he could hide. It had a potbelly stove and he slept in a sleeping bag on the floor with the mice. It was late October, red and red-brown along with the white sand and black rock and the sinuous green sea. And he contemplated the sea and the changing sky—really space. Set him up again.

Too long alone and a man begins to crave company, any company, or slide back to archaic time, become a lizard, a fish. No, no, I'm a man, he cried out. I want a woman, need a friend; I want to hear somebody laugh, hear a song; to sleep on clean linen, to feel myself part of a clan. It meant something.

Great discovery. Practically ran all the way home. And there they were, his whole family, including Abe, acting as if they'd read his mind. They had all decided he should go to Europe, to Russia and Poland and Lithuania to find the remains of the family. "Why me? I've had enough of Europe for a while. And enough trouble, too. I want to stay home." They looked aghast at him. What had happened to Solomon Gurevich's son? The wanderer? He who had most inherited the ways of the Gurevich grandfather, the itinerant peddler, the man who had walked one end of Europe to the other selling buttons, thread, needles, cheap watches, earrings, coming home only to thread the needle and sew another child's garment? " You have to go," Abe said, wiping the sweat off his face. "Besides, it will be good for you. Get Ida out of your head." Abe always knew what was good for Zeke—good for everybody, but himself. He had become so fat now, everyone said he would die from a heart attack.

"All right. I'll go."

Lenin's corpse looked like a wax doll in a marble cradle embedded in snow. Cold winter, heavy snow, exquisite onion cupolas above stark, stone, Kremlin walls, silent streets, poverty, poverty, atrocious food, red noses, red cheeks, red flags and red terror, the *Zdanovschine* picking up speed. Wearing a fur hat, six sweaters, a sheepskin coat, his nose like a railroad danger signal, he went out to look for his father's family.

What an unfortunate family. He himself had been born on the evening of the day his father's oldest sister, Esther, who had migrated from Vilna to London received the news her eldest son, Arthur, had been killed going over the top against the Hun; her youngest son, Sydney, was killed in November 1918, three days before Armistice, nine months to the day before Miriam was born with her one hand. In Buenos Aires, the day Miriam's father died, the wife of his father's oldest brother, Isidor, gave birth to twins, one of which, the boy, died of scarlet fever in his second month. What misfortunes occurred to his father's two sisters and three brothers who remained in Vilna had not been recorded by the family in the States. Abe told him the news received after VE day indicated they and their families had all been murdered by the SS, though there appeared to be a slim chance that Stalin had incarcerated one of the families in a slave camp in Siberia after he invaded Lithuania and, if they had avoided death by freezing, hunger, or brutality, might very well be living in Moscow or its environs.

He inquired among the Jewish community in Moscow —very carefully since Stalin was then in his overt delusional paranoic anti-human stage, concerned with Jewish poisoners—and to be sure Zeke was given a thin thread which he followed by bedraggled droshky and bony, sad-faced nag, driven by his guide and shadow (courtesy of Intourist), thirty miles out of Moscow into the middle ages. In a wooden hut with a dirt floor and a stall for a sickly goat, as cold as all winter, he found a daughter of his Vilna Uncle Reuben living with her son. She was a tall, gaunt woman with the large nose of the family, the square jaw, and black teeth. She was a doctor driven from practice by Zdanov, and she wouldn't kiss him since he was an American and her eyes ran frantic with fear as he approached her. He wasn't too sorry because it was obvious she hadn't washed her mouth in a month. But her fear made him quiver. There were no windows in the hut, just chinks in the wood, and the hovel was lit by a smelly oil lamp. With her in the medieval hut was a thirteen-year-old boy, her son, long, thin, dirty, red-haired, bignosed and tough-jawed. The boy, whose name was Mordecai, just sat in the corner on a heap of bedding, staring first at his American cousin, then at his mother, who stared at her visitor stiff-lipped and angry. What the hell did he want from her? When he entered she acknowledged in Yiddish the family name and that her parents—she waved her hands in despair. When he tried to carry the conversation further, she answered in Russian. No understand, he said. All they did was look at one another, mother, son, cousin, in anger, in wonder, in frustration.

At the door stood the falsely smiling guide, driver and flatfoot.

A horrible few minutes passed by in slow motion. Decided it was best to leave, so he nodded both to her and to the boy and left the hut. As he started after the driver into the rickety droshky, Mordecai lunged out, grabbed at his sleeve, and said in Yiddish, "You are my cousin," and kissed his hand.

Zeke began to cry. Mordecai stared hard at the guide and spat. Then he ran into Zeke's arms and they embraced.

Three days later Zeke found in his overcoat pocket a letter from Mordecai's mother which was translated for him at the American embassy. It was merely a note to tell him he had another cousin, Pyotr, son of his Vilna Aunt Judith, who lived. It seemed Pyotr was chief of police of Soviet Lithuania. Before Zeke had an opportunity to inquire further, he was abruptly called into another office of the embassy and informed that the Russian authorities requested he leave the country. It wasn't that they had discovered him to be the spy who was printing LET ME

ALONE! in Russian all over Moscow but that they had checked out his name with their dossier files and come up with the information that Samuel E. Gurevich was the same as Zeke Gurevich, former *cabo* in a battalion of Spanish mavericks who had shown contempt for the party commissars, especially after the latter had tried to dry gulch them during the fighting at the Ebro River while beating off a fascist crossing. Gurevich was a fascist, the Russians said, and must leave the U.S.S.R. He was zealously guarded until he reached West Germany, but still managed to leave a message on the ceiling of every toilet he visited. LET ME ALONE!

A year later his cousin and Mordecai disappeared, victims of the Jewish doctors' purge. Two weeks after their disappearance he received a letter postmarked Paris, someone's private underground, that Pyotr, the son of Aunt Judith, really was chief of police of Lithuania. He wrote to Pyotr who answered, refusing to acknowledge his kinship to the Gurevich family. "We have no relationship. I am not a Jew," Pyotr wrote.

Zeke answered, advising Pyotr to go to hell, and the Russian government, wishing to create an incident, printed his letter in *Pravda*, an example to the Russian people of American boorishness.

Another year passed, Nicola was born to Pacifici and himself, and he received word that Pyotr had vanished. Sardonic laughter. Shortly thereafter, another letter arrived from Paris, this one from Isaac, one of Pyotr's three children. Isaac wrote that he went to the Vilna synagogue whenever he had a chance. "Not because I believe (my brother Reuben believes), but because I am a Jew and will not permit the government or anyone else to legislate or terrorize it out of me."

In the meantime, Conchita Gurevich, the Argentinian

[185]

twin whose infant brother had died of scarlet fever, married a German refugee. She soon discovered he was a Nazi who had married her to use as a blind. She shot him to death and was smuggled out of Argentina by Israeli agents. Now she lived in Haifa, married, and with three children. On the morning of the birth of Vito, his second son, Zeke wrote Conchita, "The storm troopers and the commissars will come and go, but we multiply, for our blood," he plagiarized Chava Green, "is like an ancient wine, and our seed fertile and strong."

It was on his way back from Russia, in Paris, in the *Jeu de Paume,* one gray, chilly, damp morning that he met Pacifici. She stood before Manet's *Déjeuner sur l'Herbe,* a fairly tall, full-bosomed girl with reddish-brown hair, a big can and an elegant face. A foot swinging freely on a graceful heel, she was examining the painting intently, with obvious pleasure. Still, though it is an especially joyful painting, there was a sadness to her face. Zeke looked at the painting, looked at her, the painting, her. Without ever seeming to have seen him, she became aware of him, blushed slightly at his brash insistent stare, imperceptibly began to turn to another painting, firmed her lips as if she'd decided who the hell was he to make her move on, bit her finger nail, kneaded her lower lip, examined the painting further. In one hand she carried a Michelin in English. He could see he'd spoiled the moment for her, said as quietly as he could and still be heard, "Excuse me for staring. It *is* a beautiful painting, isn't it?" She was shy, and she swallowed, and said, "Yes, it is," in a soft, lovely voice. "New York," he said. "Massachusetts," she answered.

He tagged after her through the rest of the museum,

and though she was shy, and a little scared about being picked up, she began to loosen up and tell him about the paintings and their painters, and she seemed to know what she was talking about. He listened, asked a few questions, and sneaked looks at her big can, and at her nice legs, just a little off, not perfect, but right, and the soft brown eyes, deep and sad. She had large, strong, uneven teeth and knew how to laugh, and he liked her. First he liked her, because whatever she said, she said straight, with good diction, in a gentle, womanly voice. She was in her early, perhaps mid-twenties, but, though a little scared, mature. Soon he was only aware of her, the paintings be damned. Yet, strangely, he could always remember every painting they saw and everything she had to say about them.

For lunch they went to some restaurant near the French National Assembly, where she told him the deputies ate, and they became friends.

In between the soup and the ragout and the wine, they talked. But there were many silences and it didn't matter. By the time the afternoon floated away on the Seine, he was hopelessly, and happily, in love. Scared, too—but in love. "It's Paris," she smiled. "No, it's you," he answered. Later both were to admit it was because they were looking for love and happened to be in the right place to find it.

Her name was Pacifici—Pa-chee-fi-chee—Bartola Ahmed.

"Bartola Ahmed? What are you, an Italian Arab? I'm a Jew."

No, her parents were Italian. She'd been married to a Syrian boy named Rafik Ahmed from her hometown, Brockton, Massachusetts, a boy whom she'd married when she was seventeen and who had died in the war.

She'd come to Europe on the insurance money, to see where she came from, and she'd not felt a stranger at all.

"Your parents Sicilians?"

No, her parents came from northern Italy, Turin, involuntary exiles from Mussolini. "My father was an industrial worker, a blacksmith, then a tool and die maker. He was an anarchist in Italy, a Wobbly in the States."

"Okay, Pacifici. My father came from Vilna, Lithuania, and was a billboard painter. One week JESUS LOVES, the next ladies' hairnets. Fell from a scaffold and died. He was a left-wing socialist. Fought in St. Petersburg with Trotsky in nineteen-five and died before the revolution had a chance to betray him. You're quite a piece."

She blushed.

He guessed most men were scared off by what they thought was coldness because her strong-boned face had elegance and class.

In a few days he found himself in a position to say to her, "May I have *déjeuner sur l'herbe*, Pacifici? I never had an Italian knish."

She was scared. God, she was scared—and wanted to, wanted more than anything to do it. Ignoring her elegant jaw and calm eyes, he stormed in frontal attack. Taken completely by surprise, she yielded. Later, when it was easy for her to talk, she told him she could never fathom how she had got on her bottom so quickly. No man had ever dared before, she told him. "Idiots," he said dryly, said as though he were a master at love, all others mere apprentices.

She wanted love as much as he did, and she wanted to do it as much as he did. Except she was scared, and she hid her fear behind a shy little smile.

So he didn't hesitate, went straight to it, that was the

[188]

only way, and he was as gentle as he could be, because he wanted to love her and wanted her to love him.

There was want and need on both sides, but what astounded him most was that she was as hungry as he. "Hungry? Oh, yes, I'm hungry, Zeke. I never seem to be able to fill up." She kneaded her lips, bit her nails. The bivalve unfrozen, it suddenly developed a mouth with which to talk—and he loved to hear that soft, gentle, New England voice. Hunger? She knew what it was. The ugly shoes, a generosity of Welfare, the oatmeal with watered milk three times a day, for breakfast, for dinner, for supper, and that's all. The hunger to play a piano, to own a bike, and the most agonizing hunger, the hunger for beauty, thank God there were museums—the Fogg, the Boston, the Worcester. The red hat on a Botticelli boy; the sweet gentleness of a Fra Angelica, the hungering pain of Giotto. The madness of Castagno, a hunger, too. She played *Death and the Maiden* over and over again, until the record wore flat. Or a Bach cantata. *Je-su. Je-su.* It was amazing how an entire cantata could fill her head, and tomorrow not be able to recall a note. The need to form little figures with her fingers was a hunger, too. Talked about hunger, kept the fingers moving, using wax from a cheese. Calm face, nervous fingers, nails she bit to the quick. Busy, busy fingers. Sold bread in a bakery after school when she was ten—stole fresh rolls, tired to death of the stale. Packed condoms in a factory for twenty-two cents an hour when she was thirteen, the boss patting her behind till she cried; stealing condoms to leave on her papa's bureau in the hope he'd take a hint. There were enough Bartola babies. Kept the fingers moving, using soft bread centers rolled into dough, using mud, clay, anything she could lay her hands on, to make miniature caprices which frightened her father and would in time frighten her husband, Zeke Gurevich, womanlover, who could never learn to keep his hands where they belonged.

Hey, wop! the Canuck kids had called after her. Hey, wop! let me see your Roman twat, the Irish kids had laughed. Hey, wop! your father a bolshie? Can't your father hold a job? Always trying to cause trouble, that goddamn Wobbly bastard, the Yankee neighbors had sneered. Meetings held behind pulled shades—blond Estonians and Swedes, swarthy Portuguese, Italians, palefaced Jews. A new world. Sang Joe Hill songs, sang *Bandera Rossa*. Wept behind pulled shades, candles burning for Bartolomeo and Nicola the day they were electrocuted. Until she was about twelve she had believed she could remember the day they were killed. How could she have—she'd been a baby? It had been the memorial meetings every year which she remembered—the burning candles, the speeches, the weeping, the elders weeping, the kids, she too. I want new shoes, she had once cried, the bottoms of her blistered feet coming through the sides of her old ones. Everyone cried louder, and her papa slapped her. "Quiet! Shoes she wants when we weep for our murdered comrades." She cried harder, everyone cried. A comrade, a Finn from a Spencer shoe factory, gave her a red silk handkerchief. It was beautiful, soft and brilliant. She stopped crying. Tears! she had run out of tears by the time she was fourteen. Hid behind her high-arched Roman nose and New England jaw, just like her father's. No more tears, they hurt. A tear slipping down a cheek hurt more than fire. What she wanted was beauty and softness, gentleness. That red silk handkerchief gave her joy for years. When she held it in her hand it was as soft and grand as papa's cheeks after he shaved. Smooth and electric, her fingers carried the current to the pit of her stomach. Even lower. A brilliant silky red. On rare Saturdays, she hitchhiked to the museum in Boston with Giovanni, her older brother, after helping him deliver his papers in the very early morning. He would give her two cents and she would save them to buy crayons. But the colors were bad. She started to save to buy water paints, but Giovanni lost his job. Papa had made him insert copies of *The Industrial Worker,* the Wobbly paper, among the Gazettes and he'd been caught. Red bastard, don't come back again. Looking at the paintings, biting her nails, hypnotized by their beauty, she almost believed in God though papa would have killed her if he knew. He could be terribly cruel. Continually taunted Giovanni for being a sissy because he always had his nose in a book and wanted to be more than a factory worker; told her to stop making drawings, they were ugly. "No talent. Work." Or he would laugh, one never knew which. Once he was put in jail for fighting with a policeman when he refused to get off the job after being fired for agitating for one big industrial union, solidarity forever for the union makes us strong. She and Giovanni and Sophie, her oldest sister, had gone to visit him in the old stone building where the jail was. She brought papa an apple, a big, juicy, red apple, which she shined on her hole-filled sweater. She thought she would find papa crying, but no, he was laughing uproariously, and when she gave him the apple he sang her favorite song, a song he would sing to her when she sat on his lap in the evenings, the coal stove bursting with heat and her belly deep inside with that same scary wonderful feeling as when she ran her fingers over the red silk handkerchief which the Finnish comrade had given her. They ate and smelled and dressed and looked poor. But her father sang beautiful songs, and the museums drew her like a magnet, her fingers always at work with clay or bread or wax—ugly, her father would call them, too.

He was rough on her mother, but there were times when she turned him back with a double-edged laugh. Late one night she'd heard papa tell mama as they sat in the kitchen, the children supposedly asleep, in Italian English, "Mama, I am the great lover, unnerstand?" In Italian, "*Sì*, Vito Bartola. You are a great lover, have given me nine children, one, two, three, so I never see the sun but through weary eyes. We are enlightened people, Vito, we have forsaken our fathers' God. Our prophet is Malatesta, Bakunin our God. You will lead us into the new world, Vito. So, please, my great lover, go buy one of those rubber balloons." There was loud sipping of wine. "Nine children are enough. I am no slave. I want freedom." Silence. Heavy work shoes scraping under the table. "No, Angelica. I cannot bring myself to deny life." "You don't deny yourself life, my husband, it is I who am deprived of life. *I* need life. For once, my great lover, I want to see the beauty of the earth without the smell of urine and baby caca. To see the sun with untired eyes and a flat stomach. Hypocrite." A heavy male sigh. "You berate me because I am poor, Angelica." "I berate you because you fight to free man but forget your own wife." "I can't bring myself to use one. It is obscene." "My broken back is more obscene—a slave to your hypocrisy. My great lover. All men believe themselves to be great lovers. But you all make love the same way. With your hands you tear, with your teeth you bite, with your mouths you suck, and with your *macchina* you drive." Papa laughed, slapping his huge thighs, a man who when he walked always seemed to be pushing uphill. "How do you know so much about men, Angelica? You were a virgin and have never known another man but me." Silence. How many ears

[192]

were listening? "True. But I am not without some beauty, even now, round as a ball though I am, and some men have tried—comrades, friends: a hard knee, an elbow, a tender smile. 'Come, Angelica, I will give you a love no blacksmith can possibly know; come, I am a fine lover, Angelica.' " Papa laughed loudly at her mimicry, half understanding it was he she mimicked. "True, we all hold the bow the same, all rest the cello against our thighs, position our elbow at the exact angle, but some saw wood and some bring Vivaldi to life. Aie, Angelica?" Silence, as papa awaited her verdict. "Aie, Angelica?" There was a scraping of chairs as mama laughed and papa whacked the table.

Her mother gave them whatever love she had time for; papa gave love the way the wind brings rain. Blows it here and blows it there. Vagarious. Once he'd brought a little Negro girl home, an eight-year-old who'd been brought to the city by a committee to save the Scottsboro boys. Lucille was the sister of one of them. Papa brought Lucille to the house late at night and she was put to bed with Pacifici. Huddled against her, the child cried. "Why are you crying, Lucille?" "Because I have to make a speech tomorrow and I'm scared."

In the morning Lucille didn't want to go, and sobbed, and papa didn't know what to do. So she took Lucille into her room and talked to her quietly and gave her the red silk handkerchief. Lucille ran her skinny, brown finger over it. "So smooth," she said. "So beautiful." Lucille stopped sobbing and reluctantly, blackmailed, put on her hat to go with papa.

Papa hugged Pacifici so hard her bones cracked, then he went into his room and cried because his Pacifici was so good. Good. Everyone, damn them, thought she was good. Because she controlled her selfishness, her envy, kept it to herself, while they paraded it, flaunted it. Good.

"What's wrong with being good?" Zeke asked.

"Nothing. But I'm sick to death of having to wear it like a yellow star of David, the universal patsy. Oh, I suppose I just want to be left alone."

"Hey, that's my line," he laughed. "I love you, Pacifici."

"I love you, too, Zeke."

"Come here, I want to drink from you. I want to put my head up as far as it'll go. Why are you laughing? What's funny?"

"You. Your tongue is like a fish. A serpent, you're a wonderful serpent. I'm going to be as evil as I please."

She laughed. Once she'd found it difficult to laugh. Frozen face, they'd called her after Rafik died in a South Pacific jungle, because she didn't want to sleep around.

Rafik had been an organizer for the shoe union, a poetic twenty-two-year-old Syrian boy with the black eyes and oval face of a Picasso clown and the strength of a strongman. Gentle and poetic, strong and energetic, with very white even teeth, he was so strong he almost broke a scab's back throwing him out the window at a meeting—a striker caught scabbing. Hunger and fear can make a man into a beast. Idealism can make a man a killer. At twenty-two, Rafik was idealistic and violent. He despised the violence in himself. "It's not for me, Pacifici," he said, and showed her his poetry. She was sixteen then. At sixteen she'd been a woman burning with fire, hidden behind a granite jaw. All the boys were afraid of her, but love made Raf Ahmed brave. She read his poems. She'd already read Keats and Wordsworth. Raf's were very bad. But his own sweetness was fine, very fine, and he wanted to take her in his arms and was afraid and so was she, knowing the flame of her fire. They held hands. Papa had been dead a year. Heart attack. Mama slaved in the house, the top floor of a

[194]

wooden triple decker, thirty dollars a month. The nine—
no, eight; one died, Marcello—the eight went out to work
at whatever they could find. Dollars, dollars, dollars.
Food, rent, clothes. Nothing else, though it had become a
little easier; the war in Europe had started. Raf bought
her clay and they went to the park and as he rested on his
stomach and elbows, his black eyes on her lips, she
molded figures. Odd how he always watched her lips.

Thin, nervous lips they were, always biting them or her
nails with her large uneven teeth and always working her
fingers. "Reveals everything about you," Zeke said. "Energy and passion. Men are such fools. Not Raf, he knew."

Raf, observing her, couldn't keep his eyes off her lips,
wanting to kiss them. She sculpted a centaur with a sad
face and large eyes and Raf laughed. In the darkness they
lay on the grass at last touching one another, half frightened, Raf too, even though he had been to women in
Providence. But this was love. They touched one another,
the first time for her; she had entered puberty late: one
day, no breasts; next, bosoms, big, round, hard, white
bosoms with tiny pink nipples. They touched one another.
But no, Raf. Enough, Rafik. Papa will be angry. But papa
had been already dead a year. Touching was all—burning
one's fingers playing with matches. And then just like that
Raf Ahmed was in California, in the army—America was
in the war. "Please come and marry me, Pacifici. I don't
want to die without having been married to you. I need
you and want you terribly." Seventeen she was then. She
wanted to go to Raf but she didn't. She wasn't sure. Did
she or didn't she love him? She was too young for marriage. But her desire was ripe. He was sent to officers'
training school and looked frighteningly beautiful in his
uniform and she had a foreboding he was going to die.
She woke up in the middle of the night with the terrible

feeling he was going to die. Pacifici, sweet, good Pacifici, smiling Pacifici. She telegraphed she was coming. They were married at the camp chapel and walked under drawn swords as in the movies and he did it to her after missing the first three times. It hurt, her thighs held on too tightly, but he loved her and he was tender and sweet and pretended no sophistication. It wasn't bad after a while. Raf made her laugh. He would make her undress and put her legs around his waist facing him, and a two-bodied centaur they would gallop about the little house. An officer, Rafik had a bungalow. Class conscious Lt. and Mrs. Rafik Ahmed. It was no longer just a hot protuberance, it was sex, hot and hard and exciting. "Don't cheat on me, Pacifici," Rafik said after he received his orders. "Don't worry about it, Raf, I won't." "If you have to, then—" "Yes, I know. But I won't have to. I know myself." She would be able to get along without it, and she didn't like to do it to herself, it was childish. Raf was sent to the Pacific theatre of war. A play, a great drama. "Pacifici, my Pacifici will guard me." Three months later he was dead. Now he was a memory; she didn't even know if she had really loved him. Yes, she had.

Then until she had met Zeke Gurevich her body had been frozen along with her face. Cold. She could never make the first move. It took a rake to notice what was under the ice floe—a man who'd been taught by Rachel Farrell to know what girls are made of. A few had tried with Pacifici, but she had become frightened and fled. To do it without love was offensive to her. An indignity. So she was the last of the chaste; that's the way she was built, so?

"Don't apologize. I'm not complaining. Now you belong to me—I've suddenly become a *parvenu*. Don't ever cheat, I'm a jealous man and tend to violence."

"Of course," she said. "And you, too, you won't?"

"No," he said, looking straight into her brown-black eyes. And he meant it—at least he meant it when he said it. The only other woman he would ever have wanted to sleep with would be Rachel, and he hadn't slept with Rachel, except once or twice—three times—during the few years with Ida. They'd just found themselves alone and hadn't had anything to say, so they had done what was easiest. But Pacifici Bartola wasn't Ida Bitch. She was a woman to have a marriage with.

Pacifici and Zeke lived together in New York in her small apartment on Riverside Drive at 111th Street. She was taking some art courses at Columbia and he resumed his job with the union. As soon as his divorce came through, they were married.

The first night of marriage, Zeke said, "Let's throw the gadget away. I'm getting old, I want babies."

"I'm willing any time, Zeke. In fact, I can't wait."

They threw it away—it had lost its resilience anyway from over-use, night after night for a year, the time of month meaning nothing to him and finally to her, too.

The Bartolas and Gureviches were a fertile lot: Nicola was born nine months to the day.

XV

Zeke Gurevich sat on the beach contemplating nothing, an old habit; older, more intense. Like a metronome which had slipped its notch he asked in perfect rhythm without skipping a beat who the hell cares and what's it all about?

Nothing.

A slender tern over a calm sea screeched, *Mi-shu-gah. Mi-shu-gah.*

You're crazy, too, he thought, raising his head lazily to observe the tern, who screeched again, dropped a nugget, banked, and fled.

It was a quiet beach on the Maine coast, empty but for him—white sand, black rock, yellow sun. Here the land world disappeared, a mere bite of the whole.

Closed his eyes, resumed his contemplation of the void. The sun caressed his thinning red-gray pate, hot and strong. With a burst of Gurevich energy he tore himself loose, jumped to his feet and dove into the sea, embracing the freezing water before it numbed him. A wave took him by the rear, tumbling him playfully head first into the ice-cold surf. Swam a sprightly twenty strokes out and back. About to turn purple, he sprang from the sea and, dripping, reached for the towel, deep orange. Fine beach. No one there and he could swim and loll around bare. Bolicky, Pacifici called it. The beach was screened off from the dirt road by a wide stand of high yellow sea grass

[198]

which also hid the shack he'd bought years ago when he ran away from Ida. Ida Bitch. Stop lying, she ran away from you. Forget it. Soon the children would be down, the tumult would begin, and he would have to cover up. The child psychologists now said it was wrong to run around naked in front of the kids—a half-baked bohemian barbarism. Led to sexual frigidity: after all, we don't live in Tahiti. And why not? Oh, well, every twenty years the style changed.

Threw the orange towel aside, lay back on an unraveling straw pallet, closed his eyes against the sun and tried to sleep, not forgetting to cover his crotch for fear the diving tern might mistake it for a sardine. Thought of Ida again. Once he got started he couldn't stop. An ancient Gurevich disease. Why did he have to think about her? It would spoil his taste for the sun, the beach, the sea, his family—himself. Aaa, stop hating her. Enough. She could hate for two. Three. Four. Five. How much is infinity, Pop? Calm yourself. You weren't—aren't so hot. Have pity. Be understanding. Merciful. You've got Pacifici now. It had happened so long ago—God! don't start counting the years—by now it should've been forgotten. Obsessive bastard that he was, every time he came to this damn beach he remembered. The bad with the good. Can never separate them. Sermon for today: the inevitability of the bad with the good. Ida Bitch and Ocean Beach.

Tried sleeping. No good. What's the sense of pretending—he was waiting for the phone call from Matt Cahn. It would be coming any minute, any hour, any day. This wasn't going to be much of a vacation.

Zeke Gurevich and his women. Soon there'd be only one. Started counting them—realized the idiocy of it, stopped. The pleasure of having had lots of girls when you were young was the counting of them when you were old. Not yet, though damn if it wasn't getting closer.

Despite all the wanting, he often patted himself on the back; he hadn't cheated even once on Pacifici in the fifteen years or so since he met her, except with Rachel on occasion. Which was like saying he never stole anything, except money on occasion. Cheating with Rachel? With a fantasy? No. It was something else. The few times over the years they'd been alone, totally alone, they'd talked, without thinking touched, laughed, and knocked one off for old time's sake. It hadn't been love, romance, infatuation any longer; it had been like calling back some nagging, but comfortable childhood dream. A fretful harmony. After all they had counted for a lot with each other.

Rachel and Pacifici were the only ones really who had counted. Yet how different each was. With Pacifici it was man and woman, conflict, sex, love, coming home. Oh, Pacifici, I love you. You are my very own heart. You are my years of travail come to rest. You are my wife. Pacifici with the tender smile, the unfrantic reality, the nervous energy, and the iron will. Few, if any, obsessions. Except for the fingers, never stopped, goddamn them. Everything done with a fine, graceful rhythm. Only in bed was she hesitant. Afraid to face the reality of giving herself up completely. Guilt, how do you do? Was it Freud had made it up and everyone's living up to his fabrication or had it been a true insight? Pacifici had loved her father, therefore was inhibited about giving herself completely to her husband. "That's simplistic," she said. "Read the Greeks," he retorted. "Freud. Everybody knows it. It's a fact." "Theory, conjecture. It's true, I loved my father. But it's not necessary to discuss it. There are parts of me which belong to no one else but to me. Not even you." And vice versa. Still, Pacifici avoided delving into the unknown.

[200]

Perhaps it was too frightening. Those strong fingers of hers kneading clay into grotesqueries: miniature bodies with huge heads, *el Enano;* distorted, despairing arms and legs. Many times no face. Reality she looked upon with equanimity. "Don't worry," she would say (he was becoming a nag like his old lady) about some child's crisis, "don't be so anxious about him, it's only a phase. He's human, not a machine." Nicola would come out of it with a Bartola-Gurevich bounce. She smiled tenderly, spoke softly, and wounds healed. The children, he, could press her to the wall, nagging, yelling, taking advantage of her easy nature and temper—but then there was an abrupt hardening of the voice, the soft Italian eyes, brown-black, lost their smile. A Medici, a Borgia. "Enough." It would come as a shock and had an immediate effect. Pacifici had class, good taste, and had been forged by Vito Bartola, the smith, into a tough piece of iron. In the end, Zeke supposed, that's what's most important—the politics of morality, of beauty, of reason. Pacifici. And in bed, under him, the breasts flat, the belly concave, the thighs taut—conflict, hesitant. Challenging. Take me but leave me a part of myself. Perhaps it wasn't guilt at all. Perhaps it was fear of vanquishment. Don't be a victor on me. Sometimes he wanted to yell, don't be afraid of being a victim and you won't be. I'm not trying to defeat you, just make love to you. But she made no concessions. She wanted no patronizing man plowing her under. As he came to understand over the years she too wanted to be let alone, it got better. At least that was one theory of his youth which met the test of time.

With Rachel the coin was reversed. Tête-à-tête: conflict. Tit on tit: harmony. The breasts flat, the belly concave, the thighs resilient, spread wide: enter, merge, fusion, total yield. In the darkness, unseen, total fearlessness. In the sunlight, total fear. All that pretense. All that guts. All those years of fear brazened out.

They each had married elsewhere—and it was elsewhere they lived their lives. When they were with each other it was disappearing into some wilderness to escape the difficulty each found living in the world as it was. Terrible, terrifying, beastly world. Oh, balls! Each was totally aware of the filth and evil which stalked the earth—they knew themselves so well. In the rare hours they found together, they cuffed each other about, nudged, nagged, ragged, bit, snapped, pinched—then they went to bed and it was ease. The axles were oiled. Ride, boy, ride. Go, Red, go. Let that locomotive roll. I'm only a woman, I gave birth to the world.

Soon it would be over.

Late one afternoon last year he returned to his cubicle at his office. He worked now for a Negro civil rights organization on loan from his union. ("I'm not leading them, they're leading me," he told Abe. "No one can lead them anymore—they're in revolt as much against themselves as against the society which has demeaned them. It's like the time we made the Normandy landings—the war's won, the last bloody battle hasn't been fought yet, that's all.") At his desk he found a message to call Rachel. He dialed her number and she asked him to come over that night, she must see him.

"What do you want, Rachel?"

"Matt's in Europe again, covering the Common Market meeting in Brussels. Believes the Common Market's the greatest happening since Runnymede. I'm lonesome."

"I have to help Pacifici with the kids."

She whispered a husky intimacy to him, a sibilance, taking advantage of him because she knew Pacifici was eight months gone with child, their third, and had a complication which, though minor, had made it necessary for them to abstain. She knew Zeke Gurevich would be about ready to eat the paint off the walls. He needed it regularly and often. Everybody knew. His sap overflowed. Zeke Gurevich, cuntlover. Smile, when you say that, sister. Never look a gift orgasm in the mouth, buster. "All right," he said. That was the excuse he gave himself, he needed it; also, what the hell, sleeping with Rachel was like sleeping with an ex-wife, one you'd slept with for twenty years. What was the difference, one more. What crap. He was amoral about these things—as far as it concerned Rachel, anyway.

She called, he went. She lived in a Westchester town, in an antique house with a multitude of rooms, gold wall-to-wall carpeting ("It's good insulation and keeps the heating bills down," had been her lip-biting answer to his sneering smile), but the same Fourth Avenue secondhand furniture and Chianti bottle lamps, and new plush velvet drapes: only Rachel could put that concoction together and get away with it. He and Pacifici lived across the river in a house on a hill overlooking the Hudson. ("So he can look at a bit of flotsam and wander with it out to sea," Pacifici had said patronizingly.) After Pacifici took her eight-month gone belly to bed, he washed the dishes, cleaned up around, shined the kids' shoes, and after all was quiet, Pacifici's pregnant snore in perfect pitch—she had a miraculous ear—he sneaked out like a petty thief, despising himself, slipped into his secondhand Chevy which was parked on the hill, released the brake without starting the motor, and rolled down silently in order not to wake his wife. What she doesn't know won't hurt. In thirty minutes he was at Rachel's. Her door was open, it was summer, the lights were dimmed, and she stood in a thin housecoat at the foot of the stairs, waiting for him. He slipped in and she threw her thin arms about his neck, burying her head in his chest; she was feverish, trembling. The house was mostly dark, and silent, her children long since off. She smelled of fresh soap and powder, and as she leaned on him she felt unmercifully light; he led her up the gold-carpeted stairs to her room. He undressed in the dark, the old glued-together Rodin catching a star's gleam, and soon held her trembling body in his arms. Once as he caressed her breast roughly she struck his hand away. "No." Though he wondered why, he was too far from shore to stop.

Later they drank ice-cold beer in the semi-darkness of the kitchen, a hall light on, and he remembered and asked her why she was so thin and why she'd struck his hand away. She ignored his question and it was too dark to see her face. They talked about their respective children, but not about Matt and Pacifici. When he finished his beer, he stood and pressed the electric button: the white kitchen light was barbaric: she was gaunt, her huge eyes in their caverns frightened and lonely. My God, she's become an old woman. Too quickly. Her tongue moistened her lips and her eyes retreated into the darkness of the caverns, trying to conceal themselves from his. He took her long thin bony hands in his. "What's wrong, Rachel?"

"Nothing's wrong. Matt's been gone quite a while this time, the children are away, I'm lonesome, and even an old woman needs it once in a while."

"Cut it out. Who the hell do you think you're crapping? What's wrong?"

"If I say it it will be true," she said quietly, and he could feel himself become frightened.

"It's true even if you don't say it," he was merely mouthing words. They were silent. Then he asked, and he couldn't control the quiver in his voice, "When did you last see a doctor?"

Hesitant, then plunging, she said, "A year ago."

"Abe?"

"No."

"What did the doctor say?"

" 'Young lady, you have a lump in your breast.' "

A year! He swallowed hard, could feel himself going pale, fought against tightening his hands around hers. With her one had to pretend. Oh, Rachel.

"Many women get lumps in their breasts. If it's anything, they have an operation and live forever."

"If I amputate my breast, Matt will turn away from me. He can't endure the sight of cripples."

How does he manage to shave, Zeke wondered, but didn't say it. "If you don't do it, you'll die if it's malignant."

"I know."

"Why do you want to die?"

"I don't want to die."

"Then let's hope there's still time. Call Abe in the morning."

"NO!"

He wanted to beat her. Goddamn vain, cowardly bitch. "I'll cable Matt that you're ill," he said coldly. "He'll return immediately."

Her eyes retreated deeper into the caverns; she bit her quivering lips. "I knew I shouldn't have told you."

But she had called him to come and he knew she had because she wanted him to know, she wanted him to do what she herself couldn't do. "If you tell Matt," she said hoarsely, "I'll not speak to you again as long as I live."

"That may not be very long," he said cruelly. Her eyes could retreat no deeper and now implored him from their depths to help her. "Who's your doctor?" he asked.

She evaded, she dodged, she hesitated. Was death so welcome? Does the sea dry up? Would all that would be left be a salt flat? She told him the doctor's name and he picked up the phone.

"Not now," she said, defeated, "It's almost midnight."

"Tomorrow you might change your mind. You hate daylight and might prefer to die." He called, waking the poor man, and made an appointment for the morning. "I'll cable Matt."

"You're not to cable Matt. He can't stand to have his plans disrupted."

"You're totally nuts."

"Matt has a girl friend in Europe," she finally said.

Again they were silent. All her friends knew and had believed she didn't know. Now he didn't tell her he'd known because he didn't want her to think he'd pitied her all along. "He's your husband and will come immediately. He's a decent man and I'm not blaming him for not knowing what you never told him, though I have to admit to wanting to blame him."

As if she hadn't heard, she said, "He told me himself."

Of course, truth too can be a murderer. "Look, Pacifici's baby is due any day now. I have her and my children to worry about. Matt's your husband, he'll have to come home."

"My friends will help out."

"You can always put your friends to the trouble, but never Matt. This time it's different."

Her eyes flattened against the cavern depths; the lids

closed, then opened. "All right." That was, he knew, what she had wanted all along. Now she could pretend it had been his doing, not hers. Damn if she would ever curtail her husband's freedom. Fool of a woman.

"I'll cable now," he said. "It's about seven, eight o'clock in the morning in Brussels, so you need have no qualms about waking him with this news while he's in his girl friend's bed."

"For you to be so contemptuous of him is utter hypocrisy," she said hard, protecting Matt to the end. Matt was later to use the same words.

"You're right," Zeke shrugged.

The following morning he took her to the doctor and then to the hospital. The biopsy indicated a malignancy. Matt returned by jet the same day. Within two days her breast, a quarter of her side and the enlarged mole at the base of her spine were amputated. Matt Cahn lived in the hospital and walked around with a tight rectum and pursed lips. The doctors told Matt it might not be too late, a vague hope; Rachel they told she would be all right, but she told them they were liars and demanded the truth. "At least give me the dignity of truth," she said. The doctors told her. And it was taking her a year to die.

He moaned now. Gulls wheeled overhead, as clumsy as ancient bombers. A tern dove into the sea, a slender screech, came up with a silversides. Ah, get up and take another dip. He did, the icy water refreshing him. His usual twenty strokes out and back.

Then the sea calm, the sun hot, the sand shimmering, he napped, a sharp hook in his heart.

"Hey, dad; hey, dad!"

He sighed without opening his eyes. It was his son, Nicola. "Go get lost, Red."

"It's Matt Cahn, dad," said Nicola. "About Rachel. He's

on the phone. Mom's crying. Can I go to the ball game later?"

Rachel! He sprung to his feet. It had come. There's no time for *nothing* on this busy little shit of land. Rachel, Rachel.

His son observed him with intelligent unsentimental yellow eyes. "Mom was crying," he repeated.

"I understand, Nicola. Run quickly and tell her to tell Matt I'll call him right away." Why did his heart hurt so much? He had known it was coming. Had learned to accept it. No, no, one never learns to accept it—better not to.

When the boy's red head was lost in the high yellow sea grass, Zeke began slowly to follow after him. Suddenly he began to beat himself on his chest with his fists. Beat himself hard. Woe is me, woe is me. He wanted to maim himself. To cry. Rachel. But he couldn't cry anymore, except taken unawares perhaps by some sentimental pap—a TV kid's crying at the death of his dog or some such crap. To cry at anything else at this stage of the game he thought obscene. The ghosts of the past would turn their contemptuous, cold eyes on him and punch out their notorious Roman gesture.

In the china blue sky two dun and black marsh hawks made a swift graceful pass; one dived and rose with a rush of wings, a squirming black snake in its talons. A flight of six white gulls screamed past; a slender tern on a solo spin, screeching, *Mi-shu-gah. Mi-shu-gah.*

He phoned Matt.

No, she hadn't died yet. The doctor said a day or two, it was impossible for it to take much longer. "So what do you want, Matt? Get to it." When Matt called, it was to ask for something.

"Rachel wants to see you—wants you to be with her."

"Why? Your girl friend keeping you too busy to stay with your wife?" He couldn't help being nasty to Matt. Self-righteous guilt.

"What book of the Bible are you playing now?" Matt asked coldly. "Judge or prophet? You never seem to be able to decide. Still, most of your life you've been a bum."

"A hobo, not a bum. But you never could tell the difference. You're right, though, I've become a prig."

"Make the epiglottis hit it a little harder, Zeke."

"Don't push it, Matt."

"Should I tell Rachel you don't want to come?"

Blackmail.

"I'll come." Rachel dying was no different from Rachel living—put a person in the position where he had no alternative but to heed her command. He wished he didn't have to go now. He'd had enough of dying for a while. A few months before he learned of Rachel's cancer, he'd had to speak the eulogy for Michael Berg, an old Spanish civil war comrade and union brother who died of a heart attack while exhorting a sneering lot of mealy-faced, meanmouthed workers to join the union outside of a textile factory gate in Alabama. After burying Berg, he had been depressed for weeks. What can a man say that means anything for a friend who had died? In ten minutes. All you're really thinking about is how close it's getting to you. Mike died and they buried him. Then Zeke learned of Rachel's cancer. While mourning this knowledge, Rebecca died from an embolism. Broke an ankle slipping on an icy sidewalk—forty-eight hours later dead. He'd mourned her deeply. She hadn't been too bad—a nag, a show-off, but an honest sort. He'd loved her sinfully when he was a kid, hated her passionately. Always tried to show him up. His father and mother had treated her as if she'd been the only bird in the cage. Left Roger with thirteen kids and Mama Gurevich, sour pickle tycoon. The old lady went on though. Had decided to make life her permanent abode—tough as an old sequoia. Still, he felt it was closing in on him. He couldn't open *The Times* in the morning without—he caught himself. His mind was wandering again, and reality kept bringing him up short. His impulse was to say who the hell cares? But that was a lie and he had promised himself to tell only the truth to himself. Another lie—for every truth a lie—since he was well aware that promises are written in water.

He must pack; in the morning Pacifici would drive him to Portland and he would catch a plane to New York. Rachel wanted him close by as she was dying, couldn't leave him in peace.

The children seemed to understand and went to sleep without any fuss, even Rebecca, ten months old, usually a screamer, though she compensated by having the fattest little kumquat he'd ever seen on a baby girl. Then he asked his wife if she wanted to go out for a walk on the beach and she said no, it was all right, he could go alone, she had some work to do.

But before he walked out the door, she said softly, "Will you be at peace afterwards?" And he looked at her and she returned his look calmly, except she was biting her nether lip. She was thinking, he knew, tomorrow he has to go to his dying Rachel to hold her hand until she dies. Her own husband's not enough, she must take my husband's hand, too. Before he could answer, Vito, their second son, called her, and she went in to him.

It was chilly out. There were a hundred million stars in a black sky, no moon, and the sea also black, no diamonds gleaming as on a moonlit night. Just roaring and sighing, sometimes crying, never lying, the soft sea as hard as iron, ruthless and splendid, the Atlantic, our cradle, our father who art in heaven, the sea, the sea never once at rest. Will you be at peace afterwards? Pacifici had asked, his love, his wife, his children's mother. She hadn't enough vanity, so she had very little jealousy, or so at least he'd once thought. He'd learned different. He gave her lots of despair, too damn much, no peace for her, her husband with his womanloving, his motherloving, his breastloving, his assloving, his obsessions. It's true, he gave her something else—at least he was vain enough to believe he did. All of a sudden he would fall in love with an ear. Would kiss it, suck it, love it, caress it, his fingers softly tracing its shape and convolutions. Oh, your ear, Pacifici. He would make love to her ear. Or her elbow. Or her breasts. Or her thighs. Or her lovely russet hair. He would put his head on her almond, his bitter sweet almond, and caress it, pinch it, taste it, feel it with his fingers, a feel here, a press there. One never knew which part of her would next be the focus of his obsessive attention and love. Or he would be off wandering. When he'd been young, he'd wandered. Run off. I didn't run away, I wanted to see. Found some excuse, like Rachel's turning me down, or some such, and I'd go off. Saw the country. Saw Spain. Saw death and glory and no-glory. Saw IT in the center of Europe. A rotting intestine. We come from Europe, don't we? It's our heart. Isn't it? So I ran off to see IT. To tear out the rottenness—that rotting, blackened intestine. That's what he'd told her. He boasted, exaggerated—he lied. He'd been a wanderer in his youth. Hit the road, on the bum, absconded with his hurt in his stomach. Now he wandered off in the middle of a spoonful of soup. She hadn't meant would he be at peace afterwards, she meant at last.

He'd loved Rachel for most of his life. It had been a hold-over from childhood, when it had been obsessive, like an infantile disease. There are many kinds of love, he knew, but his for Rachel had been of the simplest, most common variety. He would be at peace. A little, anyhow. He had Pacifici. He would go back to the shack and take her magnificent shoulders between his two hands and shake her till she understood. Or did she understand better than he?

The sea was becoming more noisy—cracking and raging, snapping, and as he walked along its edge the cold spray shocked his face. The moonless sky with its million stars was blacking out entirely, heavy clouds moving down from the Northeast. A northeaster was shaking itself down. The shack would be rumbling. It was nothing, she was used to northeasters, coming from the edge of the Cape herself. She was probably sitting at her wooden bench molding clay, something with which to frighten him. "Hard to understand, these creatures coming from you." He wanted her tranquil and unafraid. Her husband had many fears, hidden away even from his dream world. She just kept hers hidden behind her *condottiere's* jaw and quiet brown-black eyes. God, she was a beautiful woman. Their kids, too. What would she have done if they weren't? Eaten them. No, she still believed in her own immortality and omnipotence. She would say they were beautiful and so they would become. He laughed. "One of these days," he once warned her, "you're going to come by the unhappy news that you're both mortal and powerless." "Not powerless, Zeke; mortal, yes." "You're right, Bartola, with me you're all-powerful." "Liar."

He knew she lived with the nagging fear that one day he would jump up and leave. Silly dame. That time he went off to Europe without her on a seventeen day excursion ticket and returned four days later. Hadn't he told her, "I can't live without you. Tied to your womb now. Come here, let me bite the inside of your left thigh. Couldn't sleep for three nights, daydreaming about how soft and sweet that left thigh was. Nuts, I'm nuts. I love you. You don't have to worry, I'll never run away. Might look at another broad, even go to her, but outside her door I'll stop and turn back. No more. Had enough. There's nothing like doing it to a woman you love."

She couldn't stand violence, and he was a violent man. That time he returned from Mississippi after a freedom ride and grabbed an axe, went to the garage in the back and hacked it down. Better a garage than a man's head. He was learning, wasn't he? By time. What kind of a question was that to have asked, would he be at peace?

Just because he was a foolish man. Jealous. "I love women, I know; the feel of them, that is. If I ever catch you with another man I'll beat you." Foolish male bastard. Foolish males. Must always prove their virility, such a delicate thing, can so easily be damaged. English china. They desire a passionate woman, then worry themselves sick she will give it to someone else. If she does, they respond as if their very maleness had been challenged. A not so subtle form of faggotry. Women have it, too. She admired a woman's breasts almost as much as he did. There was an esthetic unity to a woman's body that no man could ever approach. Men were all angle, she said once, till they reached middle age and began to resemble a seal. A plump fish. She had been making fun of him, his irreversible corpulence. Rachel Cahn even in her late forties had been beautiful enough to keep wanting to show it off to the world. A man's angularity, Pacifici said, became esthetic only in relation to the woman's variety of plane and curve—but a woman's body could stand by itself. It sure could, Pacifici Bartola. Still on occasion he knew she did manage to look at another man and want him, estheticism be damned. But just because she wanted, didn't mean she did. To a woman, wanting didn't seem to be as important as to a man. Even Rachel said that. To him it was, though. He said he would beat Pacifici, and he had. Once at a big party, drinking a little, convivial, a man nabbed her in a corridor and took her in his arms for a sweet, romantic, hot-tongued kiss and in the excitement of the moment, the spontaneity, hardly noticing the man himself, name vague, a nondescript man, just the kiss, hot and quick, she put her arms around him, her fingers on the nape of his neck to bring his head closer, the kiss deeper—a stolen hot sweet, and he, her husband, her baron, happened by on the arm of another lady. That didn't count, of course. There was violence—immediate and swift. On her. Damn. Still blushed. The man he merely shoved aside—it was almost comic, would have been comic, except he saw blood on his wife's lip and humiliation fragmenting her face. Gurevich, you dirty son of a bitch. "Why should I hit him? He didn't betray me, you did. He only did what I would do." "The only reason I can't do what you can do is because I'm a woman." "Naturally. Oh, all right. Intellectually I know I'm wrong, but I can't help it, my jealousy is visceral. I suppose I'm victimized by my own neuroses." "No man need be a victim," she mimicked him. "Even a slave." He had blushed with shame.

But her lip sore, her dignity shattered, at home he tried to make love to her. "Go peddle your fish elsewhere, Mr. Gurevich." Gurevich meant fisherman, he'd fibbed to her. He'd once thought Rachel was the sea. Pacifici was more sea than Rachel had ever been. Rachel had to divide her love into smaller parts because one love was too big a burden for her. Pacifici Bartola could carry the burden of love of one man—all he had to give, and more. He knew that very well. Wasn't he like Rachel? Who knew better?

Still Pacifici had once taunted him, "Some day I'm going to run off and have a love affair with another man just to see what you all make such a fuss about. It must be something special the way everyone talks so damn much about it." But, of course, he didn't take her seriously. Or another time, "What we ought to have is a sexual collective like they had in primitive societies. Ah, we'll get even on all jealous men. Our daughter, if we ever have one, will live in such a community and take as many men to bed with her as she pleases and have a collective baby and the world will have turned full circle. Good." And she laughed at his obvious discomfort. "Earth goddess. White goddess. Black goddess. Ishtar. Rachel Cahn." Dead silence. "You think I don't know?" she asked quietly. He said nothing, just waited for her to get it all out. It seemed she hardly cared. She wasn't going to envy a woman fifteen years her senior, especially one who was so obviously unhappy. Better he went to Rachel than conceding to his desire to sleep with all the girls in the world. If he slept with all the girls he wanted to he'd be a reed, a wet string; he'd have the vitality of a dying fish. Well, she didn't care, but she was jealous, she wasn't after all a stone. But how could she care? Rachel was elemental, mythical, the ideal of his youth, even her father's youth. They belonged to a different century, the previous one, the century of sentimentality and utopianism.

The Medici blood was boiling and she stopped right there and waited for him to tell her the truth.

"A couple of times."

"A couple of times. And you struck me for a silly kiss in

a hallway in a houseful of people. And every time I have a pleasant little flirtation at a party you kill me with your eyes. Hypocrite."

"All right, don't rub it in. I've been ashamed enough. Besides, I've never pretended to you to be other than only half-civilized."

"Shit! None of that phoney bohemian nonsense. When you say you're only half-civilized you say it with pride. If you're half-civilized, become all civilized."

It was then he said it, this man, this fool that he was. An honest man. "I married you, I love you, Pacifici, because you're mature and civilized, a fine, energetic wife and mother to our children. You're civilized for both. I've gone on rare occasion to Rachel to lose myself in my youth for a couple of minutes, nothing else. I know you sometimes wish you were a *femme fatale,* the passionate, sleek, blacksheathed *amorata* of all male dreams. But you'll never be one, you're too civilized. That's why I married you."

He understood he could never hurt her more than by what he'd just said. He knew as well as she that every woman, no matter how mature, how civilized, wants one time or another to be Helen, sought by every Paris. Even Andromache envied Helen her moments. He realized he had chained her to the broad marriage bed. There was venom in her face now. Her eyes were cold black. If she'd had a stiletto he'd have poured blood. Too pure to be a walking, vibrating, vagina like his Rachel. She decided then and there to strike him both mute and blind.

Matt Cahn was a very attractive man, and women could feel that when he wished he could be a sensitive lover. He came one morning and they talked about Rachel and Zeke and their elemental, eternal, ineluctable, love.

[216]

Nicola was off at school by then, Vito sprawling in the playpen in the next room, and it seems they became totally alone, aware only of the closeness of the other, and it was very sweet and exciting and she could remember her heart raging violently, and his, and they made love swiftly and defiantly, deeply, before remembrance of reality could lay its cold, heavy claw on them. Before she had a chance to revive, he was gone, and all day she had moved about with a quiet, profound trembling. And she remembered what her mother had once said to her father, "You're only the bow, my Vito, but I am the cello."

And it was true, she wasn't lying. Her husband stood before her dumb and blind and white. Murdered. And he could see she felt like a murderer, for she told him Matt never returned, had too much good taste; if he had, she wouldn't have permitted it. She and Matt had proved their point, that was enough. "One has to have the ability to say no to oneself."

He always believed he would beat her to death if she cheated, and now he knew and did nothing. He had just gotten a whipping, and finally knew enough to keep his mouth shut.

Pacifici Bartola.

Still, Rachel had made it right for all of them. A few weeks later she came to visit Pacifici. It was in the morning. For once, *she* came, the queen had ventured forth. What a queen! Pacifici liked Rachel. Rachel was open, and free, though oddly enough she had never learned to laugh at herself, and in that sense was like Matt—they could tear themselves down in front of people to the point of embarrassment, but they couldn't laugh at themselves. Too serious, both of them, self-destructive. They could throw a picnic into chaotic despair because someone forgot the pickles. Zeke told Pacifici Rachel hadn't always been like that. Matt had made her that way. "Well, my dear Gurevich, baloney," Pacifici snorted. So Rachel came to visit and Pacifici was glad to see her. Pacifici had no shame about Matt—her conscience had bothered her a bit, but no shame. Guilt and shame are not equal or synonymous; it had been neither dirty nor evil. She enjoyed Rachel's beauty—it was before Rachel became sick, of course. Rachel was beautiful and her innate goodness and honesty hadn't permitted age to corrupt her beauty. Ripe white beauty, what wondrous color, her hair long, a sinuous blackness, sparkling, deep and cavernous dark blue eyes in that miraculous head, and her breasts, at her age, heavy in their roundness with thick brown nipples which she always managed to have pressing through her bodice —all of her, ripe beauty in every sense. He'd been lucky, Pacifici told him, to have had a woman like that—and what he'd once said about her was so true, it was just right for her to have such bad taste in clothes otherwise she would have been incredible. An Ingres stepping from the canvas. She wore an orange flouncy dress with broad purple stripes, she looked like a barber pole descending from the car.

They talked about books, had lunch, and she began to sketch Rachel as they talked. She couldn't help herself, she must capture that beauty as she saw her, but the sketches were bad, she was doodling with lines. Vito was cranky, always was a cranky, colicky child. She put him in his cot and gave him a soft toy to play with. She and Rachel returned to the living room. Rachel wanted to hear a new record they'd bought, early Renaissance music, Josquin; they listened, Rachel on the sofa, Empress Theodora, as he had once called her. Pacifici got some clay and began to model her. No good, nothing worked, calendar stuff. Rachel laughed. "I used to pose," she said, "for a living. Started in Simon Farrell's class—ended up on my back. Hold it for a moment." Rachel stood, shrugged out of her ugly dress, unhooked her bra, stepped out of her panties, kicked off her shoes, rolled off her stockings, and then reclined on the sofa in the classic odalisque pose. Pacifici just stared at her dumbfounded—it had happened too swiftly and naturally to be embarrassing. How old was Rachel then? Forty-five? A year or two didn't matter. Pacifici said Rachel overwhelmed the room; the living room was too small for her beauty—that flesh, that hair, that imperial smile. She wasn't showing off, she was beyond and above that; she was an extremely vain woman, true, for herself; showing off is something one does at the expense of others. "Go ahead and sculpt," Rachel smiled her famous, white, intimate smile.

Pacifici tried with the clay, but nothing moved. She was too taken with the model. But she continued working because she wanted to look at Rachel without embarrassment. Rachel was a wondrously beautiful woman, and she thrilled to look at her. One must understand. It didn't diminish Pacifici, it made her proud. Beauty can't diminish, only enhance life, she said. But it was something more. She understood him, Zeke, better—and more of herself. She realized she had stopped working and was just staring, boldly, and Rachel was smiling. Rachel called to her and she went to sit beside her. Incredible beauty. Rachel stroked her hair. "Your hair is exquisite, Pacifici," she said, and kissed her on the mouth. A real, frankly dikish kiss, and they laughed.

"Zeke loves you," Rachel said. And Pacifici knew what Rachel was saying.

"Yes, I know, I've never doubted it. And Matt loves you, too."

And Rachel said, "Of course."

They looked at one another now with full understanding. There was nothing dirty among them. Rachel had made it right for all of them.

Tomorrow he would see her again. He dreaded it. Dreaded to see how she looked. Before he left with his family for their vacation in Maine he'd seen Rachel twice in the hospital where she'd gone for the terminal period. Unlike Matt, or himself for that matter, she wasn't afraid of death, and somehow he had the feeling she welcomed it. Not so much because of the pain—she had boasted many times she could take pain better than any man—but because of what the disease had done to her beauty. The disease and age. She had been arrogantly aware all her life of her beauty and luckier than most she had kept it to her fifties. Besides, she was just plain tired.

Still, when he'd entered her private room in the hospital just a few weeks before, she quickly opened her purse and slowly and deliberately began to paint her lips and it was ghastly because the disease had deformed her head and neck, and her face had a sickly puffiness, a result of the operation they had recently performed on her to lessen the pain. The doctors had promised the operation would not dull her intelligence, and it hadn't. When she finished painting her lips a horrible coral red, he forced himself to smile and even to kiss her on the mouth. She caressed him and he patted her rump which was now a pathetic nothing, so wasted was she. They played the old game to the very end.

Then they talked about books—she was reading a novel about Theseus—and death. "It will be such a fine rest," she said stoically in the Greek style. And he wanted to shout at her, death's for real and you're still pretending.

She had always been a fantastic pretender—especially about courage, about which she had pretended so hard all her life that it had become her most durable virtue. She fooled a great many people, though not Matt, whom she could rarely fool, but she had fooled Zeke Gurevich for most of his life, because he was a pretender too and so was easily fooled by a pretender even more practiced than he.

They were quiet for a moment. And he looked at her and wanted to run. She was so ugly he couldn't bear the sight of her. A big lump grew on the back of her scrawny neck; her cheeks were puffed up sickeningly, her body all skeleton, her skin hanging in dry cracked folds. His Rachel.

"Come back Friday," she suddenly said, it was Wednesday afternoon, "and tell me what you're going to say for me when I'm dead."

"Oh, go to hell, Rachel," he cried.

"Gladly," she smiled, her still beautiful teeth pure white against the yellow of her face. "The quicker the better."

He went home and returned in two days. Matt had been there before him, lunched with her and left. It was like old times, Zeke Gurevich following on Matt Cahn's rubber heels.

"He told me he still loved me," she said after they kissed, their hands weaving the same old pattern.

"I'm very happy," he said, trying hard to keep the sarcasm out of his voice. Dying as she was, still he found it difficult to refrain from wanting to hurt her. For years now every time they'd met they had hit out at one another. He was certain she would have loved taking him down to hell with her. But he was damned if he was ready to go.

She knew he was aware that Matt no longer loved her —hadn't loved her for years. "I'm glad he loves you. In fact I never doubted that he did."

She smiled broadly, a brilliant light in death's yellow shadow.

And he *was* glad, not only for her but for Matt too. Matt was one of those men who never lied and up to then he had believed Matt was so absolute in his honesty that he would be truthful not only if it killed himself but if it killed her too. So now in the face of her death Matt had lied.

"Can't you look at me?" he heard her say bitterly. He must have been staring into nothing. He turned again to her. The bitterness of what his eyes saw showed, because she said, "Am I that ugly?" For the first time she whined. She wanted to die, but not all the way.

"No," he said, and it was suddenly true. "Your celebrated courage is too strong for the disease."

"Disease," she spit out the word as if she'd just bit into her own malignant bile. "I hate the word."

"Yes, I know," he said. He didn't know what else to say. Someone ought to write a manual, he thought, on what to say to a friend who is dying and knows it.

She slipped from the hospital bed, her nightgown hiking up to her thighs and he pretended he didn't see what they had become. Two sticks. Those regal pillars. That Ionic crown. She wrapped her robe tightly about the remains of herself and sat down at his knees. She laid her head on his lap, and cried.

He wanted to cry, too, but no matter how hard he tried he couldn't.

She wiped her tears away on his shirt and sat looking up at him. "When are you leaving for the beach?"

"Tomorrow."

"This will be the last time we'll ever see each other."

"It seems impossible, Rachel."

"Yes," she said. "I keep telling myself I have a few days left and then I'll be dead."

His knees began to quiver and she tried to still them

with her wretched hands. He made a wrench at himself, attempted to slip from the grasp of this hideous dream. Yet he was terribly curious, wanted to know everything she felt and thought. She seemed to understand—she could always read him with fluency.

"Yet, you know," she continued, "I think I'm able to go on day to day because I don't really believe it. A miracle will happen. The doctor will rush in any moment and tell me with a great big white smile like on television that he's just discovered a cure—even for terminal cases—and I'll live forever after, if not happily. Oh, shit! I'm dying and I don't want to die. Yet I do, too. I'm so tired and ugly and fed up. My children—though—my children—"

"Like all children, they'll become adults," he said harshly.

"Yes. I feel sorrow for them—but it's really for myself. It seems the years have gone very swiftly and yet not. I've lived," she said simply.

"Yes, Rachel."

"You think so?" She wanted reassurance.

"More than most. Tell me, what do you think about all day?"

"Of Simon. I lived a myth. Of Sean—how much he hates me. Of the children. Of certain moments, unimportant ones. The wonderful moments when I slipped into bed, a clean, crisp bed, after a tiring day and knew I'd fall immediately into a strong sleep. Of all my big revolutionary talk and not once having walked a picket line or gone to a demonstration. I hate big mobs so. Matt says our kids are already making up for it. Of the ecstatic first time I stood on Quai Voltaire looking across the Seine at the Louvre. The first time I saw Masaccio's *Adam and Eve* fresco in Florence. I thought I would never catch my breath again. That first time with you when you caught

me in a short nightgown washing the dishes. Of Matt—
the rare good days. Of my lovers—everyone always
thought I had them by the score, didn't they? Just a few.
One was Alonzo Truesdale. I had to do my share for the
Negro. How false we were. I was. And Alonzo—he
couldn't even get it up, so that he had to run away in
shame. 'How could I live up to what's expected of me by
the white lady?' he cried. He was right, of course. How
could he possibly live up to our erotic daydreams and
perk up at our falsity?" She was silent.

"What else?"

"Of death. That soon I won't exist. How impossible that
the world can go on without me."

"Everyone thinks that. The world doesn't exist without
us, Rachel. When we're dead, the world's dead."

"No," she said. "The world goes on and we go on in our
children."

"So I've heard tell. But I don't really believe it."

"Neither do I," she said softly. "Neither do I."

They were silent, each with his own thoughts.

Then he asked, "Does it all seem absurd, Rachel?"

"No. Having lived doesn't seem absurd. Only the sense-
lessness of our seriousness. And the constant waiting for
tomorrow; the constant waiting for the something indefinable that never reveals itself—that seems ridiculous. The
guilt, too. Yet at certain moments it's because of the heav-
iness of the guilt that I find myself almost euphoric
about finally dying. Oh, at last the guilt will be ex-
piated."

"What guilt, Rachel?" he asked, and he could feel his
heart beating insufferably fast. Would she at the abyss reveal the secret of their lives?

"I don't know," she said, and he ate gall. "Certainly not
original sin. Not the sins we're aware of. Those we expiate

[224]

somehow. With our headaches, I suppose, or we beat our breasts, do our good deeds. But another guilt—like the waiting for an indefinable something which will never reveal itself—an undecipherable guilt, also waiting to be revealed so that we can at last grab it to our hearts and find our excuses—murmur our *mea culpas* for it."

He was about to say, try to think of it for me, it's important, please, but a nurse entered the room. Starchy ghost, tired face. "You're supposed to be in bed, Mrs. Cahn. The doctor—"

"I'm entertaining my lover, Patricia. Yes, this ugly man," and she was her obnoxious flippant self again.

The nurse puffed up the pillows and tucked a corner of the linen under the mattress, then strode from the room.

He helped Rachel into her bed and he fought to restrain the shiver of distaste at the touch of her bony body and dry scaly skin.

She stared at him from the pillow, her dark blue eyes huge in the puffy yellow face. "You didn't write the eulogy, did you?"

"Yes," he lied. "But it wasn't any good and I tore it up."

"I don't care, I didn't really want to hear it. But promise me you'll say some words afterwards. I've discussed the arrangements with Matt, he will ask you to say a few words. He will also ask you," she said coldly now, "to please not make it too long. You understand of course he is one of those men who is afraid, and he will want it over quickly, how will he sit in the chapel with that box in front of him, a brutal reminder of what will some day soon happen to him?" Now she smiled. "Tell big lies for me, will you?"

"All right, Rachel."

"Don't forget," she said softly, "I've been a good mother to my children. Though not to Sean."

"Yes," he admitted. "An excellent mother. Though not to Sean."

She closed her eyes a moment and then tiredly opened them. "Kiss me, and go away. I'm very tired."

He kissed her, thinking it would be the last time, and started for the door. He walked slowly. He couldn't say goodbye.

"Remember that time on the rocking chair and it gave way under us and we landed on the floor without coming apart?" she asked through a pitiful smile, and he turned again to her.

The image came clearly, and he smiled at her too. "Of course. I remember every single time."

"You liar," she whispered hoarsely, and held his hand as if she didn't wish ever to let go. But he kissed her again, gently, then withdrew his hand and this time reached the door before she spoke again. "It's inescapable, you know —the damn guilt, and the dying."

He had come to the end of the sand beach, the wind was a fury, the sea pounded, as it always would, and every star in the sky was hidden by black storm clouds. It was time he went back to the shack and told Pacifici, yes, he would find some peace, he had her. But not yet. Hey, wop! let me see your Roman twat. She'd learned how to handle that, she could learn to handle him, too.

When he entered the shack, Pacifici was ready for bed and she smiled secretly at him, deeply, as his mother used to smile at his father when he was a snotnosed, redheaded kid. He grabbed her breast and drew her hard to him. "My bitter sweet almond. My very heart." She smiled, and he kissed her, his tongue like a cool fish in her mouth.

"Let's go," he said. "Tomorrow I have to go to Rachel for the last time."

"The pain will soon be over for her. I suppose it will take longer for you."

"Yes."

Before they got into bed the phone rang and it was Matt calling to say that Rachel had died. She would be buried the afternoon of the day following, would Zeke prepare a few words to say at the chapel. Yes, he said, he would and they spoke to one another for a few minutes as old friends, the enmity burnt out, only ash.

He held Pacifici tight in his arms, without crying, and then he had a fierce desire for her, and Pacifici said yes. Before he fell asleep, he said to her, "I hope I don't have any of those terrible war dreams tonight," but Pacifici didn't answer, she was already asleep. When she closed her eyes for sleep, she slept. On the instant. A maddening woman.

He had a bad night. He had to speak for Rachel laid out in her coffin and he didn't have the slightest idea what he'd say. He would fall asleep, turn, waken. Then he had one of those ghastly dreams which wouldn't leave him even after he forced himself to wake. A childhood dream, everyone had them one time or another. He dreamt he was dead and went to his own funeral. Then the wind roared over the beach, the shack groaned, the sea pounded, the yellow sea grass whined in the blackness. He had to leave their bed and go out into the wind to put the storms over the windows and then to the beach to see how high the waves were rising on the shore. He saw the tide was low and knew there would be little trouble.

He returned to their bed, the wind howling, and it seemed to him the entire universe was crying, except for him. Pacifici slept peacefully, curled in a ball, breathing warmly on his back, one arm thrown over him. Thus they had slept all the years of courtship and marriage. On the other side of the partition he could hear Rebecca sucking her fingers in sleep, from Vito's and Nicola's room only deep silence. The wind was the cry of a mad owl, and the sturdy shack groaned and leaned into the gale. He wished he could cry for Rachel—Rachel, how often I cried for you and now you're dead and I can't. The years have flown and the world has changed—and in the end is the same. What will I say for you? What words will I find? Can I stand dumb before your friends and kin? Should I tell them all, Rachel? All? Better I stand dumb.

He remembered the room on Charles Street, with the sooted windows, and the books, the sighing couch on its piers of bricks, and Rodin's *The Kiss,* and Goya's *The Executions of May 3, 1808.*

Por el honor de la vida. That was for all of us, Rachel. The wind shook the shack and behind him his wife kissed his back in sleep. He smiled. How odd? It gives no guarantees, no promises, but honor it and it gives you all. For a moment. Again he smiled. The wind raged. He fell asleep.